DEAD ON TIME

DEAD ON TIME

MEGHNAD DESAI

HarperCollins *Publishers* India
a joint venture with

New Delhi

First published in India in 2009 by
HarperCollins *Publishers* India
a joint venture with
The India Today Group

Copyright © Meghnad Desai 2009

ISBN: 978-81-7223-829-2

2 4 6 8 10 9 7 5 3 1

Meghnad Desai asserts the moral right to be identified
as the author of this book.

This is a work of fiction and all characters and incidents described
in this book are the product of the author's imagination. Any resemblance
to actual persons, living or dead, is entirely coincidental.

HarperCollins *Publishers*
A-53, Sector 57, NOIDA, Uttar Pradesh – 201301, India
77-85 Fulham Palace Road, London W6 8JB, United Kingdom
Hazelton Lanes, 55 Avenue Road, Suite 2900, Toronto, Ontario M5R 3L2
and 1995 Markham Road, Scarborough, Ontario M1B 5M8, Canada
25 Ryde Road, Pymble, Sydney, NSW 2073, Australia
31 View Road, Glenfield, Auckland 10, New Zealand
10 East 53rd Street, New York NY 10022, USA

Typeset in 11.5/15 Adobe Jenson Pro
Jojy Philip New Delhi 110015

Printed and bound at
Thomson Press (India) Ltd.

To Kishwar,
who made it possible.

Author's Note

All the characters and events described in this work are fictional. For the sake of verisimilitude, the names of some real-life radio and TV personalities have been used but the words and actions ascribed to them are imaginary.

1

06.59 a.m. London

This is the Today programme with James Naughtie and John Humphrys.

Ian groaned as his radio alarm woke him up. So it was the Big Two this morning. What were they up to?

Pip pip pip pip pip peeeep.

Good morning on Monday the tenth of May. Here is a summary of the news.

International tensions are rising between Libya and the United States of America as an American attack on Libya seems imminent.

As Scotland gears up for the first elections for the devolved Parliament, an opinion poll shows the Scottish Nationalists closing the lead. We talk to Gideon Crawford, the secretary of state for Scotland.

Negotiations for Cyprus's entry into the European Union enter a crucial phase. Is enlargement a step too far? We talk to the foreign minister of Greece.

And what is the prime minister's recipe for the millennium? We ask the experts: What is the Free Way?

Today's newsreader is Corrie Corfield.

Ian drifted back to sleep as the soothing, well modulated voice washed over him. In his dream, he was surrounded by newspaper files and was trying to open a door. Someone, he could not make out who, was trying to get him to drink a glass of something dark and murky.

He lost the dream, and turned over. Hilda, of course, had been up since half past six. She did not need an alarm clock.

It was James Naughtie's voice now.

It is eleven minutes past seven. The enlargement of the European Union, when it is finished, will add eleven new members to the present fifteen. But not all are alike. While Poland, Hungary and the Czech Republic are on everyone's list of favoured new members, there are problems with Cyprus. Our European Affairs Editor reports.

Ian forced himself out of bed. He would normally linger until 'Thought for the Day' came on at around ten minutes to eight, with some bishop rabbiting on about Jesus and cannabis. But he had something else to do today, something he could not immediately recall. Something that meant he had to break his routine. It will come to me, he thought, as he splashed cold water over himself and grabbed a large furry blue towel to dry his face.

On the line from Heathrow, before he boards a plane to Vienna for the EU Council of Ministers meeting at which Cyprus is being discussed, we speak to the secretary of state for Europe, Terence Harcourt.

'*Good morning, Secretary of State.*'

'*Hello, Jim. How nice to hear from you.*'

Ian remembered. Just the sound of Terence Harcourt's voice, that polite, unctuous voice full of false bonhomie, brought him back to reality. Yes, he had to go in and do a spot of political journalism today. No foot pounding through the streets or the corridors of power, he was too old for that. He only had to wrestle with newspaper archives. Now, where was his toothbrush?

7.20 a.m. London

When Gideon Crawford arrived at the White City complex of the BBC, he was greeted immediately by an immaculately dressed young woman in a well-pressed white shirt and a skirt which was just a few stripes short of tartan. Gideon thought he heard her say her name was

Celia. He noted how bright and pretty young women were nowadays. As to what Celia thought of this tall and lugubrious Scotsman with his large beaky nose and thinning hair, we shall never know. You don't get anywhere in the BBC by revealing your thoughts about the great and the good. Celia showed just a shade of respect for his status as a Cabinet minister but no more. She whisked him through the door using her BBC pass, upstairs to the first floor to the *Today* studios, and sat him down in a small waiting room with transparent walls. It had the morning's newspapers and a machine for dispensing coffee and tea. There was a large jug of orange juice on a side table.

'Will you have some tea, or coffee?' Celia asked.

'Coffee, please. Milk and sugar, two, please.' Gideon was not into healthy habits.

A voice from behind the *Guardian* said, 'Hello, Gideon. What are you doing here so early in the morning?'

It was Andrew Merton, the well-known sociologist. Thin and wiry, with a sallow complexion, Merton wore an old-fashioned NHS frame for his spectacles. It was his idiosyncratic way of telling the world that a professor at Cambridge he might be, but he was still proud of his working-class origins. When the Beatles were all the rage, John Lennon had made the wiry NHS frames trendy. Andrew had adopted them then; now it cost him a fortune to have them reproduced.

Gideon had known him for many years. Andrew had been in and out of the party as his conscience or his latest sociological theory dictated but Gideon always regarded him as one of their own. After all, a Scottish lad can't go too far wrong, or Right for that matter.

'Well, this is a surprise, Andrew. I didn't think you Cambridge dons had to get out of bed till your first tutorials after lunch. Are you here to face the dulcet duo as well?'

Facing John Humphrys and James Naughtie early in the morning on *Today* seemed to many people an exercise in self-flagellation. Whatever you did and however clever you were, they came out on top. But it was still worth it, since the programme set the day's political agenda. To be tongue-lashed by John Humphrys or to get hopelessly lost in the labyrinthine questions of James Naughtie was the fate of anyone and everyone who ventured on the programme, but they still kept coming. To be asked to appear on *Today* meant you had arrived in the political village of Westminster.

'I have been up since half past five to get here on time. It's the Millennium Commission that the PM has set up. They want to have some fun with me about it, I think.' Andrew did not want Gideon to be confirmed in the popular view that Cambridge dons enjoyed a sybaritic lifestyle.

'Oh, Harry White's great dream project. His cure for the world for the next millennium. Well, I take it you tell Harry what to think and he agrees with you.'

'Oh, don't you believe it. Harry White is not so simple after all. He takes his Millennium Commission very seriously. He is genuinely keen to arrive at some philosophical agreement that can guide us through new challenges. To be honest, I've come to admire him while working with him on this.'

'Well, I am glad to hear that. Don't let those two make too much of a mockery of Harry.'

7.28 a.m. London

'*It is twenty-six minutes past seven and here is Gary with the sports.*' It was James Naughtie speaking.

'*Morning, Jim. Morning, John. First, the Old Firm game at Ibrox. It is a cliff hanger since the championship of the Scottish Premiere League hinges on the outcome. Celtic have to win outright if they are to win the League. Rangers, who are level with them on points, are ahead on goal average. So they only need to draw.*'

'*Isn't this the match the prime minister is attending?*' John Humphrys asked.

'Well, for fans of the Old Firm game, that will be the least important thing, I can assure you.' Gary laughed.

At the mention of Harry White, Sarah threw off her bed clothes and leapt out of bed.

Sleep or no sleep, she had to get ready for work.

7.30 a.m. London

Celia walked back into the waiting room and Gideon heaved aloft his tall, gaunt frame and prepared himself for the ordeal ahead of him. He waved goodbye to Andrew Merton, who was still waiting to go in.

The studio was next door to the waiting room. As Celia ushered Gideon in, he saw that a large round table occupied much of the room. Across at the other end, behind a glass wall, he could see the programme producer speaking into his phone. Celia directed Gideon towards the side where chunky red and blue microphones were scattered around. John Humphrys was listening on his earphones with his eyes on the producer. All the morning newspapers were spread across his side of the table. He waved a pencil in greeting at Gideon, and James Naughtie, who had been sipping coffee from a polystyrene cup, looked up and mouthed a silent hello. To his left, a woman was just finishing reading the news.

'Thanks, Corrie. It is now seven thirty-five and with me in the studio is Gideon Crawford, the secretary of state for Scotland. Good morning, Secretary.'

By some mysterious and long forgotten rule of the BBC, Scottish matters went to John Humphrys since he was Welsh and James Naughtie was Scottish. That, however, did not make things any easier for Gideon.

'Good morning, John. Good morning, Jim.'

'Now, Secretary of State, are you in trouble in Scotland? The latest poll shows the Scottish Nationalists catching up with you. How will you manage?'

'You don't want to take a single poll too seriously, John. I am pretty confident that when the day comes...'

'But we don't know the day because the prime minister will not set the date. Is he afraid of losing?'

'No, let me finish, John. I was saying that when the day comes and, indeed, it is the prime minister who will set the day, we are confident that voters in Scotland will remember that it was our party that delivered devolution.'

'But was it? It was Stan Davies who did much of the work along with Terence Harcourt. But Harry White is not the same thing, is he? Is he not very unpopular in Scotland?'

'I wouldn't say that, John...'

'But the polls say that in Scotland Harry White has only twenty-nine per cent support while the Scottish Nationalist leader...' John Humphrys was quick.

'The election will not be fought on personalities but programmes. We have a positive and radical programme for Scotland in its first Parliament. It is good for Scotland and good for the Scottish people.' Gideon had not been in politics for nothing. He could waffle his way through the few minutes he had been allotted.

'You call it radical, but it is the Scottish Nationalists who are promising to take North Sea oil into public ownership, and perhaps ScotRail as well. You have avoided any talk of nationalization.'

'All that is empty talk. It's the old way, and around the world it is being abandoned. We have to do the same. What matters is health and education, and jobs for our people.'

'Are you sure your party members in Scotland agree with this new fangled philosophy of the prime minister? Isn't this just the old Tory radicalism?'

'Well, this is what the party fought the last general election on, and we won at Westminster with the largest majority anyone can remember.'

'So what is good for Westminster is good enough for Scotland. Then why devolve?' John kept the pressure up.

'No, I am not saying that at all. Devolution is the great and glorious achievement of our party. The Scottish Nationalists don't want devolution. They want to break away. We will protect the union.'

7.45 a.m. London

'Oh, give up, Gideon,' Ian shouted at the radio. He had gone through his morning routine of shit, shave and shower, as he called it, and was getting ready for the outside world. What was he to wear? What did the day foretell? He drew the blinds and looked out. It was a glorious morning on the hills of Hampstead, which meant that by midday it would be sweaty in the lower marshlands of Westminster. No suit, then; a light combination with a tie would be apt. He might end up in the portals of Parliament after all.

9.00 a.m. London

England was not made for hot summer days. They used to be rare, which was why the poets celebrated them. But in the final decade of the twentieth century, with the global warming, such days came often. Yet no one was prepared for them. There was no air conditioning in cars or offices or homes, let alone the bus or the underground tube. New York was better equipped, as Sarah recalled from her holiday there last year this time. The subway was air-conditioned, unlike the Victoria Line on which she was now stuck.

Ian, on the other hand, was walking down Hampstead High Street to his bus stop. Hot summer days were meant to be spent in Provence, he thought wistfully. But they always went to their cottage in July. That's the way it had been done in England since the nineteenth century.

The reason was simple: in the hot summer months, the foul smell emanating from the Thames made it impossible for Parliament to function. So it recessed. Thus started the practice of summer holidays at school. When their children were still at school, Ian and Hilda could not take a holiday till the end of June. Now, though the children had grown up and the grandchildren were keener to go to America than France for the summer holidays, they still went to Provence every July. Such, Ian thought to himself, is the power of history, or perhaps just the force of habit.

It was a fraught Monday morning for both, but to look at them you would have thought that it was a life-threatening event for Ian and no more than a common cold for Sarah. Ian was furious, muttering about the incompetence of people who inconvenienced him. Ian hated being inconvenienced, or having to break his routine, even if it meant that he got handsomely paid. Sarah was stoic. As she put on her make-up for the day ahead, she appeared the complete professional. Whatever her problems, she had to look her impeccable best. This meant coordinating her printed shirt with her flaming red hair and a discrete but fashionable skirt. She wore sandals rather than high heels, but a pair with bold colours that matched her top, and the beads that she had picked up at Monsoon. She decided to put on her no-smudge lipstick, 'easy for that forbidden kiss' as the poster said. She painted her nails and toes and threw on a silk scarf she had bought in New York. She was prepared for whatever might happen. After last night, anything could.

Sarah had come home Sunday night, having spent the weekend with her sick mother in Warrington, as she had done for the last few months. Her mother was getting more difficult each week. Sarah had never got on with her in the first place. She was really her dad's girl. For her mother, Sarah was a poor substitute for the son she never had. Once Sarah's father died, her mother fell apart. She became physically frail and more querulous than before. Yet Sarah was her only support and she bore the burden of tending her mother stoically. Anything, as long as she did not have to live in the same house as her mother.

She had to think about finding her a safe, sheltered accommodation. A costly option, though. She would have to consult Alan, he was the financial whiz kid.

When she entered their flat in Islington, Sarah had found it strangely empty. Alan was not yet back from his five-a-side football game, and there was no hot pasta dinner awaiting her with his freshly made pesto. No message on the answer phone, no note. She checked her mobile for any missed calls or messages. Then she changed into a floppy salwar kameez, picked up in Delhi last Christmas on holiday, and began to think about food and why Alan was not home. Something was amiss.

She put the kettle on. She was no good at food, she usually left it to Alan. She put the TV on but paid no attention, and wandered about the flat feeling strangely desolate. When she got to her study, out of habit she turned on her desktop, and the message was there, waiting for her. A simple email from Alan:

I am leaving. Jo and I are hopelessly in love.

By morning, facing the tube ride from Highbury and Islington to Victoria, she had pretty much overcome the shock. All night she had tossed and turned, trying to understand what Alan had done to her. What had she done wrong, when had she hurt him, and how? How would she cope on her own? What of the flat they had bought together on a joint mortgage? Why had this happened to her and why now? Here she was, all of twenty-nine, looking forward to a long relationship with a caring man, someone she could have children with and marry in good time. What would she say to her mother?

As the crowded and hot Victoria line train speeded from one station to the next, the anger began to rise inside her. Jo, of all the people! She'd had no idea Alan was gay. Their sex life, while never volcanic, had been normal, and Alan had always said he loved her and found her attractive. Jo, that fresh-faced Cambridge lad—a Double First and Boating Blue—had been recruited to the policy team 'for photocopying and coffee-making', as Alan had said. Why would he take Alan away from her? Alan had talked of how nifty Jo was at their weekly game of five-a-side football. She had thought that was all Alan's friends were capable of—playing their boyish games and boring each other with news of the latest transfer of a football player and the salary he had negotiated. Sex in the after-game showers among Whitehall high-flyers! Whatever next?

9.05 a.m. London

Ian never got into the Underground if he could help it. Despite a lifetime in journalism, he was not used to taking taxis and charging expenses either. His first proper job had been with the *Manchester Guardian*. In those days, that staid newspaper was deeply imbued with the values of C.P. Scott, its greatest editor. Thrift and idealism were its watchwords. As a fresh graduate from Oxford, Ian had been added to a small army of leader writers. That was the old class divide: graduates wrote leaders and those with just a school certificate or even less education went out to gather stories. But writing editorials bored Ian silly, so he chose to go out into the field as a reporter.

Over the years, the class divide had narrowed and the pay, not to mention the expense accounts, had got better. From his first home—a bed-sit in Kilburn—Ian had now graduated to Hampstead where he and Hilda had a five-bedroom house in Frognal, a five-minute walk from the Hampstead Heath tube stop. Yet he walked all the way downhill to the bus stop at the bottom of Pond Street and took the No. 24 to his destination.

For a man who had retired from active journalism twice already, it seemed an unreasonably early hour to go to work. It wasn't as if this was America where they had working breakfasts. Ian had loved being the New York correspondent for *The News* but he never took to those early hours. Life had to be lived at a more gentle pace, he felt.

It wasn't every day that Ian was wanted at the office. They called him up for special assignments and party conferences, or sometimes when the younger set had failed to deliver due to a hangover from alcohol if not something worse. Mustn't grumble, he thought to himself now, even as he cursed young Marcus who had recently become deputy editor in charge of letters and obituaries. Not hot stuff, but they'd had to find him something to do, considering he would inherit the paper when Old Marcus popped off.

Could Ian come and do an obit of the PM, young Marcus had asked. No, no, there had been no accident, no news. Just that he had not updated his obituary since Harry White became PM. Yes, he was only forty-five and not remotely likely to die soon. But Marcus liked keeping to his new fangled automatic news updating system. Ian could, of course, input the obit from home, but he was not on the network. He did not even have a laptop. What a pity!

9.30 a.m. London

Getting angry was not very professional, Sarah told herself. Not even on the crowded, smelly Circle line on which she had to travel the two stops to Westminster from Victoria. She began to think of the day and the week ahead, as she did every Monday on the Underground.

Life at 10, Downing Street was always quite hectic but of late it had acquired supersonic speed. Parliament was frantic this week— not that Harry White cared very much for the House of Commons. As the PM's diary secretary, Sarah had to be well-informed about his movements, though she was only a minor cog in a machine that was as fascinating as it was scary. When the PM was in London, life was busy but easy. When he was abroad, or going from one summit to another, dropping by only to repack, it could get really tough.

As she stepped out at Westminster, propelled by the thrust of commuters eager to alight, the bright sunshine hit her. For once, she would have preferred the day to be gloomy and overcast to match her own mood. But then, she thought, maybe my day will be upbeat and happy. She was surrounded by people who all seemed to be buoyed by the weather. Hundreds of Whitehall civil servants, foreign tourists and idle Londoners with nothing better to do than shop and stroll had converged on Westminster. A babel of languages rose from the serpentine trails of small children clutching their guides, being hectored by their polyglot teachers as they gawped at the Big Ben before turning left towards Westminster Bridge. The smart suited civil servants showed no such curiosity and turned right to their various ministries and offices.

Sarah had her own route. She turned left out of the station and then left again along the Embankment. There were fewer pedestrians here, and a view of the Thames. Now on firm ground and with the river air inside her, she began to regain her poise. The familiarity of her routine was reassuring. Some things in her life hadn't changed, she thought, her job, her daily commute to the job, her own special way to the office. She walked along the Embankment and then passed through the narrow gap between the Norman Shaw building and the Ministry of Defence. Very few people used this gap which allowed her to emerge on Whitehall just across from Downing Street. And this way she could say a silent hello to the great generals whose statues adorned the grounds of the Ministry of Defence. There was Montgomery, the hero of Alamein, whose enormous statue caused as much controversy as the Field Marshall had throughout his life. There was Viscount Slim, the hero of the Burmese campaign, with his jolly, jaunty hat which cheered Sarah every time she saw it. Poor Walter Raleigh was there too. Sarah always felt a bit sorry for the Elizabethan hero, his statue was so tiny compared to the other two. Was he being punished because he had brought tobacco from America to England?

Sarah could, at this point, take a slight detour and cross at the traffic lights. But she enjoyed scrambling across, dodging the traffic and ending up right outside the iron gates that guarded the prime minister's house and office. She slung her security pass round her neck. A few people stopped by the gates but the policemen on duty kept them moving along. She said 'Good morning' in as cheerful a voice as she could manage and they waved her through with a smile. Her usual self-consciousness at the privilege of working at such a posh address swept over her. She may be only a lowly secretary, but the opportunities at 10 Downing Street were not given to everyone.

Sarah had landed the job the first week after the new government was installed. After many years in the opposition, the new team in power did not trust the old staff to keep their mouths shut. They were paranoid about the tabloids picking up gossip, and needed loyalists they could trust. Sarah's political sympathies were well known to her friends. After all, she had first met Alan at a Labour Party dinner in Islington. She had gone along with her flatmate Judy, who was active in the party. The dinner was at Fredrick's in Camden Passage, and Michael Cramer, the leader of the Labour Party, had been the chief guest. Judy had known Alan at university and introduced them over pre-dinner drinks. They had shared a large table and got talking. When Alan won a dinner for two with Michael Cramer at the House of Commons in the raffle, he asked Sarah to go with him.

Bloody Alan. Would she run into him today? The thought nearly choked her.

From the iron gates, the walk to 10 Downing Street was longer than it looked on TV. In the old days, before the IRA security scare led to the iron gates being set up, visitors to London would stand along the pavements, waiting for a glimpse of someone famous coming or going. Children would have their picture taken in front of the famous black door of No. 10. Now the street was deserted except for a few people who worked at one of the offices. Only when there was a press conference or some dramatic development like a sudden Cabinet resignation was the place crowded with cameras and journalists.

It was an odd choice of house for the head of the government, or rather the first lord of the treasury, as the plaque on the door informed the world. The large shapeless house was stuck in a cul-de-sac off Whitehall, where tall stately buildings stood next to each other. As a building, the house had no merit whatsoever. Why did the prime minister not have his office in the Banqueting House across the road? Now there is a building, Sarah thought, with its beautiful ceiling painted by Inigo Jones and the spacious rooms. But then, Banqueting House was also the place where Charles the First had been beheaded.

The street got its name from George Downing, who had helped Oliver Cromwell, Parliament's outstanding leader, defeat Charles the First. Then, astute politician that he was, he changed sides after Cromwell died and his son turned out to be an incompetent successor. He helped Charles the Second get back the throne and earned as his prize the large plot with the buildings on it.

The property was made famous by Robert Walpole, the first prime minister. George the Second gave it to him as a personal gift but Walpole with his shrewd sense of history decided to use it as a home while he was the first lord of the treasury. Thus began the life of 10 Downing Street as the prime minister's residence.

In the eighteenth century, not many prime ministers followed Walpole's example; they were aristocrats who owned large mansions in London and houses in the country. But there were exceptions. The hapless Lord North, who lost the American colonies, lived there as prime minister and would not quit even after he was sacked. William Pitt, who became an MP at the age of twenty-one and chancellor of the exchequer at twenty-three, had nothing better than his chambers in Lincoln's Inn. He told his mother that he would love to live in 'the best summer town house possible' if only Lord North would vacate. When he became prime minister a year later, he moved into the house and spent the next twenty of his twenty-four years there.

So it happened that the property was occupied sometimes by the chancellor of the exchequer and at other times by the prime minister. Some like Pitt and Gladstone, of course, combined both jobs. Gladstone did not like living there to begin with, preferring to live in the more elegant Carlton Terrace. He gave 10 Downing Street to his private secretary, Arthur Godley, who spent the first few years of his married life there. For this kind favour, Gladstone was rewarded by the young bride Sarah Godley with a large cup of tea and a slice of bread and butter every time the Cabinet met. The rest of the Cabinet had to watch Gladstone's evident enjoyment with envy.

After Gladstone, no one tried to do the two jobs at once. The chancellor of the exchequer began to live at No. 11 while the prime minister lived at No. 10. The arrangement was not exactly conducive to harmonious neighbourly relations. In most cases, the chancellor was a rival of the prime minister, who in turn suspected the chancellor of trying to oust him. Thus, in almost every Cabinet, the two could barely stand to speak to each other.

Harry White had revived the practice of holding both the portfolios. He had seen how every government over the past thirty years had been wrecked by the rivalry between the prime minister and the chancellor. Yet he retained the tradition of having an enemy as his neighbour.

Terence Harcourt had been Harry's rival in the leadership contest and was sore about losing to Harry. To keep him happy, Harry had created a brand new department that Terence could head: the Department of European Affairs. Terence was to be the first secretary of state of the new department. To boost his ego further, Harry threw in No. 11 as a consolation prize. Luckily for him, Terence wasn't enamoured of having Harry as a neighbour either, so he kept his family in Edinburgh and used 11 Downing Street only for his receptions and dinner parties.

As she walked into the office, Sarah remembered that Terence Harcourt would be en route to Vienna with Alan in tow. Alan was

Harry's favourite economist. Harry had hoped to have him advising on treasury matters, but Terence knew how vital Alan would be in the European negotiations, so he had insisted on having him as his special adviser—or bag carrier, as Sarah used to tease Alan.

Did Terence know about Alan and Jo? Did he, an uxorious man if ever there was one and madly in love with his wife after all these years of marriage, approve? Would the papers find out and make a fuss? No one cares in these tolerant times, Sarah thought. Bonking someone else's wife is much more scandalous for a politico than a gay liaison. And Alan is not a politician, he's a special adviser. So perhaps the tabloids would leave him alone.

Sarah knew it would be a relaxed day at 10 Downing Street as Harry White was leaving for Glasgow soon after lunch. The elections for the very first Scottish Parliament were looming, and he had to show he was willing. He had also been persuaded to attend the Old Firm game—the Rangers Celtic Derby, which was taking place today. Harry hated football and kept himself away from all the talk about football matches that politicians habitually indulged in. He had no favourite team to follow and paid no attention to scores and positions in league tables. He was a cricket fan. Indeed, had it not been for his myopia, he might have played for Cambridge.

But ever since England won the World Cup in 1966, football had become a popular sport with the middle classes. MPs had to follow the fortunes of their local team and be seen to be fanatically supportive. They often tried to get local publicity by putting an early day motion in the House of Commons congratulating their local club for some recent victory. No early day motion had any chance of being debated, so it was a fatuous exercise. But that did not stop them.

Since most towns had only one team, the MPs of that town could agree, despite political differences, to back the team. In big cities like Birmingham, Manchester and Sheffield, they had two teams, often bitter rivals of each other. So MPs had to choose which one to back and the rule was, you followed the club whose ground was nearest to your constituency. It was the same in Glasgow. Rangers and Celtic were bitter rivals and the Old Firm game was just what it sounded like—a very old tradition, and in many ways Scotland's version of tribal warfare between two sides, one Catholic and the other Protestant. Harry was not looking forward to it. There had already been much twittering about his Catholic inclinations. He had taken communion recently and there were rumours that he might become a Catholic. So the match was even more fraught than usual.

'If anything goes wrong, Gideon will have his head chopped off,' Christine had said. As the secretary of state for Scotland, Gideon Crawford was an obvious candidate for the fall guy if Harry had any trouble in Glasgow.

Christine Brown was the brains in the PM's office. She knew everything before anyone else, perhaps even the results of last night's five-a-side football game, and she told Harry sooner than the rest. She was fiercely loyal and had been so for the fifteen years they had worked together.

10.00 a.m. London

Ian was astonished yet again, as he went over the newspaper files, to note how slowly Harry had started, and how fast he had accelerated since the previous election in which his party had lost. When he looked up the earlier drafts of his obit, he could see that had Harry died in an accident ten years ago, he would have hardly rated a column. Perhaps just a mention: young MP, worthy but dull career, climbing steadily. After the usual stint as parliamentary private secretary—the juniormost job as bag carrier to some minister, even worse when it was just a shadow minister—he had moved to the whip's office, and then become shadow junior minister on the treasury team. His lucky break had come when Stan Davis, the shadow chancellor, was hospitalized for a few days.

Stan was a mountaineering enthusiast and despite the obvious dangers, he had refused to give up his hobby. England did not have any significant mountains for climbing but he had climbed the Ben Nevis in Scotland, and wanted to do the same with mountains in Wales. On a wet foggy day, he made an attempt to climb Snowdon, lost his balance and fell down. He was out for five weeks. Harry had to take over at short notice and proved to be brilliant. All the economics he had forgotten since his Cambridge days came back to him. His big chance came on the weekly treasury question day. He had prepared well for it, and tripped up Roscoe Hartley—the lazy incumbent chancellor—in a question about the yield curve. They may not have grasped the subtleties of the economic argument on the benches behind him, but they laughed and cheered and threw the order papers in the air. Harry had arrived.

The party kept losing the elections, however. Their leader Michael Cramer had tried his best to make it popular again but the press remained hostile. The polls were favourable as never before as the general election approached, but at the last moment there was a surge of support for the government.

Michael could never understand economics and at the press conference which launched the party manifesto, he got into a tangle about whether his party would raise national insurance contributions. Poor Michael. He was a horny-handed son of the soil, or rather coal mines, and had a romantic view of the welfare state. As far as he was concerned, the 1945 Labour government had single-handedly established it. His father had been a miner, and the nationalization of coal mines had saved his life. He was able to get a good pension and health care for his emphysema. For his father's generation of workers, national insurance contributions meant a weekly stamp purchased and stuck on a card. This told the world that the man had been in paid employment and had paid his contribution towards the state, so he could get his pension. To a modern generation, it was just another tax on income; no one licked stamps on to their cards any longer. Yet all Michael could talk about was how his dad had always paid his stamps, and how these contributions were the backbone of the welfare state. He missed the point of the question, which was whether his party would raise taxes if it was elected. So, when he was asked point blank whether it meant an overall rise in the tax burden, he said 'yes'. Then he denied it. The result was confusion and denials and retractions. He was savaged by the broadsheets and humiliated by the tabloids. Stan Davis was furious. All his efforts to establish the party's credentials as 'a friend of business' had been nullified. The label of a high-tax, anti-business party stuck. When the government squeezed back in with a majority of twenty-five, everyone blamed Michael for blowing the election. He had to resign.

Stan Davis became the leader and Harry was promoted to shadow chancellor. Terence Harcourt resented this since he was senior to Harry by a decade. It was he who was the darling of the annual party conference, and got elected to the National Executive Committee with more votes than anyone else each year. But he had to be content with the job of deputy leader.

Terence reckoned Harry would regret his promotion. Being the shadow chancellor was not the best job, not in the Labour Party, not while the party was in opposition. It was more of a poisoned chalice. The party was imbued with old-fashioned thinking about taxing the rich and higher public spending. But the times had changed. Now Harry had to tell them that high taxes were unpopular and any spending they promised had to be vetted by him. In any case, the answer was no to all their demands for more money for their pet projects. The normally genial Harry became sombre. His position was a recipe for unpopularity. But he made a success of his shadow chancellorship. The continuing incompetence of Roscoe helped.

Soon, Harry acquired the reputation of a serious economic thinker, thanks to Christine. She had used all her charm and old contacts at

Cambridge to put together a team of advisers who fed Harry good material. The backbone of the team was Alan Carling, who gave up his job in the faculty to come and work full time for Harry.

10.05 a.m. London/10 Downing Street

'Bloody Alan,' Sarah said.

Christine put a sympathetic arm around her, but neither said anything more. There was much to be done. The Rangers-Celtic game was being played on a Monday rather than on Saturday afternoon. Weekday games usually started in the evening at 7.30 p.m. This one, however, was starting fifteen minutes later, at 7.45. There would be a reception and dinner afterwards, so Harry would not finish till after 11 p.m. But Harry being Harry did not wish to spend the night in Glasgow. No matter how late it got, he wanted to leave for Belfast, where he had a breakfast meeting scheduled with officials and ministers.

Elisabet White could not go with Harry to Glasgow and Dublin as she had to be at the dress rehearsal for her play. It was her own translation of Alfred Jarry's *fin de siecle* comedy, *Ubu Roi*, and she was directing an all-women cast at the National. The effort of getting a first night on a day Harry was in town had meant a major crisis between 10 Downing Street and the National, but they had sorted it out. Harry was to come back from Dublin the next day in good time for the 7.30 p.m. curtain rise.

Elisabet's diary was not the concern of the 10 Downing staff. She had her own staff who liaised with Sarah, but being temperamentally theatrical, they did not always appreciate political pressures. As for Sarah, all she needed to know on any day was whether Lisa was in town or not, and if in town, whether she was available for the PM's outings or busy performing elsewhere.

Lisa was a trouper, and she was stunningly beautiful as well as charming. She had clawed her way up from poverty and her parents' messy marriage to go to Oxford, and had done brilliantly—a first in English and a play at the Royal Court before she was twenty-one. She and Harry had married quite young but had no children. Elisabet pursued her career in theatre despite much muttering by the press and other politicians. She did not care. As far as she was concerned, she could combine her career and her duties as the PM's wife. And Sarah was certain Lisa could always be relied upon to turn up trumps when she was required to.

10.10 a.m. London

Ian left the paragraphs on Harry's marriage for another day. He was ready to do the politics in full detail, but not yet the chase through theatre reviews to write about Harry White's wife. There was so much to do. He was almost grateful that young Marcus had asked him to come in. He had just come up to the time of Harry's succession to leadership after Stan's tragic death in the Alps in a second mountaineering accident. The shock had been palpable throughout the country. Indeed, many people were surprised to find that even after fifteen years in the wilderness, the death of an opposition leader could bring forth such a widespread cry of anguish from all around the country. Though most voters had become cynical about politicians, here was one man whose loss was felt by many as if someone in their family had died. Newspapers gave acres of coverage to Stan's life and his integrity and probity as a politician. They mourned the loss of a potential prime minister. It was common agreement among the pundits that whoever succeeded Stan was guaranteed to win the next election, whenever it took place.

Terence Harcourt had presumed that he would succeed Stan; he was, after all, the deputy leader. He insisted on staying in London and at the House of Commons. He wanted to be in the Chamber when tributes were paid to Stan. He sent Harry to collect the body, and immediately started his own campaign for leadership. Harry knew why he was being sent away from Westminster but gamely agreed. This act of selflessness proved providential. He had hours of TV exposure as he was seen with the bereaved family, bringing the body back. It was his face that appeared on the news headlines every time the clip was replayed.

So when it was time for the leadership election, no one was interested in Terence Harcourt's experience. The party wanted a new, fresh face, the face they had just admired on their TV screens. It did not help that Terence's team tried to insinuate that Christine was in a ménage-a-trois with Harry and Elisabet. Harry was able to reach for the high moral ground. He refused to say anything about his own marriage but had nothing but praise for Terence's family. That was clever because the picture of Dorothy and her three daughters was so cloying that it put people off. The time for the old-fashioned happy family had gone, and the trendy post-modern marriage of Harry and Lisa was what people preferred.

Ultimately, the patrician Terence Harcourt lost to the young pretender. Harry was disturbingly handsome. Anyone who came in his presence felt the force field of his charisma. And when he began to speak, people forgot how young he looked. He could move mountains as well as Parliaments. They didn't care that Lisa never had the time to campaign, nor that she was a Catholic. Harry won the leadership and when the election came, he carried the party to a spectacular victory.

Once in office, Harry dealt with Terence Harcourt deftly. He had promised a new deal on Europe with Britain at the centre of things and with a positive attitude rather than the Europhobia of the previous lot. So now he created a special department and made Terence the secretary of state for Europe. As shadow chancellor, he had learnt that the treasury could destroy Labour governments. So he hived off all European economic issues from the treasury and gave them to Terence's new department. He gave all the foreign aid issues to the new Department for Human Development, which too he created. The reduced treasury was thus manageable and he retained it for himself.

For someone who had been in office for scarcely two years, Harry had not done badly. Having Terence Harcourt on board was not a recipe for a happy government but Harry was his own chancellor and had made quite sure that Terence would behave himself by encouraging Alan Carling to become Terence's confidant.

There had been some controversy when Alan 'defected', as Ian recalled, but it was something got up by the hacks. In public, there was sweet unity in the Cabinet. Most of them had never enjoyed the fruits of ministerial office, being too young to remember the last time the party was in power. It was only a few oldies like Terence and Gideon who had been ministers then. Now, they were the leaders of the party's old mafia whom Harry had to watch.

Yet, once Harry became prime minister, it was pretty much life as before. Ian had seen them come and go. They always started with a lot of hope, a promise of renewal, an obeisance to the middle classes, a distancing from the traditional heartlands. This was the hopeful beginning. Ian well remembered Harold Wilson, who shared not merely his initials with Harry White, but also his penchant for the new. They both had a gut feeling for the worries and hopes of middle England that was uncanny. Poor Harold Wilson's reputation had started high, but despite four election victories, had ended up in the mud. Like Harry, Harold Wilson had had to deal with very little opposition within the party in his first government. But then had come defeat in 1970, with much discontent and dissension among the MPs. Even when he won power back in 1974, Wilson did not enjoy either the authority or the popularity of his first years in office. Would Harry go the way of Harold, Ian wondered.

10.30 a.m. London/10 Downing Street

Christine could, even now, after all these years, feel a tingle in her nerves when Harry came down from the flat upstairs to the office on the ground floor. He always stopped by the various offices and said hello. It was a small gesture but it made all the staff feel valued. The first stop, of course, was Christine's office.

She heard him coming and instinctively looked in the mirror on the desk to make sure her long blonde tresses were neatly in place. She had put on a pale yellow shirt with golden highlights which went well with her hair and her favourite scarf which set off her smooth fair skin and almond eyes. She knew he noticed what she wore every day at work but even if he didn't, she wanted to show him her best side.

Harry was, as always, impeccably dressed. He had remembered that his day in Scotland meant no blue suit, no blue tie. He was in a white Armani shirt, with a Versace tie which had hints of red rather than pink in it. He gave her a peck on her cheek as he always did, his arms warm around her. Christine's office door was always open so she could keep an eye on what was going on around the place. Her own office was like a fishbowl. So Harry stuck to the minimum. Then he moved on to the other offices.

He said hello to Sarah, and asked how Alan was. Sarah just made a face and shrugged. Harry moved on, but he did notice that Sarah looked quite fetching.

Christine gave Harry a couple of minutes to settle down in his office, to log in and check his email. Then she knocked gently and went in. Harry looked at her and said, 'Nice scarf.'

Christine blushed. She had put it on specially because it had been his present for her when he came back from Italy after his first visit as PM. It was not his first present to her, nor even the latest. But Harry's first visit to Italy as PM meant a lot to Christine, whose father Piero

Bruno had come to England from Italy soon after Mussolini made his pact with Hitler.

Harry did not let her dwell on the compliment but merely asked, 'What's with Sarah and Alan?'

'He has left her for Jo, that young Blue from Cambridge.'

'Alan? Never knew he was gay—well, there's a surprise for you, isn't there?'

'Yes, but it only puts him more in Terence's grip, doesn't it?'

'Terence could hardly blackmail Alan after what we know about him,' Harry said.

'You still believe that old canard?'

'I have heard nothing against it yet. Thank heavens no one has raised it. But then, Chris would beat them up physically if they dared.'

Terence's PR man, Chris Mott, had been a bouncer in his youth before he got into the trade union movement. He fancied himself as an amateur boxer, especially when he was not sober, which was frequently the case.

Christine did not smile. She had no time for Terence and even less for Chris. She did like Alan, though. I hope he is not totally lost to us, she thought in passing, her mind on more urgent matters. This was their fifteen minutes to discuss the day's agenda. Christine handed Harry the brief on the Scottish situation. It was all there, down to the number of times Celtic and Rangers had played each other and the outcome each time and the clichéd jokes which he would no doubt be told ad nauseum. Harry had to be neutral and could not be seen cheering either side too much. This was easy for him since he preferred cricket anyway. Still, it would be better for his image if he could manage to look interested in the match.

'Has Gideon got any special problem with this visit?' Harry asked.

'Nothing special. Just the normal problem that we are only five points ahead of the Nats. You saw yesterday's poll, they are catching up fast. Gideon was crap on *Today*, and of course, he is universally hated within the party there.'

The Scottish Nationalists were a big problem for Harry's party as they were pushing for total independence for Scotland rather than just devolved power. They were also a left party, full of radical policies, and posed as the leading alternative to the Labour Party.

'Why do you think he is so unpopular?'

'Well, he did rat on Terence when he voted for you in the leadership election.'

'He says he voted for me, but how can I be sure of it?'

'That is what he says.'

'Would you trust him?'

Christine raised an eyebrow but remained quiet.

'I think he may not have voted for either of us. He was hoping for a second round in which he would run himself. Remember, Gideon's grandfather narrowly missed being leader. He wants to reclaim what he believes is his heritage.'

'Over my dead body'.

'Or mine,' Harry replied.

Superstitious Christine immediately reached for the cross she wore and said a silent prayer. Harry got out of his chair, came around and took her in his arms. Without a word, he kissed her eyes and then her mouth. They had not been so close since before Harry and Lisa went on their vacation to the Seychelles.

'Why are you not wearing your new contacts?'

Christine's question was a gentle but firm way of getting back to business. Ever since the leadership campaign, Harry's myopia had posed a problem for his image-makers. At that time he had refused to give up his thick bifocals and dark black frame. But his dedicated spin doctors had persisted in trying to wean him off his thick glasses. They got him varifocal lenses and rimless frames. Then they asked him to switch to contact lenses. He hated them. He kept losing them;

he had nightmares about dropping them on the floor and having to scramble around looking for them. They finally got him disposable contact lenses. But while he was in his office, Harry still preferred to wear spectacles.

'Later,' he said, 'when we are within camera range.'

'But will you remember?'

'You will be there to remind me if I don't.'

'No, I am not in the Scotland party today.'

Harry looked at her quizzically.

'Too much to do. We haven't sorted out the pile from Easter and I must start work on coordinating the various bits for the Queen's Speech. If we don't start now...'

'Rhubarb.' He put his finger on her lips. 'You are afraid, aren't you?'

'Not afraid, worried.' Christine knew that an overnight trip together was fraught with danger, both on account of her own weakness and the ever vigilant tabloid press looking for dirt on Harry. No one had forgotten how the press had hounded Harold Wilson for the way he listened to his secretary Marcia Williams on political matters. There was not even a whiff of an affair between the two, but still there were endless stories about whether she had power over him and why. Harold Wilson himself had become paranoid about these stories. He came to hate the press but could never ignore it. They had to ensure that Harry's relations with the media did not go that way.

'Well, don't be. But I will let you off this time.'

Christine was almost at the door when Harry asked, 'So who is coming with me?'

'Well, Oliver of course. And Gideon said he would bring a team from the Scottish office to brief you.'

Oliver was Harry's press officer, clever and ferociously loyal. Harry could be quite sure that his trip would be well flagged in *The Scotsman*, *The Herald* and *The Record*. Oliver was probably waiting now, to tell him more about the mess that awaited him in Glasgow.

11.00 a.m. London

Scotland, Ian thought, would show whether Harry White would end up as a great prime minister or not. As an Englishman, Ian held the simple view that nothing would ever make the Scots happy. They would always want more and they would always hate to pay for it. But Harry had little choice in the matter. Stan Davis had sold the pass when he became leader. He had needed the Scottish votes to win and so he had come to an arrangement with Terence: Scotland would have its own Parliament with a first minister.

After Stan's death, Harry could not go back on the promise. So one of the first pieces of legislation he proposed was the Scotland Bill, which provided for limited autonomy to Scotland. Certain areas such as health were devolved entirely to Scotland and others such as agriculture and rural affairs were shared. Scotland even had its limited freedom to change the basic rate of income tax up or down by a few pence in the pound. The trick was to give Scotland some autonomy without creating a federation in the United Kingdom.

Whatever the demands of the Scots, Harry was convinced that the Union of Scotland and England forged in 1707 by Queen Anne could not be broken up. That was what the Scottish Nationalists wanted and every other party was against. So Scotland got a nice deal on the amount of public spending, much more generous than what fell to England or Wales. That way, Harry hoped, his party would get a majority in the first elections for the Scottish Parliament coming up in the autumn. He may not like Scotland, but it was vital to win it. For that he was willing to do a great deal, even watch a football match.

It was time for a break. Ian had worked solidly for nearly two hours and made copious notes. But he was dying for a smoke, which in these modern times meant that he had to step out of his office, either to the cafeteria with its plastic chairs and Formica tables, or outside the building itself. He opted for the latter: it was a hot day but at least he would get some fresh air. So that was how Ian found himself standing on the side of the road, lighting his cigarette.

He also found Rodney Page, an addict of news and gossip, a constant fixture in what was once Fleet Street. Rodney had made the rounds of practically all the London newspapers. He had never wanted to do anything else. Neither radio nor TV had any attraction for him.

Roddy's once handsome face was ravaged by too much drink and too many late nights. Yet, the thump on Ian's back was hefty and startled him.

"What on earth are you doing here, Grandpa? Shouldn't you be sitting on a hot beach in Costa del Sol at your age?'

Before Ian could even open his mouth, Roddy put his arm around his shoulders and dragged him to the pub next door. The Raven and the Bat was the local pub for journalists working on *The News*. Fleet Street used to be full of such pubs, each with its distinct clientele. Now the newspapers had moved away from Fleet Street, but every newspaper still had its own favourite pub where the journalists hung out.

Most of these pubs were modern and more like cafeterias. The Raven was an exception, with its large Viennese mirrors and some lovely old prints of Victoriana. There were pools of sunlight by the large window, where tables stood overlooking the main road outside. Away from that front, the pub was dark and cool. Roddy left Ian in the sunny quarter while he went to order the drinks. It was too early to drink but Roddy was not one to take orders from anyone. Ian got a large malt whisky and Roddy's voice boomed in his ears.

'So what are you up to, you miserable lefty troublemaker?' Roddy had known Ian for many years but could never forgive him his radical past.

'Young Marcus asked me to come and touch up the PM's obit.' Ian did not rise to Roddy's bait.

'What's happened? He has not, has he? I didn't hear.' Roddy was immediately agitated.

'No, he is all right. This is just a routine updating. I expect Harry will be around, man and boy, for another few years. Who knows, he may even break Maggie's record of ten years as PM.' It was Ian's turn to wind Roddy up.

'Now there is a depressing thought early in the day. Is there no hope of getting rid of Harry? Is there no chance of an internal revolt on the back benches? God, the party is so gutless, and the opposition isn't any better. Perhaps nature will do its magic and he will have a heart attack. Maybe someone will take a contract out on him, you reckon?' Roddy's imagination began to run away with him.

'No one is going to kill Harry White and he is unlikely to have a heart attack, though I admit that's more likely than a party revolt against him. As for the opposition, they are still in denial.'

'God, politics has become dull. Mind you, even if you got rid of Harry, there is hardly anyone you would find to put in his place.'

'I thought you were a Terence Harcourt fan.'

'Me? Never.' Roddy was emphatic.

'You mean, not for the last twelve, fifteen months or so. Didn't you write a fiery article in his favour in *The Spectator* at the time of the leadership election?'

'They pay handsomely at the *Spectator* and to be honest, all they wanted was to foment more trouble for the People's Party.'

'That is what they used to call the party. Now it's the Pretty People's Party. So what are you up to nowadays, Rodney?'

'Investigative journalism. Consultant to his Lordship for his many newspapers.' Matt Drummond, the American media lord in question, owned the largest selling tabloid, and the oldest establishment newspaper, plus a television channel in the UK. He also had media interests in Europe and America. Since several newspaper owners had titles, people began to refer to him as Lord Drummond, adding to the gallery of Lords Beaverbrook, Rothermere, Thompson. As an American and a republican, Drummond didn't much care for a title, nor did he qualify. He wanted influence, not titles, and to buy influence, he was willing to spend money. Roddy was quite happy to come by some of that money.

'You mean, gossip columnist anonymous.'

'Dirt digger and muck spreader more like. Gossip is much too pleasant a name for what I do. But the shoddier the news, the better the money. Listen, why don't I buy you lunch at Nico's in Park Lane?'

'You have gone upmarket, Roddy.'

'It is the expense account that my Lordship affords me. Fancy a bite today?'

'I'd better stick to a pint and a pasty. I have work to do.'

'Oh, don't be such a miserable old sod. Look, young Marcus will pay you twice as much if you knock off now and come back another day. He would never dare insist that you work after lunch as well.'

Ian was tempted. He had done the basic work, but he was short on the colourful bits, which Roddy was bound to know more about. But still, a three-hour lunch at Nico's, even if Roddy was paying, was bound to wreck his regime. He thought guiltily about his significant other. Being a GP, Hilda never stopped warning him about the need to avoid rich food and heavy lunches. But this was really in the line of duty, wasn't it?

'Ok, but only if you give me the low down on Harry to use for my obit.'

Roddy was about to say something when the pager in his pocket beeped. He took it out, looking rather grave, and said to Ian, 'Stay here. I must make a call. Back in a tick.'

With this, Roddy put his pager back, pulled out his mobile and went outside. He looked grim but excited. Ian could lip read to the extent that he guessed Roddy was at the receiving end of some juicy gossip. He could also see that there were others who could not abide

The News cafeteria, and were now trickling into the pub, desperate for a smoke. He waved at one or two, making it clear that he was happy sipping his whisky alone.

He saw Roddy hail a taxi. Then, as he was about to get into it, Roddy seemed to remember that he had left Ian behind. He rushed back in.

'Sorry lad, must hasten. Something big has come up. This is going to be the grandmother of all bust-ups when it hits the fan.'

'Tell me quick.'

'No way. This is mega. This is the sort of stuff that Cabinet crises are made of. Tell you later. And I owe you a double lunch next time I see you. Cheers.'

With that, Roddy rushed off at a pace Ian thought was athletic. Saved from a large lunch he did not quite want, he abandoned his whisky and went back to his labours with the life of Harry White.

11.30 a.m. London/10 Downing Street

Christine turned around and said, 'Would you like Sarah to come with you? It would give her some experience and cheer her up.'

'Not a bad idea,' said Harry. 'Can she be ready in time?'

'I am sure. I'll get her on the tarmac. The rest is up to you.'

Christine gave Harry a look as she went out. He just smiled. He had a crowded day ahead as usual and no time to decode Christine.

No sooner had Christine departed than Oliver burst in. He never came in gently, never knocked, and certainly never wasted any time.

'Ok, item one, the no-hopers of the Keir Hardie Group want to see you, mainly to talk about the US policy in the Middle East. You agreed before going off on the hols. Mistake then, waste of time now. Fob them off. Next is the completely disastrous Pamela, your culture secretary.'

Oliver spat out the words Pamela and culture. Harry wasn't quite sure which he hated more. Pamela Meade had been the failure of the

Cabinet. Harry had been warned about her competence—or lack of it—but she had been crucial to his campaign for leadership. When the women MPs had accused him of being a chauvinist pig, Pamela had stood up for Harry and swung the sisters around. Then there were only nineteen of them; now there were one hundred and forty women MPs. Pamela had airbrushed out his chauvinism and a softer, gentler Harry, devoted to his wife, had been constructed. They loved Harry, all hundred and forty of them, or at least the new recruits did, since the older bunch, now labelled the Seven Sisters, had seen through Pamela's ploy.

The one thing Harry dreaded was tears and Pamela always threatened to flood the place. He looked at Oliver helplessly.

Oliver chuckled.

'But thanks to the Libyan crisis, you have to be in a video conference with the presidents of the US and France and the Secretary General of NATO. So, if you want, we can tell Pamela to get lost—very gently, of course.'

'But she will come back.'

'Yes, but tomorrow is another day. You are in Belfast in the morning and you go to Dublin in the afternoon. Then you are at the play at the National. Luckily, it's a short play. There will be a reception afterwards but we have made arrangements so you can pop back at division time, if you wish. Which means Pammy can only see you in the division lobby. Ok?'

Harry went into the House of Commons as little as possible. But every evening at ten o'clock there would be voting on some of the day's motions. As a motion came up, those in favour would go into the Aye lobby to be counted by the tellers. Those against would crowd into the No corridor. This ritual brought the party together and gave many backbenchers an opportunity to meet Harry or some other Cabinet minister whom they wished to importune for a favour, a job, or a contract for some businessman in their constituency. That was one reason why they all voted the way their whips told them to. Maybe not all, but most of the loyalists in any case. There were some perennial troublemakers in Harry's party, such as those in the Keir Hardie group, but thankfully, Pamela was not one of them.

'Then I can sack her from the Cabinet in public,' Harry said.

'I'll hold you to that'.

Oliver was one of the few—Christine was another—who knew the real Harry. Even Elisabet was not on that list. Soon after Harry got into Parliament, Oliver had been sent to do a hatchet job on the new MPs by his editor. He had all the chips on his shoulders—no university education, not even A levels. Left school at thirteen, went to a borstal and as soon as he was eighteen, he returned to prison. It was there that he was obliged to put in some time working in the prison governor's office. That changed his life. He was trusted, given responsibility. He had to sort out the incoming post, open it and make separate piles according to the subject. He also had to arrange for the letters going out to be posted, with the appropriate stamps. So he had to practise his literacy, and learn to read and write properly. He came out and got a job at *The Herald* as a messenger boy. From then on, he rose fast, moving from one paper to another until he landed a plum job with *The Daily Mail*.

Oliver had been expecting Harry to be a stuck-up toff, with his public school and Cambridge education. He had read up what he could get on him. But, on the day of his interview with Harry, it all went pear shaped. Oliver's car broke down. It was raining and he couldn't find a taxi. Then, miraculously, Harry drove by on his way to their meeting at Westminster. He saw Oliver and gave him a lift. Oliver was surprised that Harry even knew what he looked like. Harry just turned his car around and took Oliver back to his terraced house in Clapham and helped him dry out. They even matched shirt sizes. Oliver was not only well dried but also restored with a good malt whisky, which marked Harry in Oliver's eyes as a real drinker. From then on, Oliver was sold on Harry.

Harry was obviously pleased to have made Oliver a friend. He even helped him write a mildly negative portrait which showed him to be not a fire-breathing socialist but a man fond of the Opera, the theatre and good food which is to say, almost a Tory. *The Daily Mail* was not read by millions of women for nothing. Oliver and Harry had managed to hit the G-spot as it were.

Together, they conspired to build Harry as if he was the latest perfume—pretty, precious, and potent to the real purpose: in the case of perfume, seduction and in Harry's case, power. The quiet, unassuming Harry was a hard, ambitious plotter. Oliver was stunned to find out much later that Harry had been following him that morning of their first meeting, just watching his every step. Harry left nothing to chance. Even the bottle of malt whisky was the label Harry knew Oliver liked. He himself was a Martini man.

Just as the polls closed after the last election, Oliver had asked Harry the one question he had been curious about for a long time.

'Why did you join the Labour Party, Harry? Didn't the Tories offer you a seat?'

Harry did not even smile. He accepted the question as a serious one. After all, he knew he was about to become prime minister, and Oliver was bound to be keeping a diary of all conversations and events.

'I looked at the position in 1980. I examined the age distribution of Tory MPs and then of Labour MPs.'

'Not the liberals?'

'I wanted power, not a warm bath. I saw that the Tories had a much younger age profile, full of Cambridge and Oxford graduates only a couple of years older than I was. But Labour had many who had entered in 1945 or 1950 and were still around. They had come to power too soon and they couldn't stop quarrelling after 1951. Even when Harold Wilson brought them to power in 1964, they kept fighting each other. I reckoned I needed two Parliaments to get near the top. The chances were much better among the Labour dinosaurs than among the prowling Tory cats. And then Maggie, bless her soul, gave me even more time.'

'So it wasn't ideology then?'

'Only as an aftershave to stem the blood and keep off the true scent. I am after power, I want to do things. I can buy ideology from any of those think tanks which are full of sincere chaps. Cheaper that way.'

Oliver did not know if he loved Harry more than Christine did. But their love was different. Christine had sunk her emotional and physical energies into helping Harry get to the top from his early days as an MP. At Cambridge, they had been friends and briefly even lovers. But after graduation, they had gone their separate ways. Harry was not seriously into politics, though he often spoke in union debates. Christine was a passionate socialist. He went to work in the City and she joined various political movements on the left fringe. They lost touch. Then suddenly one day, years later, Christine got a call from Harry. He was going to run for Parliament, would Christine like to help him? Christine was surprised that Harry even knew where she was. But she was happy to give up her dead end job at the *Tribune*. It was a small circulation Labour weekly very much in the dissident tradition. There was never enough money to pay workers proper wages. They all worked for the cause, but no one could tell what the cause was. The paper monitored the endless quarrels of various factions in the Labour Party. After all, *Tribune* had been born in dissidence when Stafford Cripps and Aneurin Bevan founded it in 1937. They had both been expelled from the party, only to bounce back as Cabinet ministers and in Bevan's case as deputy leader. That was the complex maze of Labour politics Christine was steeped in, and she was quite happy to quit when Harry asked her.

Harry valued her extensive network in the party; Christine had other plans. She would direct Harry to the left wing of the party, or so she thought. She became the core of Harry's staff, the first and foremost. But working for Harry was for Christine more than just a job. She still had her political ideals, her pet dreams about reshaping society, and Harry was the instrument. Also, her fling with Harry at Cambridge had been brief but passionate. She was emotionally committed to her ideals and to Harry, and the job soon became her life.

For Oliver, working as Harry's PR man and press officer was a superb career move. Like Harry, he had a sceptical, if not cynical, outlook on politics. He wanted the authority to control the flow of information in and out of Harry's office. He wished to make Harry invincible against attacks from journalists. They were all reptiles, he thought. He should know; he had once been a reptile himself. Had he stayed in the media, he could have been editing a tabloid by now. But he wanted a change, an adventure.

It was Harry the person rather than the politician who interested Oliver. They were almost the same age and even similar in size and appearance. Oliver was a bit rough while Harry had a smooth baby face. Theirs was a great bond between two robustly heterosexual men, all smell of jockstraps and after-match showers, and whiskies and Martinis to sink into late into the night and even till the morning after. Oliver knew all of Harry's secrets, or so he thought. Though Harry was such a charming bastard, you could never be sure.

Of one thing, Oliver was certain. If Harry had any scandals to cover up, it would be about women. Because Harry was a sex addict. When he travelled in those early days, he couldn't stay away from prostitutes. When the pubs shut, Harry seldom went straight to bed. Oliver had to tell him to stick to escorts and avoid the floor mops in the back streets. And as Harry rose in the public eye, even that had to stop. So Christine always accompanied him if Lisa wasn't there. It was all very discreet, and Lisa did not mind. She needed the security of Harry for her life and her career. Fidelity was not important to her. She had made it clear to Harry—no divorce ever. As a Catholic, she was willing to live with a harem of mistresses but not divorce. Christine was also Catholic. Harry was happy with the arrangement, and so was Oliver.

Oliver's mobile rang.

11.45 a.m. London/10 Downing Street

Christine went round to the cubby hole where Sarah sat. It used to be a broom cupboard in the old days, but now that the staff in the prime minister's office had expanded, every bit of space had to be harnessed. So the cupboard had become an office. It was enough for Sarah's state-of-the-art computer, which sat at the other end from the door, on the wall-to-wall desk. Sarah believed in a paperless office, no mess, no files. Everything was in diskettes, neatly arranged in a box. A slim but expensive glass vase with one rose in it was an interesting new addition. Christine wondered who had brought the rose today. Alan always sent one over—perhaps he hadn't cancelled the order.

Sarah turned around as Christine came in. Christine could see that she had tried to dress especially well, as if to show Alan what he was missing. She didn't look sexy or vulgar, just someone you would want to take to lunch in an expensive restaurant in the hope of future favours.

'Hi. Sorry to disturb you, but this is important.'

'No problem. How can I help?'

' Can you go with the PM to Glasgow and then on to Belfast and Dublin, back tomorrow evening?'

'Aren't you going?'

'I must stay and do some work for the Queen's Speech. It has been mounting up. The Libyan crisis has taken up so much time. I'd be ever so grateful if you could. It might even be fun.'

'I'd be terrified. Who would be there? What would I wear?'

'Nonsense. You know all of them. Oliver will be there and Gideon with his gaggle of young Scots lads. You will be in the director's box at Ibrox and then at the reception. Belfast early next morning and Dublin for lunch. Back in time for supper in London.'

Sarah looked both thrilled and petrified. 'But...' she began.

'Oh, just go and buy some new stuff at lunch time. Charge it to us. Buy a suitcase as well, handy for such a short trip. We've all got to get used to quick changes, ok?'

'Oh yes.'

Christine smiled and turned to go when Sarah said, 'Oh, and thank you for giving me the chance.'

Christine's smile became positively enigmatic. Sarah's phone rang. She picked it up. It was Oliver.

'Can you come in for a minute, Sarah?'

'Yes, of course.'

Christine looked questioningly at her, and Sarah explained that it was Oliver. She was about to head off to the stairs to Oliver's office, when Christine said, 'He is in with the PM.'

Sarah had not been inside Harry's office, except when he had a large formal gathering. She had no time to check how she looked. It would be too embarrassing in front of Christine, but then the latter did something very sweet. She put her arm around Sarah for the second time that day and whispered in her best French falsetto, 'Courage, mon ami.'

12.00 p.m. Belfast

The English think it always rains in Ireland. The French, of course, think it always rains across the Channel. It is a subtle form of one-upmanship. Sunshine civilized, rain backward. Yet, today it was as bright and hot in Belfast as it was in London. Inside the Orange Billy pub though, it was dark and cool. At this time of day on a Monday, there was just the one odd regular whose job did not start till after one o'clock.

Alice Mason knew Derek and she also knew that he was about to do his delivery jobs. But one pint never did anyone any harm, she thought. She had just finished polishing the brass handles of the beer pump behind the bar, which she would be pulling several times later. For now, her job was to tidy up and get the place ready for the lunchtime crowd.

The door opened and there was a sudden brightness from the street for a brief moment before it closed again. When Alice adjusted her eyes, she saw it was Kenny, the young plumber from the Ardoyne. Kenny's dad used to be in plumbing before he got blown up in one of those quarrels that went on in the province. His uncle had found Kenny, seventeen years old and a school dropout, his apprentice job as a plumber. Alice knew that Kenny's heart was not in plumbing.

He looked like a kid as he stood there now, with his acne and his pale skin and greasy hair. She knew he was up to no good, but then she was not his mam, so why should she care. He silently asked her the question she was expecting. She just nodded her head and pointed to the staircase at the back.

Upstairs, Kenny knocked gently on the door and a gruff voice said, 'Aye'. Inside, there was a long table, which was bare except for a revolver in front of which sat a man who was clearly the leader of the four others gathered there. All of them were solidly built, with clean-shaven heads and tattoos visible to the naked eye. Their leader was of medium height and stringy. He had thin lips and lanky red hair. He wore a black shirt under a light grey jacket. There were rings on two fingers of his right hand, and one on the index finger of the left hand as well. On his neck you could just see the beginnings of a tattoo which went over his shoulder.

'Kenny boy, did you get it?'

'Yes, Red, I got it.' Kenny held out the rucksack he had been carrying on his back.

The man smiled.

'Good lad. Are you ready then to come with me?'

'I'm looking forward to it, Red. It's not often I get to go to a big match like this.'

'It's not just any big match, lad. It's the Old Firm game. It is our civil war against the papists in just another fashion.' Red was laughing now.

Ken produced an envelope from his rucksack. There were airline tickets in it for each of them. They all got up and silently put on their jackets.

'We better give Kenny all the hard stuff. All the guns and knives and the dope you may wish to get rid of at the other end. He will go through security separately from us. His Nan works there so she will see us through. Let's go.' Red was decisive as he led the group out. No one said anything as they got out through the back door of the pub to avoid the few stragglers now giving Alice something to do.

Red got into the driver's seat in the van.

Safely away from any danger of being overheard, Ken asked, 'So what's the plan, Red?'

Red looked back and glowered at Ken. Ken realized that he had overstepped the mark. He was not supposed to ask such questions.

'Sorry. Forget I said anything.' Ken's heart was thumping loudly.

The four others in the van laughed.

'Don't you fret, lad. Red won't kill you. He is always gentle with his kind. Not as if you are a papist.' It was Ritchie, large and obviously the man for heavy duty, who spoke. He wore a blue flak jacket even in the heat, beneath an open-neck orange shirt.

'Well, as you are new, I should tell you something. Just so we don't get into trouble if you get caught on the other side and the bastards shake you out. You, Kenny, don't know the names of Eddie, Ritchie, Rob and Des, if the police ever ask you. You never met them until the game. You are all going to enjoy the game, the most glorious game on the annual calendar. It is us against them but in Glasgow, not here.

Here we do it with bombs; there they stick to footballs. My purpose is simple. I shall not be so much watching the game as going after my quarry.' Red was expansive now.

'Don't ask who. He will tell you if he feels like it,' Ritchie warned Ken.

'No, I'll tell you. It's that bastard, Harry White. He is coming here tomorrow and as we now know, he will be signing his surrender to the PIRA. He calls it a negotiated settlement but we know he is selling Ulster to the boys down south. He has swallowed their promise that they will decommission, but he is a fool. They'll just hide their real weapons elsewhere. For a long time, I didn't mind that he was canoodling with the boys in Dublin. Each of them, when they get power in London, starts selling out. That is, till we lay down our marker and then they come to their senses. I thought Harry White would be just the same. But once he had taken communion along with that foreign wife of his, I knew he was beyond hope. He is supposed to be there tomorrow at lunch time after a meeting here, and if he gets there, we can kiss Ulster goodbye.'

'Except that he won't get there,' Ritchie added helpfully.

'Aye, I intend to stop that papist bastard in his tracks tonight. The time has come for some hard measures.' Red turned around as he said that and nearly drove off the road.

'Whoa, Red. Wait till tomorrow before we go off the road,' Ritchie shouted.

'Aye, lads. Tomorrow we will celebrate the decommissioning of the prime minister.'

Ritchie laughed. 'Don't ask how, lad. Wait till you see what Red has planned as part of the post-match celebrations in Glasgow. You just make sure your rucksack makes it to the other side and Bob's your uncle.'

Ritchie had known Red for nearly twenty years now. They had been in many scrapes together. They had been bloodied in the big

strike when the Protestant shipyard workers of Belfast stopped any
compromise of the London government with the nationalists. In
those days, things were quieter. It was just the SDLP, and they were
a lily livered lot. It was later that the PIRA got into the act. They
were a seriously murderous lot. The only way to fight them was with
gelignite and bullets. So Red formed a gang and they called
themselves Carson's Irregulars after Red's hero Carson, who had saved
Ulster from being swallowed by the Catholics. They freewheeled
across the province as they saw their chances. Ritchie and Red had
been in and out of the Maze a few times. They were marked men but
they were also dedicated loyalists.

Red drove on, more carefully. Getting caught in an accident,
especially at this time, would do him no good. The RUC would love
to lock him up even for a minor offence. They always said it was for
his own good but Red did not believe them. It was not like the old
days when you could rely on the RUC to protect its own people. It
had gone soft. It was all performance pay and the diversity bullshit.
Mind you, things had started going bad even before Maggie had
gone. It all had to do with fear. When the bastards blew up the Tory
conference at Brighton, even Maggie relented and gave in to Dublin.
Now they were galloping along at a very fast rate towards
Armageddon, and Red reckoned he had to do something desperate.
Something as big as what the bastards had done to the Tories, so
they could generate panic in the London mob. Only then would
they come away from their foolish ways.

He had to get Harry White somehow. When he heard that Harry
was coming to Glasgow and to the Old Firm game, he could not
believe his luck. Glasgow, and especially the Ibrox crowd, were his
family. He would much rather get at Harry on the mainland than in
Ulster. Why not a bomb deftly planted under the prime ministerial
car? The INLA had managed to do it to Airey Neave in the car park
at the House of Commons. Surely Red could manage it in the open

parking lot at Ibrox. With such a big game on, everyone would be watching the action and not the car park.

12.15 p.m. London/10 Downing Street

When Oliver answered his phone, he knew they were about to run into a problem. Apparently Matt Drummond was in town for the day and wanted to lunch with Harry. He was not around London, or Britain for that matter, very often. He had to stay out to escape taxes, though he still kept a close eye on his empire. He had flown in from his yacht near the Balearics for the afternoon and he wanted to speak to Harry.

Harry was annoyed. He had arranged lunch with members of his Commission on the New Millennium. The Commission was Harry's favourite project. It was to give the British people a new ideology, a new map for the millennium. It was also a ploy to secure Harry's place in history. The Archbishop of Canterbury and the Chief Rabbi were co-chairs. The Duke had graciously agreed to be chief patron. Andrew Merton, the Max Weber Professor of Sociology at the University of Cambridge, was to be its principal theorist and Maxine Murtagh was the token woman. She had spent her life in the probation services. The other two members of the Commission were Abu Obiah, the fiery Black poet whose streetwise pronouncements were popular among the politically correct, and Barry Carrick, who was the David Hume Professor of Moral Philosophy at the University of East Anglia and a leading humanist. Harry had been looking forward to this cerebral gathering and now Matt Drummond had turned up.

But Matt was insistent. He had to talk to Harry urgently about something and no, it could not be said on the phone. No, he was not free at any other time but lunch. No, he could not come to Glasgow, Belfast or Dublin, he had to be in San Francisco tomorrow. Matt was not to be denied. He had secretly funded Harry all these years. He had paid for all those escorts and undermined Terence Harcourt's campaign by spreading rumours that he had been a paedophile in his younger days.

That was where Sarah came in. Harry had his contact lenses on now so that his blue eyes could work their magic.

'Come in, Sarah. You know Oliver, of course.'

'Yes, Prime Minister. And...'

'Listen, Sarah, you have to do something special for Harry,' Oliver said.

'Hang on, Oliver. What were you going to say, Sarah?'

'Just a simple thank you for the rose you sent me.'

Oliver tried his best not to look at Harry. The bastard, he thought. Here we go again.

'Don't mention it. I just thought it would cheer you up after what Alan did. But Oliver is right. We are in a bit of a fix and I would like you to do me a favour.'

'Whatever you say, Prime Minister.'

'Oh, call me Harry, please. No formalities here. But you know the lunch today?'

'With the Commission?'

'Yes. Can you cancel it?'

'Now?' Sarah looked at the big clock in Harry's office. There wasn't much time left. 'Of course, whatever you say. Though I am not sure I can find all the invitees to inform them.'

'Well, try your best. If they turn up, we'll just have to send them away. But Sarah, it is very important that you don't tell them I cancelled it. '

'What can I say?'

'Well, the simplest way, though not the most pleasant for you, is to say that you got my diary wrong. Tell them any story you like, but if you don't mind terribly, can you say you goofed up?'

'If you say so, Prime... Sorry, Harry. '

'That's marvellous. I look forward to having you with us on the Scotland trip.'

Finally the penny dropped for Oliver. So this was the new recruit.

'But...'

'What, Sarah?'

'I hope it won't go on my record.'

'Not at all. No one will mention it after today.'

12.20 p.m. London/10 Downing Street

Christine saw Sarah coming out of Harry's office. She was white as a sheet. Christine got to her door and silently waved her in.

'What's the matter, Sarah?'

'Well, I have to cancel Harry, I mean the Prime Minister's lunch.'

'Which lunch?'

'The lunch today, with the Archbishop and all the other members of the Millennium Commission.'

'Why?'

'He didn't say. He said I was to tell them that I had got the diary mixed up.'

'Really? But who is he seeing instead?'

'I was not told. I had better get on with it. There are so many people to contact.'

'Of course. Do you need help?'

'No, this is my job, I'm afraid.'

'Yes, of course. Anyway, don't stay on the phone forever, remember your shopping.'

'Well, who knows about that now...'

Christine was curious. What were those two concocting? Who could Harry be seeing that he was standing up the Archbishop and the Chief Rabbi? Something was cooking and Harry wasn't going to tell her. It was something that Oliver had obviously hatched. She was going to find out, but how?

12.25 p.m. London/The Slug and Lettuce, Docklands

The noise in the bar was deafening. But it was essential to Roddy's transactions. He was looking at some photographs in the dim light thrown by the garish jukebox. The Honourable Adrian Andrew, as seedy a toff as you might get to see, was standing by with a sherry. He was tall and stood a head above Roddy. His straw-coloured hair had not yet thinned, and his handsome good looks, once ravaged by drugs, had clearly stood him in good stead. He had given up drugs and even hard drink since his time in detox, hence the sherry. Roddy was aware of Adrian's history and despite that, still liked him.

Adrian was the younger son of Lord Summerfield. He had a title but no money. He went to Rugby because his father had been there, but he refused to learn much. On leaving school, he had an attitude but not much aptitude for anything. So he tried the City and then he tried exploring for oil and diamonds and had a go at running specialist tours in remote parts of the world. Nothing worked to earn him the sort of money he thought he was meant to have. Then he met Rachel Stoner of the family that owned the Stoner supermarkets.

Rachel was devastatingly beautiful, a porcelain doll. She'd had a wild upbringing, having been sent off to a finishing school in France after the usual routine of being expelled from several schools in England. In Adrian, she met her match for wild living. Then a maiden aunt left her money in a trust, with peculiar conditions attached to it: she had to be twenty-one before she could get her hands on it, and even then only *inter vivos*. She could not pass it on to anyone else.

As soon as she was twenty-one and could claim the money, Rachel married Adrian and took off for travel around the East. Their interest was not in the religions or the arts but in the drugs they could buy, and they blazed a trail from Goa to Varanasi, Kathmandu and Bangkok. In India, one could freely get charas and ganja and bhang, all variants of cannabis. Soon they were into heroin in Kathmandu and by the time they reached Bangkok, cocaine as well. Rachel could not cope with it as well as Adrian. Her drug habit killed her before she was thirty.

Adrian's life was now in shambles. He had no wife, no money and no future. He had to do something to get himself out of the hole he had dug. He came back to England and tried to make a living. He had picked up photography as a hobby when he was at Rugby. His family knew many of the rich and famous and he exploited his connections. He became a celebrity as a photographer snapping other celebrities. When the glossy magazines took off, he was in clover, supplying them with pictures of posh weddings. He could get to weddings from which most ordinary fashion journalists were excluded. For a while, he had spending money, if not serious wealth. But then his cocaine habit drove him to a crisis. He was referred to City Roads, a 24/7 drug rehab charity located in Islington, near the Angel tube station. A small outfit, it had a dozen beds in which to treat drug addicts and rehabilitate them. This was his saving.

He came out of rehab and found that the magazines did not want him back. It was one thing to be on drugs but quite another to be plunged into a crisis and need treatment. So he had to explore other avenues. That was how he met Roddy. There was a lot of money to be made, Roddy told Adrian, if he could get pictures of the famous in compromising positions. It was every paparazzi's dream to catch a famous singer with someone other than his wife, or the police commissioner's car parked outside a brothel. Footballers were even better quarry. The newspapers paid enormous sums, multiples of what magazines did, if they could run a scandal.

This was how Adrian became Roddy's instrument.

He knew that Matt Drummond had a complete hatred of Terence Harcourt. The origins of this hatred went way back to the 1970s when Terence was a junior minister in the Board of Trade in charge of competition policy, and he thwarted Matt in one of his takeovers.

Matt got what he wanted from the Tories who came back into power when the government fell, but he never forgave Terence who had refused a large bribe to bend Matt's way. Terence did not need the money, thanks to his wife's largesse, and so could afford his left-wing conscience.

Matt Drummond began a whispering campaign against Terence. He'd had a tip-off about some sexual peccadilloes of Terence but was short of evidence. Once Labour came back to power, Matt could not wait any longer. He had let his papers hint for some years off and on that Terence was a paedophile. Now he went big with a full Sunday spread. Terence sued, and the case was rumbling on through the courts. Roddy had taken on the job of finding the evidence and this was where Adrian came in. He promised he would get some evidence on Terence though he would not say how. Roddy did not care about Adrian's methods or his morals. He wanted the bullet to get at Terence Harcourt.

Roddy looked at the pictures now with rising excitement. 'This is dynamite. But it is filth.'

'Yup. You buying?'

'I think so. Can I talk to the boss?'

'Only from here. Now that you've seen the pictures, I can't let you out of my sight.'

'You can trust me, Andrew.'

'No way, if you can't even remember my first name.'

'But you have two first names, you bastard.'

'Be that as it may, you call your lord and master from here. And don't give me any bullshit about not knowing where he is. He checked into the Ritz at eleven this morning.'

'How do you know?'

'Never you mind. Call him.'

At that moment Roddy's phone rang. It was Christine. Roddy put a hand to one ear and shouted, 'What is it?'

Christine and Roddy had been lovers briefly, long ago in their Stalinist youth, when Christine was ready to go to Vietnam to fight for the Viet Cong and Roddy was the intellectual of their local branch. They never spoke of it.

'Is Matt Drummond in town?'

'Happens he is. Why is everyone interested in his whereabouts?'

'Don't worry. Thanks. You're good as always.'

Christine rang off. Adrian looked at him with contempt.

'Now will you call that American toad and get me a proper price?'

Roddy had no choice.

12.30 p.m. London

As soon as Ian got back to his office, he ran into Edward Shorthead, the young tousle-haired editor of *The News*. Young only when compared to Ian, of course. He had been in journalism for some twenty-five years now and had built a reputation for combining quality journalism with fiery political editorials. He had revived the fortunes of *The News* and made old Marcus very happy indeed.

Edward was clearly agitated. He needed to speak to Ian.

'Ian, good to see you. Are you free for lunch?'

'Yes, of course, but isn't it a little premature?' Ian gestured hopelessly at the work that awaited him.

'No, I need a rather long chat with you. How about I buy you lunch at the Garrick? You are a member, aren't you?'

The Garrick was the club that most journalists and actors frequented. Located in a street with its own name, it had stood on the edge of Covent Garden for decades. It was a convivial watering hole for its members, who were partial to long boozy lunches. Ian had gone off the club ever since the public fracas about women not being admitted to its membership. He had not minded as long as the issue had not been raised but now he felt a trifle embarrassed.

'I don't like its misogynism,' he said now.

'Oh, sod that. I have to speak to you about this mad policy Harry White is pursuing on Libya. You know his mind, I am sure, and you were so brilliant on Vietnam, as we all remember. You can tell me how to think about it.'

Ian may have escaped Rodney's big lunch but there was no way out of Edward's invitation. Libya was beginning to look worrisomely like Vietnam thirty years ago. British prime ministers had always had a weakness for things American and especially the White House, regardless of who the president was, or which party was in power.

The way Ian looked at it, the Americans were constantly looking for cheap and reliable suppliers of petrol to drive their big, fancy cars. Towards the end of the Second World War, they had made a deal with the Saudi princes, that in return for American protection, they would supply oil to America for ever. Soon the entire Arab Middle East and North Africa were being used as a source of oil. The Arab princes and sheikhs were happy to pocket the millions of dollars that the Americans spent on petrol. Then came Colonel Gaddafi who overthrew King Idris of Libya. He was a fire-breathing Arab nationalist. There had been others like him before—Egypt's Nasser, for instance. They wanted to fight Israel and help the cause of Palestine. Nasser was defeated soon enough but Gaddafi had oil, and hence a guaranteed flow of money. Soon, he became the leading anti-American Arab leader. When oil prices quadrupled in 1973, he became even more of a nuisance, and the Americans began to look for some way to remove him, or at least contain his influence.

At this point, a young English policewoman called Yvonne Fletcher was killed outside the Libyan embassy. It was suspected that the bullet which struck her had been fired from inside the embassy. Then followed the crash of Pan Am 103 in the Scottish village of Lockerbie, where again Libyans were among the suspects.

Currently, the long running soap opera of Colonel Gaddafi and the US was having another one of its episodes. The president was convinced that Gaddafi was trying to wean the Saudi princes away from the US by getting them to endorse extremist policies. If the Saudis went against the Americans, the oil market would explode. This was not a risk the Americans could take lightly. There were accusations of terrorist activity originating in Palestine but with Libyan financial support. It was a murky issue with many doubts about the bona fides of the CIA, which was issuing the reports that named Libya as the source.

But the Americans had little patience. They needed a *casus belli* one way or another. Then a military satellite picked up activities in the Libyan desert which looked suspiciously like preparations for a nuclear explosion. They traced the nuclear connection to Pakistan, where there was a sizable technological and scientific expertise. It was obvious that blueprints of nuclear bomb technology had passed from Pakistan to Libya. The CIA picked up contacts in Zurich where the deal had been closed. As far as they were concerned, there was a clear need to do something quick and effective.

Harry White was in the loop from the very beginning. Given the death of Yvonne Fletcher and the Lockerbie connection, he knew that the British public would back him on any tough action against Libya. Some in the US State Department wanted to go to the UN Security Council. But Harry advised the president against it. By the time the Security Council had a debate and came to its usual inconclusive resolution, which would then be vetoed by France, China or Russia, Libya would have moved the facilities elsewhere and the element of surprise would be lost. He urged immediate bombing of the site; they could face the UN later.

'Come, there is no time to lose. I have told Andrew Merton we will meet him there. You know Andrew, don't you?' Edward grabbed Ian by the shoulder and hurried him along.

'By reputation, though not personally. I read his book on post-

Marxism way back when no one was even thinking about it. But since then I have only read him in the weeklies, not between hard covers.' Ian was trying furiously to recall what he had read most recently by Andrew Merton.

'I think Andrew is one of the great thinkers we have today. Harry White has inducted him into his Millennium Commission. I guess he hopes Andrew will write the report for him.'

'If the Archbishop and the Chief Rabbi allow him to get a word in edgewise, you mean.' Ian's cynicism was intact.

'They can do the three-minute package on Thought for the Day, but surely not any sustained thinking. Doesn't God always get in the way?'

'So you think the Millennium Commission report won't be just the Thought for the Day spread over three hundred pages?' Ian was not letting go that easily.

'You have to ask Andrew that when we see him in a minute or two. Actually, it's a happy chance that Andrew is free for lunch. He just called me. We've known each other since our college days, so we keep in touch as and when we have the time.'

They were in the hall of the Garrick now. It was small but impressive, with its splendid sweeping staircase and brilliant portraits of actors and writers from the past. They were now getting up to the bar where Andrew Merton was waiting for them. He must have arrived earlier and found someone to buy him a drink. The man he was with, Robin Capstone, was in Ian's view an obsessive bore. He had had a brief career as MP and even became a junior minister in a previous Labour government. But his hopes of going higher up had been frustrated. He had lost his seat and no one had thought of putting him up for a peerage. So he had recycled himself as a columnist and for reasons Ian could not fathom, editors and publishers kept giving him space to display his prejudices on any and every occasion. Perhaps the only thing to be said for Robin was that he could write twelve hundred words on any given topic in quick time, and hard-pressed editors love anyone who can do that.

'So you have found yourself a drink, Andrew. Thanks for looking after my guest, Robin. You all know Ian, I take it. Ian, what will you have? Robin, Andrew, are you ready for a refill?' Edward took over the occasion immediately. He was, after all, the host.

'Thanks for agreeing to meet me at such short notice, Edward. A very strange thing happened. I was supposed to be given lunch by the PM and we were going to have a meeting of the Millennium Commission. At the last minute his diary secretary, some daft woman called Sarah, cancelled it. Apparently she had got his dates completely wrong. Such bloody incompetence, I tell you. There's a lot to improve in our bureaucracy.' Andrew was quick to get that off his chest.

'Anyway, it's Harry White's loss and our gain, Andrew. I bet the food is far better here than at No. 10. Thanks a lot,' Edward said, collecting the drinks from the bartender.

'Mind you, it could be like a diplomatic cold. I recall when Henry Kissinger was in Pakistan in the early seventies, I think it was 1971 but I could be wrong, there was a news item that he could not attend the dinner given in his honour by President Yahya Khan. It turned out later that he had hopped across to Beijing to meet Mao. That was the beginning of the Nixon-Mao relationship. Mind you, had he left without putting out a press release about it, no one would have noticed. So he was obviously giving a signal, don't you think?' Robin could go on like this forever.

'Let us hope Harry White has not hopped across to anywhere far away. Shall we go to our table? Why not join us, Robin, if you are not lunching with anyone in particular?' Edward asked, much to Ian's dismay.

'Thank you, Edward. You are a generous host and who knows, I might learn something from your discourse', replied Robin as he fell in with them.

12.30 p.m. London/10 Downing Street

The bastard. The filthy bastard. Christine was beside herself with rage. She had never liked Harry's arse-licking of Matt Drummond. It was not so much that years ago the Drummond rags had attacked her active role in the campaign for nuclear disarmament and pried into her private life. That had all been long forgotten. But Matt Drummond was a poisonous, evil person whose agenda was money, money, more money—and Matt Drummond. In the run up to the election, Harry had suddenly shifted his media strategy and opened a hotline to Matt. This had led to a big split in the campaign team. Christine was for the first time ranged against Harry and on the same side as Terence Harcourt. But Harry had talked her around by taking her off with him on an eight-day trip to the US. Their 'honeymoon', as he called it. He had wined and dined her in style. Oliver had protected them ferociously, provided perfect alibis. Even the White House staff had been squared so they could spend a night together in the Lincoln bedroom.

But when the sweetness continued after the election, Christine suspected that Harry's relationship with Matt Drummond wasn't just strategic. He might actually be in agreement with Matt. She looked for any chance to wrest Harry gently from his clutches. She encouraged him to talk to other papers like *The News* and *The Guardian*. Harry indulged her but she could never be sure.

So Matt Drummond was in town and in such a hurry that Harry had cancelled his big lunch to be with him. What were they up to? Christine started surfing her way around recent news to pick up clues to Matt Drummond's agenda.

12.35 p.m. London/The Slug and Lettuce, Docklands

'Two fifty,' said Roddy.

'No way. I want half a mil or there is no deal.'

'But we may not be able to use them. They are very close to the bone.'

'You'll use them alright. You may not print them in your papers but that is your lookout.'

'Ok. How about two fifty for use and three fifty if we publish them?'

'Don't be silly. You know you have been looking for this ever since your master shot off his mouth, especially with Terry's cases still pending against you. This will let you off the hook, and you know it. Half a mil. You have his permission, I can see that in your face. So pay up. Take your cut from someone else.'

'But we must have the negatives and we must have exclusive rights.'

'Leave all that school boy stuff, Roddy. Where do I pick up the cash?'

'Come with me.'

12.40 p.m. London/10 Downing Street

Sarah was on the phone all morning, trying to find people. The Archbishop was on his way to the lunch, and was not answering either his pager or his mobile. But the brilliant ladies at the Downing Street switchboard were legendary for their ability to track people down. Finally, Sarah got the message to him via the station announcer at Euston where he was to arrive from Manchester.

The Chief Rabbi and the Cambridge professor were mildly cross at their schedule being upset but Sarah was profusely apologetic, and the Very Important Persons turned out to be mortal and flexible. Despite the lateness of the call, Sarah's charm and a promise to reschedule the lunch soon satisfied them.

It was Barry Carrick (Hara Kiri as he was known to his less kind friends) who proved difficult to track down. His office thought he was at a seminar in University College London, after which he would come to Downing Street for lunch. But no one at UCL could help. His wife thought he was in Glasgow and was not going to be at their Norwich home until late that night. He did not believe in pagers or mobiles and did not send or receive emails. As a moral philosopher, he said he could ply his trade with the same tools as Thomas Aquinas. All he had to do was think.

And cheat on his wife. Sarah concluded that this was a classic case of a man with a mistress sending contradictory messages to his wife and his secretary. The simple rule used to be that you did not lie to your secretary even if you did not tell your wife the truth. Barry Carrick had gone one better. He had lied to both. The secretary, Sarah concluded, must be an ex-mistress.

It was five to one when Sarah gave up the hunt for Hara Kiri. Christine had said they would look after anyone who turned up for the lunch. Just having been inside 10 Downing Street would mollify their egos. Sarah, on the other hand, had to do something drastic to restore hers by buying some decent clothes in the lunch hour. She tidied up her already tidy office, left an email message for Christine, and dashed out the front door.

12.57 p.m. London

Harry and Oliver were going out via the back door. After some quick thinking, they had decided to let the plainclothes security guard drive Oliver's car while they both slumped back behind smoked windows. They were to get into the Ritz by a side door and then up a service lift to where Matt Drummond was waiting for them.

1.00 p.m. London/2.00 p.m. Vienna

Alan was waiting for lunch to finish. He was with Terence at the table where all the finance ministers were seated with their advisers. The Austrians combined German efficiency with a French love of good food and wine. No one seemed to be bothered that a tough working session was to start immediately after lunch.

Alan wanted the lunch to end so he could steal a few moments alone with Jo. Poor Jo. He had no status and was eating in the cafeteria along with the junior officials from the embassy, while Alan was in

the closed-off, posh area. Jo was a bit overwhelmed by his first
European Union encounter. This, plus the suddenness of Alan's
decision to leave Sarah for him, had made him giddy. Since the early
morning when they arrived at the VIP lounge in Heathrow, till they
got out of the car bringing them to the Imperial Palace where the
meeting was, Alan and he had been unable to keep their hands off
each other even for a second. Terence was quite liberal and let Alan
sit with Jo, although they had to talk the policy through. Alan had
promised Terence that once they got into the meeting, he would stay
with him throughout the day.

Alan knew all the highways and byways of EC/EU budgetary
negotiations. Olives, he had told Terence, were going to occupy most
of the afternoon. Cyprus had olives and so had Greece, Italy, France,
Spain and Portugal. They wanted Cyprus in, but couldn't face the
glut of olives which would result when Cyprus joined and began to
enjoy the Common Agricultural Policy subsidies.

By the time the main course arrived, all the jokes about extra virgin
olive oil had been exhausted. There remained the prospect of a hard
slog. Alan just wanted the lunch to get over. Stuff the olives.

1.15 p.m. London/The Garrick

'So tell me now, Ian. Can you make any sense of Harry White's foreign
policy?' Edward wanted Ian to sing for his lunch.

'Why? What is wrong with his foreign policy?' Andrew asked, ever
the loyalist.

'Don't start Edward on that one, please. We will be here until after
dessert and he still won't have finished. In brief, Edward is upset
about the impending crisis in Libya,' Ian interposed.

'Surely the crisis is not so much in Libya but somewhere in the
mid Atlantic. With our so called special relationship, I mean. Harry
is not like Anthony Eden. He's unlikely to get on the wrong side of
the Americans, though I grant you the Americans were in the right

then, one of the rare occasions in the post-war years when they have done something right in the Middle East. However...'

Before Robin could go any further on his excursus through history, Ian interrupted.

'You have to understand that Harry is a man who sees the world in black and white. There is truth, freedom and liberty on our side and out there is nothing but darkness. His friend President Rob Roy is a cynical man and will use Harry as a shield if he can. Harry thinks this is a just war against Libya but Rob Roy only wants to look after his Saudi friends and their ample oil supply.'

'No, I think you misunderstand our PM. I know he is aware of the Christian doctrine of just war, but that is beside the point. He is a man of rational analytical habits and he is immensely well read for a politician, I tell you. He was asking me the other day to give him references on the history of Islam and of the schism between the Sunnis and Shias. I am sure he knows what he is doing.'

'In my view he is the most right-wing leader the People's Party has had since Ramsay MacDonald. How he became a leader when we have a perfectly good and solid man like Terence Harcourt is beyond me. Why doesn't the party get rid of him? He just does what Matt Drummond tells him to do.'

'I think that is going a bit far, Robin. Even I, critical as I am of Harry White, would not agree with you there. I think there is something to what Ian says about a Manichean world view, all black and white, Good versus Evil,' Edward intervened.

'It has to do with his Christian beliefs...'

Ian was about to explain when suddenly Andrew said, 'Speaking of Christian beliefs, look who is here.'

The Archbishop of Canterbury was approaching their table to say hello to Andrew.

'What a rotten shower, eh? So you ended up here as well,' Andrew remarked.

The Archbishop shook his hand, silently nodding assent, and moved on to his table.

1.20 p.m. London/The Ritz

Harry said he would have a dry Martini American style—very dry and with an olive. The waiter in Matt's suite came back with a perfect specimen of its kind. Dry, with just a dash of vermouth, and a fat green olive staring up at Harry from the bottom of the glass. Matt had his pint of lager, as always, and Oliver for once stuck to tomato juice. He had decided that someone would have to stay sober.

Oliver held up his glass now and decided it was best to start the proceedings.

'Cheers, and welcome to London. How's tricks, Matt?'

'Awful. Margaret has decided to go public with our divorce and she is going to fight for control of King Korn and half of my assets.'

Clearly, a split of his assets upset Matt more than the end of his forty-year marriage.

'Why does she want your money? I thought she didn't care even for her own,' Harry asked.

'Well, you know Margaret has cancer and has only a couple of years to live. She found out about Asha—and now she thinks if she dies and I get her share, it will all go to Asha and her daughter. She can't bear the thought. So she wants a divorce and half my assets. She wants to give it all away to charity.'

Asha Chan was the daughter of a Chinese father and an Indian mother from Malaysia. She was a bright young tax lawyer when Matt first met her and very much his match in her love of money. Like Matt, she came from a poor family, though much poorer than Matt could imagine. And she was very clear about her goal: she wanted to amass a large fortune as soon as she could and towards this end, she would strain every nerve to avoid paying tax. Tax law was not just a profession for her; it was her religion. She took up Matt's tax problems with a relish few could understand. The more complex the problem, the happier she was. She had rapidly risen in her Chambers, the first woman and the only non-English barrister to reach the number two position.

Matt's life trajectory was very different, as Harry well knew. He had known Margaret since their school days. They had married the day after they graduated and joined the radio station her father owned. Matt was a simple farmer's boy while Margaret was sophisticated and urbane. Her father used to take her to Europe for their holidays while Matt had to help his dad with the dairy cattle.

Someday, he had thought, I will get to Europe and show them.

And indeed he had. Working in the local radio station, he had showed a flair for business that surprised them all. He saw early on that even small towns in the American Midwest would soon have their own TV stations. He worked out an ingenious deal with the local bank and its New York counterpart, and won a franchise from CBS for their local station at a hideously high price. But Matt knew that if he could have even two hours of local broadcasting time, the advertising revenue would make it worthwhile. He saw that it wasn't the thirteen-and-a-half minutes of programming that was the heart of TV, but the one-and-a-half minutes of commercials. So he added fifteen minutes of local news to the CBS news and soon expanded that to thirty minutes. He helped Lew, Margaret's father, buy up other local TV stations and start new ones. Soon the revenue began pouring in from local business dying to advertise on TV.

Lew Drew had no sons, only two daughters, of whom Cherry headed for the bright lights of St. Louis and Chicago, while Margaret chose to stay in Cutler City, Kansas. Margaret loved broadcasting. She loved the arts, the music, the culture she could deliver from radio. TV bored her. She thought it was a shallow, brash medium. But she loved Matt and admired his business acumen.

Not as much as Lew did, though. In Matt, he found the son he had always wanted. He treated Margaret much more like a daughter-in-law once Matt arrived on the scene. Lew was an old newspaper buff who had drifted into radio. Within five years of their marriage, Matt and Margaret had made him a multimedia owner—newspapers, radio, TV. It was only after Lew died that Matt ventured abroad. On their honeymoon in Paris, he had noticed how badly run the local radio and TV were. But they were state owned. So he cast about for newspapers to buy. To be on the safe side, he started buying up English newspapers—small-town newspapers, miles away from the glare of London publicity. These local sheets made money because of advertisements. They had small staff for the local news stories and bought in a lot from the bigger services such as Reuters and AP. But there were more advertisement pages than news.

Then came Radio Caroline, the pirate radio broadcast from a ship anchored in the North Sea. This was the time of the pop revolution, with the Beatles and the Rolling Stones rocking the baby boomers. Radio Caroline could play non-stop pop, unlike the BBC. This broke the BBC monopoly of radio, and private commercial radio became big business. Privatization was soon to become even more popular. On both sides of the Atlantic, the Conservative Revolution began to triumph. Matt took full advantage of this. He was well known as a large donor to the Republican Party in America, and now he also began to give secretly to the British Conservative Party. The other Margaret became his sought after prize. He wanted to champion her cause and link up with her friend, Ronnie.

But Margaret, his wife and lover of all arts, especially music and theatre, began to see in the free market philosophy everything that she disdained. She could see that provincial theatres and small-town art galleries and museums were losing their meagre support; they had to beg for commercial sponsorship. Margaret had the money. The company was, after all, her father's and she had inherited it, though Lew had given Matt a thirty per cent share.

As Matt chased newspapers, radio and TV stations, Margaret helped out small-town repertories, struggling artists and writers. She put money in the Lew Drew Foundation. While Matt came across the Atlantic to buy up British media, Margaret came to admire British theatre. She helped out young companies by purchasing theatres and leasing them back at peppercorn rent. Matt made money, Margaret gave it away. Matt thought of money as the one thing he never had as a farmer's boy in the prairies. Margaret had grown up with money in every sense of the word. As she got older, her fortune got larger and larger. She did not know what to do with it.

But a shrewd instinct told her not to let go of her share in the Lew Drew News Corporation. Matt begged and cajoled and finally persuaded her sister to sell him her fifteen per cent share, making him the owner of forty-five per cent of the company. Margaret, thanks to Lew, continued to have a majority share. That was one thing she would not discuss with Matt. She had no intention of letting him control LDNC or King Korn, as it was affectionately called in the prairies.

Then Matt got obsessive about tax. He could not bear to pay income tax or corporation tax. He began to live on his yacht, *El Dorado*, shunning permanent residence in any one tax regime. Margaret did not mind visiting him, but the idea of choosing a home with the sole purpose of tax avoidance appalled her. They had no children to keep them together and it wasn't long before they began to drift apart, meeting only when they were together on one of their many company boards.

That was how things were when a beautiful, dark-eyed half-Chinese, half-Indian woman beckoned Matt closer. He was more than willing, though he was clear that he would not divorce Margaret. Asha knew that; she concurred that the tax loss would be horrendous. She had her daughter Matasha, and Matt stayed married.

Harry had known about Matt's pending divorce. Elisabet was a great friend of Margaret's and had told Harry how Margaret had promised her company a large endowment in her will. The prospect of Matt being left with only a couple of billion did not seem such a tragedy to Harry. Still, he thought he'd better take an interest.

'So what are you going to do? Play for time and hope that Margaret goes before the divorce comes through?'

'Jesus, Harry. You are more cynical than I thought. But that's it, really. I have to fight it for as long as I can. I could do without the hassle. But to hell with this mess. Let's eat.'

A table had been laid for four in Matt's suite. As Harry was wondering who the fourth place was for, Asha came in punctually, on the dot of one thirty. She was simply but expensively dressed in a purple Karl Lagerfield top and trousers that showed her dark skin to great advantage. Her long hair and high forehead atop a compact torso made her look taller than she was. She shook hands with Harry and Oliver, pecked Matt lightly on the lips and sat down.

'To business then,' said Oliver.

'I want you to throw Scotland,' Matt said.

'What do you mean?'

'Lose the election. Let the Nats win.'

The Scottish Nationalists were beginning to irk Harry. He had heard Gideon being grilled on *Today* by John Humphrys. Now Matt was bringing them up as well.

'Whatever for? That would be madness. What is more, it would cause a lot of problems among our Scottish MPs. If they lose up there, they will lose in the next general election. I doubt if we could keep our large majority.'

'Or any majority,' Oliver added.

'Well it's like this. We have looked at the Scotland Act. Your mob is bound to put the tax up and go on a spending spree.'

Scotland's autonomy was rather restricted since all the major powers were retained at Westminster. After much debate, the

Scottish Executive had been allowed to alter the basic rate of income tax by three pence in the pound up or down.

'And you think the Nats won't?'

'We know they won't. Their strategy is to cut the tax rate by three per cent. Spend the money and cause a budgetary crisis by running a deficit.'

'How does that help you?'

'Well, for one thing, your mob will want control over the media and will want to promote local, Scottish owned companies. On top of that, they are still Old Labour and hate me passionately. Anything they can do to punish me for my support of the poll tax, they will.'

'But hang on. They can't just do anything they like. They are subject to Westminster.'

'Culture is a partially devolved subject and media will be covered within that. You retain the control of telecommunications at Westminster but that doesn't help me. What with a likely referral to the Monopolies and Mergers Commission down here, restrictions on cross board ownership up there, and an extra three pence in tax, I can't afford your lot in Scotland.'

'It's not easy to lose Scotland. In any case, my Cabinet will revolt, Terence especially. Scotland is his fiefdom. He wants his own man to be first minister, and Gideon is dying to have the job. He is all set to resign down here.'

'We calculate that a Labour victory in Scotland will cost Matt's group fifty-five million pounds extra immediately and seventy-five million pounds in the long run,' Asha intervened. She had listened quietly thus far. She now spoke with confidence and a clinical precision that left little scope for argument.

'And I stand to lose my leadership to Terence, and the next general election to the Tories, if we lose Scotland.'

'Don't worry about Terence. We can take care of him.'

'What do you mean?' Oliver perked up.

'We have enough on him to destroy him. If we publish the stuff, he will have to resign immediately.'

'What on earth are you talking about, Matt?' Harry was beginning to lose his cool.

'I will say no more. But if it is Terence you are worried about, rest easy. We can put him out of any leadership stakes overnight, as and when we choose.'

'You mean blackmail?' Oliver asked.

'No, just investigative journalism. Remember the motto of *The Herald*—Truth Holds No Terror For Us.'

'And when do you intend to do this?' Harry asked.

'As soon as we reckon you require it. Our only concern is to protect you when you throw Scotland.'

Harry was appalled and fascinated. Getting rid of Terence would make his life so much easier. He would lose a Cabinet minister who was admired all across Europe but also a bitter rival who had never been a friend. Terence with his conventional marriage and his three snotty children had a lot of appeal inside the party. He controlled Scotland and was laying careful plans to challenge Harry the moment he faltered.

Harry was aware that Terence and his wife Dorothy hosted a lot of parties at 11 Downing Street for MPs and their wives or partners. Dorothy made Terence send each one of them a birthday card, even the spouses. She remembered their children's names, and sent them birthday presents. Elisabet, bless her soul, had little time for the MPs or their partners. Her parties were full of actors, pop singers and sculptors—luvvies and druggies, as *The Herald* called them. Losing Scotland would definitely lead to a challenge to Harry's leadership. But if Terence were out of the way, no one else would dare to take him on. Harry was tempted, sorely tempted.

But then, he thought, why should he do Matt's dirty work? He had received a lot of help from Matt, no doubt. Including an easy provision of escorts. But now he was the prime minister with one of the largest majorities ever. Matt had no other friend in the party and the Tories were in a shambolic state with the smarmy, oily Peter Portugal as their leader.

Harry tried to catch Oliver's eye but for some reason, Oliver was looking intently at his plate and refusing to look up. Then Harry twigged. Oliver was not eating, but he had placed his knife across his fork. The message was clear—no deal.

'Sorry, Matt, I can't oblige you on this one. Winning is part of politics. Leaders have to win elections, especially big ones. This will be the first Scottish election and we owe it to the party and to Stan's memory to win it. What I can promise to do for you is make sure they behave themselves. You would have observed that we have weeded out all the troublemakers from our candidates' list. We will bully them about taxation, perhaps make a promise of no extra taxation. But win we must. The risks attached to losing Scotland are too high. Of course, we can't be sure that we will win, but I have to lead from the front, whether I like it or not—and you know how I loathe Scotland and the Scots.'

Matt didn't respond, neither did he bother to hide his annoyance. He could never understand why politicians were so naïve. He had the perfect plan to get rid of Terence and shore up Harry's leadership in the party. All for the price of a provincial election in which the turnout was bound to be under thirty per cent if the previous record was anything to go by. If the Nats were to win, they would follow an adventurous course, but they would be completely ineffective. That would suit Matt, and if they got an independent Scotland, even better. In Matt's experience, the smaller the country, the easier it was to buy it. Anyway, he had no intention of abandoning his plan. He would have to bring extra pressure on Harry somehow. Perhaps the new dirt on Terence would be the trigger. But for now, he had to seem reasonable.

'Fair enough, Harry. Win some, lose some, that's what I say. I can see that you have to be seen to be doing your best. But I hope you won't mind if I don't wish you good luck on this one.'

'Fairly put, Matt. No hard feelings. I know how much you have helped me along the way and within limits, I am happy to oblige, as you know. I did help you on your German bid and put in a word with the president about your takeover bid for *The New York Times*.' Harry began to account for all the big pay offs.

'Don't mention it. I won't speak to you of Scotland again. There will no doubt be other fish to fry.'

There seemed to be little point in lingering. Matt was a spartan eater at lunch time and so was Harry. Oliver got on his phone and told the car to come round to the same place, then they were on their way, leaving Matt and Asha together. Would they work out the tax consequences of the lunch at the table or on the four poster in the suite, Oliver wondered as they got back into the car.

1.30 p.m. London/Knightsbridge

Sarah did not have much time as she wandered around Harvey Nicholls, but she knew she had the money. Buying an outfit for later that day for a posh do, albeit in a directors' box at a football match in Glasgow, was the main thing. She chose a sleek black dress with a halter neck which would leave her shoulders bare and would be easy to slip off, if and when the moment came. That done, she bought a sober pastel pink shirt and a matching light tweed skirt for the next day in Belfast and Dublin. After all, the day would be spent with the prime minister rather than with Harry. That left only the crucial night garment. It had to be sheer and seductive, if only for the short time it would stay on. Sarah found a silver-grey nightdress, diaphanous and with a floral design, which would show her cleavage to advantage. Oh yes, and a spare pair of shoes and tights, and extra make-up. It was hectic, but she was in and out in a little less than an hour and a half.

At the last minute, she added a small bottle of Samsara to her purchases, feeling rather wicked as she did so. But what the hell. This was her first trip with Harry. She kept saying Harry to herself, just to get used to it. She would have to figure out for herself when to say PM and when to get informal with him.

And to hell with Alan, she thought, as she tried to flag down a taxi. She felt alive and vibrant.

2.00 p.m. London/Drew House, Docklands

Fleet Street had been abandoned by the print media. Most of the newspaper offices were now housed in the beautiful tall buildings which had come up in the Docklands. Matt Drummond had commissioned a forty-story steel and glass building as the principal location for the Lew Drew News Corporation. It had been designed by Norman Foster to look like a giant corn on the cob as a tribute to its Kansas roots.

On the thirty-eighth floor of Drew House, Rodney Page was deep in an editorial conference with the editor of *The Herald*, Alexis (Lex) Pritchard. Matt had picked Lex up from a local newspaper in King's Lynn and brought him to London as his latest editor. Lex's main attribute was a total lack of taste or backbone. He was willing to do whatever Matt asked him to do. He even called up every day to check: was Matt happy with the tabloid's front page, the nooky page and the editorial page, such as it was? Lex was proud of what he called his nipple count. He had to outclass his rivals in nude and semi-nude photographs every day; his four million readers depended on that.

But this time even Lex was taken aback. Rodney had brought in Adrian Andrew's photographs. He had cleared with Matt that they would pay the half million. The cash had been delivered early by the LDNC emissary in a smart leather case. Adrian had counted the contents of one pile and then the number of piles. He had worked in casinos and knew how to count cash quickly. He seemed happy and then without so much as a thank you, he swept it up and left. Lex saw to it that Rodney escorted Adrian out by the back door and that no one saw him.

Now there were just the two of them. The pictures were disgusting. How Adrian had been able to shoot such intimate photographs, Lex couldn't figure out. Rodney seemed to be sure, Lex did not know how, that the pictures were authentic. He kept on about the black mole visible on the hip and how he had seen it once, while playing rugby years ago with Terence.

'Jesus, we can't print these. We are a family newspaper.' Lex always had his hypocrisy armour on.

'The choice, as you know lad, is not thine to make. All we do is obey orders and it is the order we await. Our maker knows best and I am sure even at this moment, he is working out the answer.'

2.00 p.m. Glasgow/Strathclyde Police HQ

Chief Constable Douglas Mackie was looking forward to the evening. The prime minister was going to be in Glasgow and he would get to meet him at the dinner this evening. He wanted to bend Harry White's ear about how wrong Glasgow's image was and how much it had improved, in terms of crime especially, under his leadership. He had hoped to have him tour one of the police stations but the PM's timetable was too crowded for that. So the Old Firm game it had to be.

Douglas was a rugby fan and Hampden Park was more his scene. In his considered opinion, rugby fans were well behaved while soccer fans were animals. Hopefully, they would behave themselves today, though if they didn't, his team was ready for anything. Superintendent Richard Erskine was in charge of the G district of the Strathclyde police area and Ibrox was part of his territory. Richard was a fine officer, so Douglas Mackie had nothing to worry about.

His phone rang. It was Richard Erskine himself.

'Richard, I have just been thinking how nice the evening is going to be, thanks to your efficient control.' Douglas didn't wish to rub it in that it was he and not Richard who had been included in the dinner guest list, but he couldn't help it.

'I am sure, sir. I wanted to report that the RUC just called and told me that they saw Red boarding the flight for Glasgow. You know, Redvers McGann of the Carson Irregulars.'

'Do you think he is coming to us at Ibrox?'

'Well, if he does, we will keep an eye on him. I will post his picture at every entrance to the stadium and tell our boys to be on the look out. He hasn't done anything as yet to be arrested, but we have to be vigilant. He is probably coming for the after game punch up, which will follow, no doubt, as night follows day. The game always attracts coachloads of supporters from Northern Ireland as you know, sir. But we are used to that. Leave it with me.'

'I always do, Richard, with full confidence.'

Now why would Red come to the game if it was not to cause trouble and what kind of trouble was he planning? Douglas prided himself on his university degree and his superior brain power. This development, he reflected, required some serious thought. It was more than just policing.

2.15 p.m. London/The Ritz

Within minutes of Harry and Oliver's departure, Asha took over. Matt could never figure out how such a clever, brainy woman, barrister at law, first class honours from the LSE, knew so much about sex. When Margaret and he made love in their young days many years ago, it was fast, hurried and quick. Just doing it was fun. They knew little about foreplay and knew of no positions except the only one they thought was not indecent. It was some years before Matt realized it was called the missionary position. By the late sixties, when erotic magazines could be published in the US, they had lost their urge to explore anything new. They were far too busy and usually retired exhausted to bed. Matt never regretted this because sex did not interest him.

Until he met Asha. She was his junior by thirty years. He was old enough to be her father. Indeed, he was older than her father would have been had he been alive. But Asha seemed to know precisely how to please older men, or at least, one old man. She recognized his hesitations, his fear of failure, and his seeming disdain for sex which arose from this fear. Matt used prostitutes when he felt the need for sex; he did not have to pretend with them and they did not mind, nor would they talk. Asha was different. She had this knack of lovemaking which seemed to make it last for eternity. Yet, each time they did it in London on a normal working day, she managed to make it to her next appointment on time. She would swiftly undress both of them and get him going exactly as she wanted. She played the little kitten, the lethal Lolita. Thank God Matt did not have a daughter. It came pretty close to incest, the way they played their games.

Gradually, Matt's heartbeat returned to normal. Asha was waiting for this moment to slip out of his arms. As she picked up her clothes one by one and put them on, he watched her, free to think of other things.

'So what do you think, Ash?'

'Miserable sod. After all you have done for him.'

'But what about Terence and the pictures?'

'I say publish them. If Harry won't throw Scotland, let's help him lose. We publish those pictures and they can kiss Scotland goodbye. So Harry stays clear and we get Terence. Harry will come round in good time.'

'Do we publish or do we threaten Terence?'

'Threatening Terence will only mean he will resign and the Great British Public will never know why. It will all leak out slowly and you could hardly publish your evidence after that. We don't care about Terence. We want to lose Scotland and this is the best way.'

'Good thinking. I wish I could get that bastard Harry, though.'

'But who else is there, if he goes as well? No one will elect Pamela now.'

'Yes, you're right. What a waste of money Pamela was. After all that we invested in her, she flopped as a Cabinet minister.'

'I say embarrass Harry, don't bring him down. Show him who's boss.'

Now in her full barrister gear, Asha bent to kiss Matt deeply one last time and left. He allowed himself a couple of minutes to recover, then forced himself to get out of bed. He had work to do.

2.30 p.m. London/Drew House

Anthony Otto-Trevelyan was back from his lunch at the Garrick. He liked the club and could rely on meeting other members of his profession there. Thank heavens it still excluded women, or Elisabet White would have been there. Today, by chance, he'd had a sudden call from the Archbishop to say he was available for that much promised, frequently arranged but cancelled lunch. Apparently, Downing Street had stood him up. Some incompetent secretary had booked a lunch though Harry White was occupied elsewhere. The Archbishop could not stop talking about it. Anthony tried to cheer him up by saying the food was far better at the Garrick than at 10 Downing Street. He knew; he had tried both. But the Archbishop refused to be mollified. He was going to complain to the Cabinet secretary, he said.

As the editor of *The Daily Chronicle*, the leading daily, indeed the establishment newspaper, Anthony kept an eye on everything. He made a mental note to check on the PM's appointments. He smelt something fishy about such a sudden cancellation. For the moment, he focused on persuading the Archbishop to write a three-part essay on Ecumenism and the Church. He wanted to know how he evaluated the Pope who had had such a long innings.

After lunch, just as he was getting to his thirty-sixth floor office in Drew House in the LDNC building, he ran into Vera Drinkwater. Vera was an old hag, with her tobacco stained teeth, bulging eyes popping out of a horn-rimmed pair of glasses, and a beaky nose to boot—but she was the nation's agony aunt and was paid a fortune (twice Anthony's salary) by *The Herald*. Vera, of course, insisted on kissing 'dear Tony'. Anthony could not stand such vulgar abbreviations, nor the unwanted physical contact. It was an affectation people had picked up from the French, and Anthony had no time for the French. He wondered what he could find to say to Vera on the short ride up on the elevator. Luckily, Vera could not stop telling him how thrilled she was to be invited to Elisabet White's opening night at the National and the party afterwards at No. 10. Vera loved Elisabet and adored Harry and thought Anthony should stop being horrid to the PM. Anthony let out a deep sigh as he got out, leaving Vera to go up two floors more. Just then, his mobile rang. It was Matt.

'O.T., I have some news for you.'

Somehow Matt could not call Anthony by his double-barrelled last name and he knew Anthony hated being called Tony (as did Vera, of course). So he had settled on O.T. as an abbreviation that was novel, and Anthony had not been quick enough to take umbrage.

'Surely you are not going into journalism, Lord Drummond.' This was the one joke Matt allowed against himself.

'Listen, I want you to publish a simple factual report that the prime minister had lunch with me today at the Ritz. Don't make much of it, just report it.'

'So that is why the Archbishop had his lunch cancelled at such short notice?'

'I would not know about that. You can spin it if you like.'

'What if they deny it?'

'A couple of grainy photographs of the PM getting into and out of a side entrance at the Ritz are on their way to you in a plain brown envelope.'

'Brilliant. Will do. Why are you back in London?'

'I am staying here for a couple of days, but that's not printable.'

'Understood.'

A small factual paragraph deep inside, maybe on the Parliament page, and perhaps a diary item about the Archbishop's cancelled lunch. That would do the job, Anthony thought. The wise in Westminster village would grasp the connection. Though he'd better spell it out to Peter Portugal so he could use it at PM's question time. Being a Tory was hard work. Anthony sighed.

2.40 p.m. London/Drew House

'Lex?' It was Matt.

'Yes, boss.'

'Go with it.'

'Do we tip them off?'

'No, let them see it in the early edition.'

'Understood.'

Lex began to think he hated his job. He could see Rodney's eyes light up. That filthy gossipmonger. He thought about the front page and the four-page spread with its slab of purple prose. Then the editorial with its sanctimonious humbug about family values. Lex could do it in his sleep. But he had better bring Vera into the picture or there would be hell to pay. After all, Vera was in charge of the nation's morals.

4.00 p.m. Vienna/The Hofburg

The subject of all this attention was bored. They had sat there for an hour now, the good lunch almost forgotten. Terence was sick of olives and all people who grew, stored, shipped or ate them in solid or liquid form.

In international law, only that part of Cyprus that was ruled by Greece had recognition as a legitimate state. The Turkish part was recognized by Turkey alone. The rivalry between Greece and Turkey was ancient and Cyprus was a bone of contention. If you look at a map, Cyprus is nearer to Turkey than Greece. But for many years Cyprus was a British colony and the rival Ottoman Empire had its capital in Istanbul. So the British kept the Turks out and let the Greeks flourish in Cyprus. Greece itself was a colony of the Ottoman Empire and became free only in the late nineteenth century. During the time that Cyprus was a colony, Greece dreamt of taking it over. But when it tried to do so after Cyprus became free, all hell broke loose. Turkey intervened by sending an army. When the fighting died down, Cyprus got divided into two, one Greek and the other Turkish. This problem had to be resolved before Cyprus could join the European Community, but it was so difficult that the negotiators had decided to leave it for a while. As committees are prone to do, they invented another problem which could be an even more divisive issue. This was the problem of Cyprus olives.

Every country within the European Community received protection for its farmers in the form of the Common Agricultural Policy. Farmers could grow the crop of their choice, and their surplus produce would be bought off them. The farmers of course overproduced because the price they got was way above the international price of what they grew. The result was mountains of wheat and butter, and lakes of wine. Now, with Cprus, they were about to get an olive island. The only issue was, who would pay. The cost of purchasing surplus Cyprus olives without taking any money away from the other olive growers of Europe exercised everybody's minds. Dark olives and green olives, olives on trees and olives in storage, olive oil of various degrees of virginity.

The French and Italian delegations wanted all the adjustments to come from the Greek quota. But Greece was the poorest of the olive growers in the EC, its national income was below the income of Portugal and Spain. Thankfully, Ireland, thought Terence, was not able to grow olives. The three poor countries wanted the two rich ones to bear the burden; the total output of olives—or even the unsaleable surplus—was irrelevant. The only criterion for burden sharing had to be the national income or, even better, national income per capita, since Spain had a large population.

Alan had already worked out a formula that would reduce surplus in the future without burdening the EC's budget. But Terence knew that the time for the correct formula had not yet arrived. Exhaustion had to set in first. After a long afternoon, with flight deadlines looming, Alan would broach his solution.

Terence did not mind the delay. He, like Alan, was staying overnight. Terence wanted to have a good excuse for being away when Harry was in his hometown of Glasgow. That way, if Harry made a gaffe, Terence could not be blamed. Harry's contempt for Scotland was badly hidden at the best of times. They had to vet his speeches but even then, he slipped up when he ad-libbed. Such as the time when he told an Aberdeen audience how sad the whole country had been (he meant the UK, not Scotland—first fatal error) to see England not make it to the quarter-final of the World Cup. Not a word about Scotland and its brave exit from the competition, which meant it did not even qualify in the last sixteen. Or when he talked about Braveheart but could not remember William Wallace's name. Terence had to nudge Gideon, who stuck his elbow into Oliver's ribs to pass the message on. Harry then cleverly wove it into his speech. Honour saved all around.

So let him slip up again, Terence thought. He was happy to be in Vienna. It did not matter if the meeting finished late. Vienna was a twenty-four hour city. Terence liked the Austrians, their bars and nightclubs, the women out on the Gurtel in their fishnet stockings, unafraid, relaxed. It was a sexually frank society with no inhibitions and all tastes catered for. Terence looked forward to a taste of Vienna's night life. After all, Alan would be busy with Jo, so he was free to wander.

Alan, on the other hand, could not wait for the meeting to finish. He kept looking behind him at Jo. Poor Jo. He had to sit at the back because that was what his position entitled him to. They could not sit together, next to each other, and rub legs or touch each other, much less kiss. For Alan, it was pure torture. He hated olives, he hated Cyprus, he hated Europe.

Jo was fascinated. He had never been anywhere like this. He understood that in some irreversible sense, he had entered the inner sanctum. He himself may not be important but he was with important people. And important people had one weakness—they always wanted to be told they were important. They were afraid of being treated as ordinary, unimportant people. You had to stroke their egos as Jo had stroked Alan's ego. He had spotted Alan's anxieties early on. Alan was important, but not enough people knew that. He was forever worried that Sarah would treat him in some humiliating way in public. Not mimic him or anything, but just treat him like an ordinary person. Sarah had known Alan before he became important. Alan had tried to impress on her how important he was by wangling the Downing Street job for her. Sarah, however, thought it was her ability that had got her the job, and a bit of luck. Poor Alan.

So Jo always made much of Alan, and listened to his brilliant analysis of economic problems, his devastating pen portraits of the famous, his vicious gossip. And, of course, he admired Alan's good looks. Jo had to give that to Alan. They made a good pair. This Vienna trip was their honeymoon. He was determined to make sure that Alan would stay with him for a while. Jo needed a leg up in his career and he knew who would give it to him. For a price.

3.15 p.m. London

As far as Asha was concerned, she had not yet arrived where she wanted to. From the outset, it seemed to her, every time she achieved something, the ground seemed to slip away from beneath her. After a secure childhood in Kuala Lumpur, she had lost her father when she was just twelve years old. Her mother Krishna had been bereft, not knowing how she was going to bring up her daughters.

Krishna was the only daughter of a respectable Tamil Brahmin family of Kuala Lumpur. Many poor Tamils from the rural area of Madras Presidency had migrated to Malaya, as it was known in the nineteenth century, to work on rubber and coffee plantations. They came as indentured workers but continued to live in Malaya even when they had been freed from their contracts. As they settled and married and had children, these poor people needed their priests to perform the rituals of birth, marriage and death. Krishna's great grandfather had come for that purpose, and after many decades, the family had become prominent in the Indian community in Malaysia, as it was now called.

Krishna had gone to college and also acquired some proficiency in Bharatanatyam, the classical Indian dance. She had performed her arangetram when she was only eighteen. But soon after, she met a handsome Chinese firebrand. Chan was an eloquent speaker, a political agitator and a very bright academic. Her family was appalled that their precious daughter had fallen for a foreigner. Their hopes of getting her married to a respectable boy from back home in Madras were shattered.

But Krishna was adamant. She broke off all relations with her family to marry Chan and gave up her dance and any thought of a career for herself. Chan was everything she could have wanted.

Then suddenly Chan died. They discovered that he had cancer, and between diagnosis and death there were only three months.

Krishna was left with their two daughters—Seetha who was just eight, and Asha who was fourteen. She could not possibly go back to her family. Chan's pension was meagre and, in any case, as a widow she only got half of it. So Krishna fell back on the one skill she knew she had. She decided to teach dance. There were enough Indian middle-class families in Kuala Lampur for her to hope for something.

She went to see Natarajan, her former teacher. She remembered him as a strict but kind man, one of the new stars of Bharatanatyam in India who, for some reason, had decided to make his fortune in Malaysia. Whether Natarajan was his real name or a stage name, she never knew. Seeing him after nearly sixteen years was a shock. The slim, well- built man whom she had held in awe had begun to lose his hair and gain a paunch. But he was still her guru. He had taught her all she knew, and she had to get his blessings before she could start to teach.

Natarajan was pleased to see his former pupil. The young, shy girl had now matured into a voluptuous woman. She was, of course, still in mourning for her husband, but Natarajan could not fail to be moved by her beauty. And so it started. He helped her set up a dance class in her house. He promised to come once a week, which was a special day for Krishna and her students. They loved his teaching and, after the class was over, Krishna usually persuaded Natarajan to stay for a meal. She always cooked something she had bought specially for him. Lovely, plump, dark aubergines or tender green beans. She would grind fresh coconut chutney and cook his favourite tamarind rice. Krishna was popular as a dance teacher but she gave all the credit to her guru. Natarajan became a regular visitor. He also got to know Asha and Seetha as they hovered around their mother, helping her.

Asha, at fifteen, was growing into a beautiful young woman. She could sense her mother's guru eyeing her. She refused to join the dance classes, despite his frequent invitations. Krishna was surprised by her daughter's reluctance but Asha explained that she didn't want anything to distract her from her studies. She was getting a small scholarship that paid her fees and helped her buy textbooks. Krishna was happy to let her be. Asha's bit of cash often paid for their food at the end of the month, when the money had run out.

Then, one day, their quiet life came undone. Seetha fell ill and Krishna had to take her to the doctor. It was Natarajan's day to teach, so Krishna was reluctant to go. She knew that it would take a while to get to the doctor and there could be a long wait before Seetha was seen to. She prepared all the ingredients for Natarajan's dinner, leaving it to Asha to do the final cooking so the food would be freshly made and piping hot.

Asha came home from school while the class was still going on. She let herself into the house quietly in order that Natarajan would not have to interrupt his teaching and come to the door. She went to the room she shared with Seetha and changed out of her uniform into her usual simple dress of a blouse and a petticoat—both rather short as she was growing fast. Then she went into the kitchen. The food was ready by the time the class was over. Asha heard the girls taking leave of their guru. Now was the time for his meal. She set out the thali, the stainless steel jug and glass of water. She took out the pickles and the precious ghee. There was a small mat on the floor, on which he sat. She would serve him sitting on a low stool nearby. She did everything the way her mother usually did. Then she went into the living room, where the class was held, to invite Natarajan in.

When she got there, he was sitting on a chair, fanning himself. Before she could speak, and without any warning, he reached for her and pulled her close. With one hand, he loosened his dhoti and with the other he fumbled with her clothes. Asha pushed him away with all her strength and the guru lost his balance and fell, his head hitting the floor. He let out a howl. Asha was appalled, seeing this large, half-naked man as she had never seen him before. Instinctively, she bent to help him up. But as her hands brushed his body, to her astonishment and fear, she saw his huge stiff penis rise up from beneath a lot of hair and brown skin. He grabbed her hands and made her hold it. It was hot and throbbing and somewhat oily. His face contorted into a strange expression. Only much later did she recongnize it as pleasure and a desire for more at once. On that day, she merely fled into the kitchen, sobbing.

All this could not have taken more than three minutes. Asha was stunned, confused, frightened. She tried to control her tears by fussing with the pots and pans. She drank some water but her heart was still thumping. She could hear movement next door. Natarajan was saying something to himself. The next sound she heard was of her mother coming back with Seetha.

'Why haven't you fed guruji yet, Asha?' Krishna asked.

Asha quickly wiped her face and got off the small stool she was sitting on.

'The doctor was very quick, and then Naidu auntie very kindly dropped us off in her Ambassador. She is such a nice woman. Come, let me do this, you look after Seetha. She has to take these tablets,' Krishna continued.

When Asha and Krishna entered the living room, there was no sign of what had happened. Natarajan, fully clothed, was dashing into the bathroom—ostensibly to wash his hands before eating. Her mother removed her own light coat and Seetha's shoes and coat. Asha smiled at Seetha and took her into their room. She was especially solicitous of her little sister that night and Seetha was happy to be looked after.

Then Asha heard her mother call. 'Asha, come and give these tablets to Seetha.'

Asha was loath to leave her sister and pass through the living room into the kitchen where her mother stood, waiting. Krishna called again. Asha rose and started towards the kitchen. Waiting just outside the bedroom was Natarajan. He had a ten ringit note in his hand

and, placing his fingers on his lips, he whispered, 'Amma, don't say anything. Take this.'

Krishna was calling again. Asha took the note and deftly slipped it inside her blouse.

3.25 p.m. London/10 Downing Street

Christine ushered the delegation of MPs into the Cabinet room. That seemed the easiest way to keep them out of the way until Harry returned.

Eric Thor was his usual immaculate self, tall and patrician, and with a pipe stuck in his mouth. He was always well mannered. Once he had been Christine's idol, indeed he had been everyone's idol. In those days of the Vietnam war and CND, he had inspired them all. He had been a Cabinet minister in the Harold Wilson government in the 1960s. Many thought he would succeed Harold, for Eric was very much in the same mould. He loved technology and was always going on about the power of TV in modern-day politics. He had read science at New College, Oxford, so he was also a fan of computers long before they got small and user friendly.

As it happened, Eric did not succeed Harold Wilson. Instead, he became the focus of the opposition within the party to everything the Wilson government had stood for. He had to be given a Cabinet post at a time when the party was in office without a majority, because he carried fifty votes with him. Those were difficult days, and Eric's friends waited for the next election. They had laid their plans carefully, not to say conspiratorially. They would capture the committee that was entrusted by the party to draft the manifesto on which the election would be fought. For Eric's friends, the manifesto was the key to influence. The party's long held socialist principles would be reflected in the manifesto. There was to be no compromise with the middle-class softies. The party would get back to its working-class roots which Harold Wilson had betrayed. They would move the party decisively to the left. They had time, Harold was good for a few more years. Meanwhile, they concentrated on winning seats on the National Executive Committee, and building links with the rank and file of the party.

Harold's sudden resignation threw all their plans into disarray. Eric had no sympathy with the new regime, and his feelings were reciprocated. He threw a massive tantrum and went on the back benches to fight the battle for succession the next time around. He had the parliamentary shock troops on his side, and he was the darling of the Conference, superb speaker that he was, and a socialist to boot. There weren't many in the Cabinet even in those days.

With Eric that morning were five other MPs, and as Harry bounded into the Cabinet room, Oliver and Christine close behind him, they all got up to shake hands with the prime minister. Eric spoke first.

'Prime Minister, we are a delegation from the parliamentary party, and we have come to express our concern to you about the government's stance on Libya. We believe it will be a breach of the UN Charter to bomb Libya as we believe you are planning. We think it is not only illegal, but also immoral. It will cost many innocent lives.'

'Now let me get one thing straight first, Eric. You are not an official delegation elected by the parliamentary party, are you? I am certainly not aware of any such delegation being elected.'

'No, Prime Minister, we are not. But we do represent, we believe, a strong back bench strand of opinion, and we have a lot of support in the country.'

'All the readers of *Tribune* and a few of *The Guardian* as well, you mean. You know that our policy has been supported in the parliamentary party and there is all-party support in the Commons. We are liasing with our allies and I can assure you that if Libya behaves itself and complies with the UN Resolution conditions, there may be no need to bomb.' Harry was trying to keep calm.

'With respect, Prime Minister,' Eric broke in. Oliver looked at the ceiling and then at his watch. This would have to be wrapped up soon. They had a plane to catch.

'Look Eric, I understand that some of you feel strongly about this. I will read this memorandum you have given me, and I will take up the question on Wednesday at our party meeting. If you like, we can put our policy to a vote. But this afternoon I am afraid I cannot give you much more than five minutes. Does anybody else on the delegation have anything to add?'

'Prime Minster, you know I have a large Muslim presence in my constituency,' Jimmy Cord said immediately. Harry found Jimmy's accent hard to fathom but perhaps it was because he did not want to listen to him. Jimmy had one of the safest seats in Lancashire.

'My constituency has written to me in very strong terms about our Middle East policy. They think we are following the Americans blindly in their anti-Muslim policy. They may all vote Conservative if this goes on.'

Oliver quickly calculated that Jimmy's majority was larger than the Muslim population in his constituency and he was in no danger, which was a pity of course. Maybe we should bomb Libya and render his majority smaller, then he would behave himself, he thought.

'I thought the Muslims in your constituency were Shias, and Libya has a Sunni leader. Isn't that correct, Jimmy? I thought they sided with Iran, not Libya.' Harry's response caused Oliver and Christine to look at each other. How did he figure that out? Who told him?

'Well, Prime Minister, we have to fight this imperial legacy of divide and rule, and unite the Muslims of different sects, you know,' said Jimmy.

'You mean, unite them so they can fight us better? Are you serious?' Harry interjected.

'The point we are making is that our government should not be engaged in any armed adventure. We should not use armaments, we should not export them, we should not produce them.' Alex Little was another with a safe seat, but then in Wales they were all safe.

'Have you any idea how many jobs would be lost if we did not produce and export arms? Are you willing to argue for an extra 750,000 people on the dole? We could lose twenty Labour seats in the Midlands and the North.' Harry played his trump card.

Christine listened to Harry and was proud of him. She had forgotten her pique at his lunchtime escapade. She could see he had the left cornered and beaten. She sat back and touched her scarf, since she could not touch him.

'Thank you all, but I must go. As I said, I will read your memorandum, and I promise you we will have a discussion on Wednesday morning. We will put it to a vote. Ok?' Harry wound up the meeting.

Eric was his usual elegant self as he shook Harry's hand and thanked him for receiving the delegation. Harry said his goodbyes quickly and left the room. He had things to do.

4.30 p.m. Vienna/The Hofburg

Alan had nothing to do except to wait patiently and silently, while everyone around him bored their way through the olive problem. He tried for a while to amuse himself by looking at each delegate around the table and imagining how good they would be as lovers. They were not an attractive bunch. Perhaps Benoit Fuchs, the French minister for agriculture, was the best of the lot, with his jet black hair glistening with some oily mousse applied that morning, his trim black moustache and rather delicate hands. Alessandro Amadeo was fat and had pudgy hands and small eyes. No, he would be intolerable. The young Greek minister Olympia Costakis was the only woman at the table, and she was stunning. But Alan was certain now that he was beyond all that. He let his mind drift to Jo again and thought of his body. He cursed his job. This was Euro mega boredom.

Terence, on the other hand, was very calm. He did not have a lover waiting at the back of the room. He was confident that, when the late evening came, Alan and Jo would go their way and he would be free to roam the bars of Vienna. Terence had nothing against gays, really, honestly. He just could not see the point of it. With so many female forms available in a variety of tantalizing shapes and sizes and ages and colours, he could not see the attraction of his fellow male.

Terence had grown up in the highlands of Scotland. But he was not truly Scottish. His father came from a long line of Anglo-Irish Protestants who served the Empire faithfully as soldiers or engineers. They were the brainy sort beneath their bluff exterior. The English hated any sign of intelligence in their officers. But the Ulstermen got to know how to feign to be simple and yet be given the tricky jobs. Terence's father had been a medical officer in the army and was posted to India during the war. That was when he met and fell in love with Stevie, Terence's mother. She was a nurse, and a Catholic, and it was only when they got back to Ulster that they realized neither of their families would speak to them any more. They found it difficult to settle in Ulster, facing naked prejudice at each turn. Finally, when Terence got beaten up at his nursery school by some helpers, they decided to move.

So Terence grew up in the highlands of Scotland. Donald and Stevie chose an obscure village in the western highlands, not far from Malaig. It was a harsh place but the people were friendly and Donald's services were needed far and wide among the scattered cottages and crofts.

There was never as much money as they had got used to in India. But it was a beautiful countryside, rugged in the hills and lush in the valleys. The sea was not far away and the islands of Mull and Skye were a short boat ride away. Terence went to a local school, a three-mile walk from home. There was no secondary school nearby so he had to be a day student in Fort William. This meant he spent the weekdays at school and came home each weekend.

Terence was in his early teens when he first became conscious of his sexual self. In every film or painting that he saw, the women aroused him with their sexuality. His imagination would run riot. But he was also afraid. Was he ever going to be big enough and strong enough to please these women, whose naked flesh seemed to be so hungry for him? Would he be able to make it on the day, or would he fail? Not that there was much he could do to realize his fantasies. That came much later when he was a university student at Glasgow. The pill had come, and his was the generation which believed it had discovered sex. There was sex, pot and pop music. On college campuses, there was a lot of radical protest, and an impatience to challenge all norms and taste every forbidden fruit.

But the young college women talked too much. And it wasn't sex they wanted, it was a relationship. It took a long night's conversation about Kafka and Existentialism and Bob Dylan before he got to the real thing. What he actually wanted were pliable young women, girls almost. He wanted to be in control mentally and physically. Women in their twenties were too assertive, too bolshie. They were too demanding and fussy. They bored him. Anything slow and elaborate, anything that meant he had to think and empathize and play, tried his patience. And he needed all his patience to study law, which he saw as a perfect entry point into politics.

Terence wanted to be a parliamentarian. He had a long range plan well laid out. But those early days were hard as he could not risk his reputation by being seen in the seedier parts of Glasgow. That was also when he learnt the importance of a European holiday. In Europe, he could go where he liked, and do what he wanted. The European cities had few inhibitions, and practically no prohibitions. He explored Amsterdam and Paris, Berlin and Vienna. He knew then what he liked, and how easy it was to find the source of his pleasure. Along the way, he also became a keen student of European politics.

Terence met Dorothy Portman by chance. Her grandfather had been a pioneer in packaging in the early years of the century. From small local shops, England was moving to big department stores in the cities. The British Empire was prospering, and even working-class families were able to afford the comforts of life. And they liked their comforts well packaged. Their purchases had to be wrapped in paper and cardboard and silver foil. They did not like dowdy brown paper or worse still, old newspapers; they preferred something clean and pretty. Often, they liked their packaging in different colours.

Julian Portman was the man who responded to this need by supplying all the shops, small and large, with a variety of new packing material. He made a fortune. His wealth multiplied twice over when the First World War broke out, and the demand for new durable packaging material shot up. Julian Portman met the army's needs for well packaged soldiers' rations, containers for water, beer, spirits and chemicals. Along the way, he also got to know the politicians.

At the beginning of the war and for nine years previously, the Liberal Party had been in power. Herbert Asquith was the prime minister. He was a fastidious lawyer with an aristocratic air but little talent as a war leader. It was his chancellor of the exchequer, the wily Welshman Lloyd George, who emerged as the inspiring figure that Britain could look up to in wartime.

Early in the war, the Liberal Cabinet was reshaped into a coalition with Lloyd George as munitions minister, and later war secretary. As the Allied effort floundered, people became impatient with the government. Lloyd George conspired with his Tory colleagues to throw Asquith out, and became prime minister himself. The Liberal Party became bitterly divided; the Asquith faction loathed the upstart Welsh Wizard. The war was won, and Lloyd George emerged as a hero, but with a divided party. When it was time for the next election, and Lloyd George was looking for financial support, Julian Portman came into the picture. His contacts in the Liberal Party relied on him for help in fighting the Khaki Election, as the general election was called because of the colour of the soldiers' uniform. For this generous aid, he was rewarded with a baronetcy.

A baronetcy, as Portman discovered, put the man receiving it above a knight and below a baron. A knight can carry the title Sir before his first name, but only during his life. A baronet can be called Sir, but so can his eldest son and his heirs forever after.

When the Lloyd George liberals started selling honours, the response was one of shock. But that was just snobbery. Buying and selling honours had a solid pedigree. James the First had invented the title of baronetcy to raise money for his ventures at the beginning of the seventeenth century; Lloyd George was only continuing the royal practice. Henceforth, Julian Portman would be called Sir Julian, as would his eldest son and heir after him. He was happy with that. A peerage would have meant giving a much larger sum to the Liberals. Too costly, he thought. He would much rather invest his money in acres of land and a modest title than a grand title and a pretty garden.

Gradually, Julian came to be a landlord of significance in the highlands. He built a castle for himself and entertained in lavish style. He organized hunts and balls and parties, bringing all his English and some Scottish friends to his feasts.

His son James inherited the baronetcy, the lands and the business. Plastics were revolutionizing packaging, and the new Sir James Portman understood this. The family's fortunes continued to grow. James enjoyed his Scottish possessions, as also his country house in Hertfordshire and his flat in Cadogan Square. His family was large, and among his children, it was not his four sons but his daughter Dorothy who was his great favourite.

Sir James was a happy, fulfilled man, though he had been widowed soon after Dorothy was born. He never remarried. He had his business in England and his acres in the highlands. Life was perfect, or nearly perfect, except for one irritant. Sir James did not like the ramblers and walkers who invaded his acres in the highlands. He did not want any intrusion on his property. The ramblers argued that they had ancient right of way through his lands, but James was determined that they should be challenged. He hired Terence, who was recommended to him as a rising young barrister in the Edinburgh legal circles. It was a tricky brief. As a highlander, Terence's sympathies were with the ordinary people who wanted to have access to their own countryside. But as a young barrister, he knew he was lucky to get the case. What he did not know was that his life was about to change.

As the only daughter in a family with four sons and a widower father, Dorothy had had a lonely childhood. She was teased and bullied by her brothers. Her father, whom she adored, had much love but little time for her. She treasured the few moments he spent with her, when he would come and snuggle next to her, cuddle her, and kiss her good night. In every other matter, Dorothy was privileged. She had been brought up to be a lady of leisure. Sir James Portman had envisaged a titled husband for his daughter, and he was willing to pay her troth. She had grown up beautiful, with a large round baby face, a flawless skin and a slim figure. Her golden blonde hair crowned lovely pale green eyes. Dorothy had been educated in England, and had been to a finishing school in Switzerland. She could ski and sketch and sing. She had a simplicity of nature, as if some part of her did not want to grow up.

It didn't take Terence long to realize that here was the perfect answer to his problems. She was like a young bud with innocent looks, indeed his ideal sexual type. Marrying Dorothy would give him happiness as well as the cushion of money he needed to reach his goal. He now saw that with a bit of luck, he could aim higher. He could be a Cabinet minister in a future Labour government and, who knows, even prime minister. The question was, how could he win Dorothy?

Luckily for him, Terence had the gift of the gab. The Scots talk more than the English, though perhaps less than the Welsh or the Irish. Terence combined the inheritance of the Ulster Irish with the storytelling loquacity of the Scots. And the lilt of his highland accent clearly appealed to Dorothy.

She met Terence at one of the dinners her father gave at the family castle. He began to tell her about his dreams for the future. He told her about his father and his days in India and how the Ulster Irish had done so much for the Empire. He told her how his parents had come to Scotland to escape the sectarian prejudices of Ulster and how he had grown up in the highlands. He also told her the history of the highland clearances, of the cruelty of the English as they evicted thousands of crofters and cottagers to make room for the large holdings of the English interlopers.

Dorothy was fascinated. Her social life was restricted to London, where she met highly eligible public school boys who were always 'something in the City'. They were also usually supercilious and immature. They had no hinterland. Terence could talk to her about things she had never even been aware of. She felt a bit guilty as an English interloper in the Scottish highlands and was ready to pay her dues to right ancient wrongs.

Thus it was that Terence met and married Dorothy, the daughter of an English baronet and lord of thousands of acres in Scotland. James was pleased that he had found a young and clever barrister for his daughter. He knew Terence's career plans, and he was willing to bankroll him. He gave his daughter away in splendid style, and set the happy couple up with a large house in Edinburgh in New Town.

In Venice, on their honeymoon, Terence discovered to his delight and amazement that Dorothy was more than he could have wished for as a partner in pleasure. Simply put, Dorothy loved sex. For her, it fulfilled the emotional vacuum that a family of five men had left in her life. Terence became her sexual mentor and a father substitute. With him, she could remain the little girl that she wished to always remain. He, on his part, had always searched for the younger girls, the immature ones, during his wanderings in Europe. It was a union made in heaven. He dominated her. He asked, and she gave.

Then the girls came, one after another. Rowena and Susanna were born four years apart. Dorothy's looks matured, as did her body. She no longer looked, or felt, like a young girl. She was as passionately in love with Terence as before, but she was no longer the woman Terence fancied.

Dorothy realized that Terence's eye was wandering. He was an MP now and had been promoted early to junior minister. He was an expert on Europe and his role became prominent in the big debate that was taking place in the country on Britain's place in the European Common Market. This meant he was away a lot, and Dorothy did not always know what he was up to. But she knew what he wanted. She thought of the nannies who had looked after her when she was growing up. Now the world had moved on, and there were au pairs. These young girls came from Scandinavia or Germany in their teens. They were blonde and pretty and young, and they were perfect for keeping Terence home on the weekends.

Dorothy understood that Terence had to have his bit on the side. It was quite cosy, really. She let him have a free range at home and outside. Even when he stopped being a minister and began to spend more time in Edinburgh at the Bar, she was happy to turn a blind eye. If the au pairs complained, they were replaced with others. Dorothy always chose the type she knew Terence fancied. They never spoke about it. How and when he got around to his peccadilloes, she did not wish to know.

Meanwhile, the girls were growing up to be beautiful lasses.

Dorothy was proud of them, but she also nurtured a fear deep within that her little lambkins would be set upon by horrid boys. So much so that she felt uneasy when even workmen or servants came into the house.

Soon Susanna got to an age when an au pair was no longer necessary. Terence was now spending more time in London. His career was going well, although the party could not win elections. He was more prominent in the public eye, and Dorothy knew that he would not want to be caught in any compromising situations. Around this time he began to pay a lot more attention to the girls, fussing over them, bathing them and taking them off for a swim. Rowena and Susanna were getting to be the same age as the au pairs were. They had their mother's good looks. She knew the danger signs, and one day she told him in no uncertain terms that if he misbehaved with their daughters even for a second, she would divorce him and tell the world. Terence vehemently denied that he would ever lust after his own daughters. He accused Dorothy of having a dirty mind. He said she was no longer in love with him. If she wanted to leave him, he would go away, though he would miss her and their daughters. They quarrelled, but eventually made up. Each needed the other more than they could admit.

Like all such reconciliations, this one too had its aftermath. Catriona was born twelve years after Susanna, at a time when Rowena was going through the worst of her teenage angst. Dorothy was happy at this sign of Terence's abiding love for her. She was now emotionally even more dependent on him. Terence had her under his control, and soon Dorothy realized she could not stop him. She told herself that this way, at least the girls were protected from those horrid boys who were their schoolfellows. The newspapers were full of teenage pregnancies and assaults and rapes. Terence was a good father, and he would be gentle with the girls. In due course, they would get married and leave home, so what harm was there if their father loved them as well.

Still, she made sure that she was always with him and the girls, in London and in Edinburgh. It was important to fend off curious journalists and gossipmongers who were always looking for dirt.

For Terence, having Dorothy around all the time was a small price to pay. He was very careful with the girls. He started ever so gently to initiate them. His years of experience with young women across Europe had taught him a great deal about the psychology of young girls. They needed reassurance and tenderness. There was to be no fear and no consequences. The act had to be safe and unhurried.

Terence had his den at the top of the Edinburgh house. The attic was above anyone else's window level. He had it soundproofed and fitted with luxurious furniture. No one could see him, and no sound could escape outside.

Rowena led the way. She adored her dad. What she gathered from the magazines and her girl friends was disheartening. There seemed to be a lot of fumbling and a risk of failure with raw young lads, who were often needlessly hurtful. With her father, she felt no guilt. There was ample time, and she knew he would not hurt her. When she went to university, however, she chose to go to Durham rather than Edinburgh or any other Scottish university. That way she was away from home, but not too far. Susanna slipped into her place, and there was no fuss. Rowena had told her how wonderful Dad had been for her. Now that she was older and had some experience, Rowena's relationship with her boyfriend was fantastic.

Dorothy told herself that Rowena was normal and happy in every way. She married her barrister boyfriend, Malcolm, and Terence played the perfect father of the bride. Susanna and Catriona were bridesmaids. Susanna was now an undergraduate and with a boyfriend in tow, while Catriona was growing up to be pretty like her sisters. Looking at them, Dorothy saw that Terence was a good man in every sense of the word, a good husband and now a good, caring father.

All he lacked was political success. He was hoping for an election victory and a rapid rise to the top. Dorothy began to help him by coming to London more often. She took interest in his colleagues and invited them to dinners and parties. Her training in Switzerland had equipped her to be the wife of a busy corporate or political leader. She brought that into play. She used her money to engage a secretary. But Dorothy did not want a young woman anywhere near Terence. That way lay trouble.

So she took on young Adrian, son of Viscount Summerfield. He worked for her in the London office. He kept Terence's diary and was willing to help out at dinners and parties. He also regularly photographed MPs and their families, and Dorothy diligently sent these photos on. Adrian had no attachments. He had told her he was gay, though he had been married once. Dorothy was surprised, but such revelations were no longer shocking. At least this meant that her daughters were safe with him. And he was as happy to come to Edinburgh as work in London. Thus, he became a part of the family.

3.35 p.m. London/Heathrow Hilton

Adrian was starting the best holiday of his life. He had the case with the cash. It had been hard work, but worth it.

Adrian had chosen his target carefully. He had first made himself useful to Dorothy. She had placed a small advertisement in *The Spectator*, for a helpful person to look after the complex diary of a prominent politician. Adrian's friends at the Tory weekly had tipped him off about who it was. Adrian knew that beneath the demeanour of an MP's wife, Dorothy was an English snob. As expected, she hired him. He regaled her with stories of what the aristocracy were up to, and who was getting off with whom. In turn, he picked up useful hints about skeletons in other MP's cupboards, which would come in handy sometime in the future. He had a free run of the houses in London and Edinburgh, especially during the holidays when Terence, Dorothy and the girls were in their favourite Tuscany. He figured out that Terence preferred the Edinburgh house to the London one for his assignations. He soon discovered the den in the attic, and fitted hidden cameras in it.

Adrian could sense that Terence was impatient. He had been restless since he lost the leadership contest to Harry, and very frustrated that Harry showed no sign of weakening. By now, Susanna had gone to college. Adrian got some pictures of Rowena on her visits back home, but she was a grown-up girl. Adrian waited patiently for Terence to move on to Catriona. She was only nine but was a very pretty girl with curly blonde hair and eyes like her mother's. She was big for her age, and nearly as tall as Susanna. Adrian could see Terence eyeing his daughter, fussing over her, and trying to shove Dorothy out of his way when the three were together. Adrian was invisible as far as Terence was concerned, and he hovered around waiting for his chance. He knew Terence would slip up some day. Sure enough, he did.

Dorothy had to be in London to attend the centenary celebration of her old school. It was to be a giant hen party of friends who had not met for long time. Terence was excused as long as he promised to be in Edinburgh and look after Catriona. Terence had the field clear with the older girls away, and Dorothy in London. He could not hold back any longer. The hidden cameras did the rest. Adrian's ship had come home.

4.40 p.m. Vienna/The Hofburg

When abroad, Terence had his routine, depending on which country and which city he was in. Vienna was the least problematic. So what if he had to wade through a lot of boring stuff about olives, he didn't mind. Terence had always taken keen interest in matters European.

Europe offered an alternative career path for the enterprising politician, when national politics got frustrating. Roy Jenkins had gone off to be president of the European Commission when he could see that he would never lead the Labour Party, or become prime minister. Terence was not giving up hope yet, but keeping good relations with European colleagues never did any harm. He had learned to wait until he got the perfect version of whatever it was that he wanted, be it food, sex or power. He could handle minor frustrations along the way, but he did not want to settle for second best. He never believed in being so hungry that he could not wait for a gourmet meal.

Idly, he started listing all the MPs he was sure would back him in a leadership challenge, if Harry was ever to falter. Harry was not invincible. He was about to take a very unpopular decision on Libya. The party would not stand for such slavish acceptance of America's will. The hard left had voted for Terence in the leadership elections, and Terence kept in touch with them. He made a mental note to speak to Adrian and set up a meeting with Eric Thor tomorrow, when he was back in London. A little bit of party trouble would add spice to his life.

3.45 p.m. London/Drew House

Normally, Lex felt elated with a scoop. His blood raced, and the adrenalin pumped in his veins. The whisky bottle, opened by lunchtime on those days, was never put away. But this was different. He had to choose from among the rather disgusting pictures Rodney had bought. He thought it best to take the less explicit and more suggestive ones, but hated that he had to do it.

In his scabrous, sanctimonious way, Lex regretted that by the time he got into this profession, scandals had become hard to come by. The reading public had become unshockable. Extramarital affairs were small beer. Gays were out in the open, and those who were privately gay could not be attacked—not unless you were a gay rights weirdo like that sanctimonious git who went around outing bishops and MPs. But children were a different matter. National outrage was ready to be tapped on the issue of paedophilia. That was the last barrier. The Great British Public, four million of whom bought his newspaper every day, bless their souls and wallets, would not stand for tolerance of paedophiles.

Lex was aware that he was sitting on a mega scandal. It breached barriers which were even beyond scandal. He had to consult Vera. It was urgent, he told her. Unfortunately, as soon she walked in, he knew she was pissed. Also, he couldn't abide the filthy cheroots she smoked. Where she found them, he did not know. Probably handmade in Turkey. He strode across and threw open a window. Vera pretended not to notice.

'What is the problem, Alexander?'

Lex hated this elongation of his name. Vera had decided that Lex was short for Alexander, not Alexis, which was what his parents had named him. Why had he not been born an ordinary mortal with a name like Tom or Bob, and gone on to have an ordinary nine-to-five job that brought him 25k? Why did he have to be called Alexis, make 200k and be talked to like this by a batty old fruit?

He explained the situation to Vera and showed her the pictures. Rodney had discreetly slipped away. His presence, he knew, would have inflamed Vera, who was as horrified by the pictures as Lex had been. But she could see that Lex would not have called her if he had a choice.

She looked at them for a few minutes, really hard, and very professionally. Then she said, 'Do the decent thing, love. Do this one with lots of blacking out and keep the rest.'

Lex saw that she had chosen the one photograph in which Terence was clearly recognizable but not the other party. Vera was protecting the victim. She had sound instincts about the tolerance of the public.

'You think…'

'Don't worry, love. This will bring him down. We don't need to bring more filth into the public eye. This will tell him what we know, and it will keep that poor thing from being hounded all her life.'

'Will you do a front page edit piece?'

'You bet. You do the full page editorial on the politics. Leave the morals to me.'

'You are the works, VD.'

'I won't say it's a pleasure, but I know such problems don't come our way all that often. Extra print run of a million. Not less in any case. Let's get going.'

Lex knew that he had to be careful about the timing of the first print run. BBC2's hard hitting programme, *Newsnight*, which went on air at 10.30, showed the headlines of the next day's editions just before going off the air at 11.15. Should he release his first edition in time for that, or just tip off a few insiders? He would have to alert Peter Portugal's office, but what about Terence Harcourt? Should he tell Chris Mott, his press secretary? Lex had known Chris as a fellow journalist many years ago, when as two juniors, they used to get pissed on cheap booze. And what about Oliver, should he be kept out of the loop? Harry White was in Glasgow that evening, watching the Old Firm game, so Oliver would be with him.

Lex had many things to do and not enough time to do them in.

3.50 p.m. London/10 Downing Street

Nor did Oliver. Harry had just gone upstairs to do his packing. Elisabet had left already, so there was no one to say goodbye to. Oliver was happy to see that Sarah was back, a bit flushed but all set with her newly acquired suitcase packed and ready to go. She had put on fresh lipstick, tidied her hair, and smelled of Samsara. They did not exchange a word, since Sarah didn't want to talk about the cancelled lunch and Oliver wanted to avoid any mention of the lunch that had taken place. He silently thanked her for her discretion. Let us hope she won't make a fuss when she is thrown over like the many others before her, he thought.

Harry came down, all spruced up, contact lenses in place and fresh aftershave on. So, obviously, Oliver sat in the front of the car, leaving Harry with Sarah in the back as they sped off to Northolt. Harry sat well back to escape attention. Sarah took note and did the same. Harry patted her hand.

'Don't worry, Sarah, you will enjoy this.'

'I am sure I will, Prime... Harry. But I will be glad when the day is over.'

'And I hope you will look back on it with fond memories.'

Those blue eyes are devastating, Sarah thought. How will the day end?

3.55 p.m. London

It was her large brown eyes that men found most attractive about Asha. But back in Kuala Lumpur, she had also understood the lure of other parts of her anatomy, and she kept them well guarded from the roving hands of Natarajan. When he offered to move in with Krishna, Asha knew why. But her mother was so happy, Asha thought it best not to spoil things. By now, Asha sensed her power over the older man. He was marrying her mother, but he wanted Asha. She had gleaned enough from school gossip and from the magazines she read to sense that there were barriers she should not cross too early. She knew too, that she had the ability to please men with some very simple moves, and after that first incident, she knew how she could make Natarajan pant for more.

She varied her theme. She could be coquettish, but he liked it more if she was cool and detached, doing him as if her mind was on something else entirely. For some obscure reason, this gave him a more powerful erection. She never let him touch her and she only touched him where she was most effective. And he always rewarded her for that.

Asha figured she would have to leave home as soon as she could. She had decided to win a scholarship to some British university— LSE would be the best. The money Natarajan gave her was useful for getting better books, and made her life a little easier. Even Krishna did not question the source of Asha's spare cash. She told herself that it was Asha's scholarship money. She did not want to know more.

Asha was determined to leave before matters came to a head. And she had her way. She got a scholarship to study at LSE when she was seventeen. She was already an expert on the subject of men, older men, that is. She knew how to master them with a deft little turn of her supple fingers. When she entered the legal world, she started with at least this advantage to offset the obvious disadvantage of being both female and of non-European origin. In a profession dominated by old white men, she had an expertise that allowed her to forge ahead. Her legal acumen made a significant but small contribution to her advance.

'Good afternoon, Miss Chan. Nice lunch?' her secretary asked. Linda was very useful in arranging Asha's busy and complex schedule, and she was totally loyal. Asha could trust her.

'Good food, lousy company. Most of it anyway,' said Asha as she went into her room. There was as usual a mountain of stuff to do, but her brain also had to work out a solution to the one problem that was proving difficult—Harry White.

Asha had to find some sort of a solution to Matt's tax problem, if Harry refused to co-operate. She wasn't sure whether he was bluffing or just playing for time. It had not escaped Asha's watchful eyes that Oliver seemed to be Harry's guide in these matters. This meant they had to get something on Oliver, but another prong of attack on Harry was also required. As Asha worked through the papers on her desk, at the back of her mind, various wheels were turning to find the answer.

Linda knocked and brought her tea. Asha indulged herself when she was in the office, every evening at four o'clock, with a large pot of freshly brewed Darjeeling tea.

'Thanks ever so much, Linda. Just what I need. Will you do me a favour, please? Will you run a check on what we know about Oliver Knight, the PM's press secretary, and will you please find out whether our friend in Glasgow is available for a word? Thanks.'

Linda knew that when Asha demanded something so politely, it was urgent. Often, Asha preferred Linda to access information, so that her name would be kept out of any fallout. Linda had a way with accents, and often made phone calls pretending to be an old lady from Shropshire or a housewife from Cumbria. People were so gullible.

4.00 p.m. London/Lyttelton Theatre, Waterloo

It was always going to be a risky proposition to stage *Ubu Roi*. It was a controversial play when it was first staged, and remained so even after a century. The occasion was a godsend for columnists and cartoonists. Here was the prime minister's wife staging a play about an arrogant, boorish and stupid man usurping power, ruining his kingdom and getting thrown out by a people's revolt. And he had a perfect shrew for a wife! What was Elisabet doing?

But then, as Harry knew, that was her style. To make it even more controversial, Lisa had decided to do an all-women production. Then she had chosen the glamorous and well-known French star, Anne de la Manche, to act the part of Ubu.

Lisa had met Anne at one of those summits she had to go to with Harry. This one was in Rambouiellet, and Anne was part of the 'culture' for the summit. Lisa and Anne hit it off immediately. After that, it was only a matter of time before they did something together. They were very much alike. If the Great British Public had problems understanding Harry's wife, the French were dismayed that a woman as beautiful and sexy as Anne should be a lesbian.

The tabloids had great fun when the cast of Ubu was announced.

Anne was in London then, and there were pictures on many front pages of her and Lisa hugging. *The Herald* lived up to its reputation with the headline 'Lisa Lesbo Love Lark'.

Now Lisa sat in the darkness of the Lyttelton Theatre, watching the dress rehearsal. She was particularly happy because her good friend Margaret had come specially for the occasion. Margaret would be present at the first night tomorrow, but this was an extra treat.

Margaret and Lisa had become great friends despite, rather than because of, their husbands. Harry disliked the arts slightly less than Scotland or football. But the artistic community had naturally been thrilled that Lisa was a professional theatre director. The luvvies had fallen over each other trying to get to know Harry. They had hopes of largesse after decades of Tory meanness and Labour's economic incompetence. What was more, in Kim Carpenter they had a trendy heritage shadow minister. Kim had been a don briefly at Oxford, having written an obscure and swiftly remaindered study of Robert Herrick. But at least he could read and write, unlike many MPs of the People's Party, or so the luvvies reckoned.

Alas, Harry had dashed their hopes. The government had come into power in the wake of a financial crisis. Battens were hatched down and, if anything, Harry had proved to be an even greater philistine than his predecessor, whose tastes did not reach beyond Trollope and tripe. Kim Carpenter had great ambitions of moving on from his heritage portfolio, which he felt was a dead end. So he played along with both sides. He slunk from one media event to another with his (once) perfectly shaped boyfriend. But being dunked in champagne by the lions of theatre was not his idea of fun or duty. At the first sign of a Cabinet reshuffle, he begged to move on and was now in the arid deserts of Transport and Regions. Pamela had replaced him. She too flattered the trendy crowd of artists and actors for a while, but then she found she was ignored completely by Harry and Terence. If there was one thing they agreed about, it was the neglect of the arts. So Pamela was left to struggle with the portfolio.

This was where Margaret came in. Unknown to their husbands, Margaret and Lisa had hatched a plot. Margaret was to set up one of the largest endowments for the arts that the country had ever seen. She was to leave a billion dollars to the Lew Drew Arts Fund, which would be set up in Britain. And just to put the boot (or an elegant stiletto) in, it was to be located in Glasgow.

Lisa had helped Margaret with the plans. She knew about her friend's cancer, and while she prayed for Margaret, she knew that time was short. She had, of course, hinted to Harry that Margaret might leave her an endowment. She had not spelled it out, but Harry being Harry, she couldn't be certain as to what he knew and didn't. Margaret did not tell Matt, nor did she care if he knew. It was her money and she was determined to blow it rather than give a red cent to him or his Malaysian mistress.

The play was going well. Lisa could hear the select guests invited for the dress rehearsal laughing and cheering. She had had the novel idea of flashing words like 'blast' and 'pow' electronically at crucial stages, so the play looked like a comic strip come alive. Everyone had been encouraged to camp it up outrageously. There was no point in playing Ubu as if it was serious or deep. It was a scatological political cartoon.

Annie was brilliant. Margaret passed a note to Lisa: 'He is a pompous fool, just like Matt.' Lisa read it in the semi-darkness, leaned over and whispered, 'I modelled him after my Harry, not your Matt.' They giggled helplessly, loud enough for the stage manager to demand silence.

The laughter in the theatre got very loud in the scene where the bear attacks Ubu and his straggling followers. In another brilliant move, Lisa had asked the ultra thin, almost anorexic model Kath Ross to play the Bear. Kath had agreed, knowing that it would lead to some interesting publicity. Now here she was, swaddled in a heavy padded costume that made her look fat and ugly.

Everyone was laughing and hooting and getting into the spirit of the play. Lisa was relieved. She had worked hard on her Ubu. This was her first production at the National, oops, the Royal National— Lisa had to be careful about such trivial matters of protocol, she was after all the PM's wife. But she could now prove that she was at the National on merit and not because of Harry. Tomorrow the world would know that Lisa was someone to reckon with.

4.20 p.m. Glasgow

Roger Birch had the kettle on, and the aroma of tea and toast rose in the air as Dorothy pushed the door open. She was surprised to see him up and about, and all dressed up.

'What's with you then?' she asked.

'Got a job tonight. A good one at that.'

'Where?'

'At the club.'

'Are they playing?'

'Och, aye.' Roger had picked up the lingo in the time he had spent with her.

'So how long will you be?'

'They want me to serve drinks at the bar. So I reckon I will be done by midnight, like. They pay well, Ibrox do'.

'Midnight? That must be something special.'

'Och, aye. It's Harry White, the prime minister, coming down to watch the big game. The directors have a big do for him, drinks and food and all. All the biggies will be there, I reckon.'

'Oh, I hate that Harry White. I wish he would drop down dead.'

'Whatever for?'

'He is a Tory bastard, he is. Not a penny for us workers, and millions for his rich friends.'

'Oh, come on.'

'Don't you come on me, remember that nuclear deal which got him a million?'

'Not him, his party.'

'Who cares? It's all the same. It's the rich who talk to the rich when the money is good. If it's the poor, the money is always tight.'

'He is coming up here for the election.'

'I hope he loses.'

'Well, all I have to do is mix his drinks.'

'Poison him for me, will you?'

Roger was startled. He had never known Deirdre to express such a strong opinion. He had his own reason for hoping that she did not mean it, but now was not the time to explain why. So he turned and started for the kitchen, saying only, 'Easier said than done, Dee.'

Roger got her a cup of tea, then set his own cup down and began to put away the groceries. He was like that, Deirdre thought. Considerate. He made her uneasy, truth to tell. She was not used to men being gentle or good. He was not normal, not natural, like.

Deirdre had met Roger when she went to the public library one afternoon to see if she could get any books to help her daughter Samantha with her maths.

Roger was the temporary assistant librarian, and he was very helpful, so different from the regular ones. He was willing to spend a lot of time with Deirdre and Sam, talking about mathematics and making it interesting by telling Sam stories and puzzles. He found books for her to read. He even offered to come around on weekends and tutor her. One day, Deirdre cooked him a lovely roast. That was before she found out he could do wonders with pasta and sauces and steak, and even stews and vegetables.

So Roger had become a part of the ménage, three years ago. He was unlike anyone else Deirdre had known. He could be stroppy, but he knew ever so much about everything. He had smooth skin and hands.

He taught Sam and helped her pass her exams. He could even fix the windows. But it was the classical music he had on constantly, on Radio 3, that intrigued her most. He knew all about those composers and conductors. He hated pop music but he adored jazz, and he knew just the kind to turn her on.

No, Deirdre couldn't complain. Sam was getting a college education in culinary science and food therapy—making chips and telling people it was bad for them, as Roger described it. She had a job that she wasn't unhappy about. She had no idea where Roger had come from and how long he would stay. But he was good about money, and did not beat her up. That, for Deirdre, was the works. Occasionally, he cooked her a fabulous meal with herbs and spices, and bought fancy wine. She suspected he had known better days, but as far as she concerned, he was here and was available. And she could only thank her stars that he wasn't a randy, hard drinking bastard like the rest of them.

She came out of her reverie to the sound of his voice. 'You know, Dee, only one British prime minister has ever been assassinated. It's not like in America, where they're forever shooting their presidents. Spencer Perceval was prime minister in the days of the war with Napoleon. He was shot by a bankrupt businessman from Liverpool, John Bellingham, who blamed him for his troubles. Right inside the Houses of Parliament. Not the present building. It happened before it burnt down, and they had to build a new one. But you know something strange? Ever since, they don't let anyone die there—not in the Palace of Westminster. Even if you die, they say you died at St Thomas, which is across the river. They have a thing about palaces. As if the people inside are immortal.'

How typical, thought Deirdre. Roger was always so keen to educate her. Ask a question and you got a lecture—not boring, mind you.

'Drink your tea,' she said. 'I'll do the stacking in a minute.'

'It's nearly done. Anyway, I must gulp and go.'

4.30 p.m. London/Lyttelton Theatre, Waterloo

Lisa's mobile signalled a message, and the stage manager shouted, 'Mobiles off!' She looked at the message and smiled. It was Harry saying he was off to Glasgow, and would call her later. That meant he was feeling guilty about something. Lisa wondered what it could be, or rather who? Christine was not travelling with him, Lisa knew that because she'd had a long chat with her that morning. So a new affair, but who could it be? Her thoughts were interrupted by a great roar and applause. The run through was over.

Margaret had to go. She gave Lisa a fond hug and whispered, 'It's great. See you tomorrow. I am sure you'll wow them.' She gave her hands a squeeze and was gone in a trice. Lisa looked at her and thought how her tall, big -boned friend was getting even more beautiful as age and the dreaded disease took their toll on her. She said a silent prayer for Margaret, wishing her a long life and much happiness.

4.35 p.m. London/Bell Yard, Off Fleet Street

Not if Asha had anything to do with it. She wanted Margaret gone, and soon. It was not just about the money that she was sure Matasha would inherit. It was the sheer irrationality of Margaret's attitude to money that infuriated Asha. Not to have it, to have to struggle for it, to save and skimp, and even to blow it on personal luxuries, that she could understand. But to give it away to the tax authorities when you could avoid doing so, and to throw it away on some nambypamby charity was more than Asha could stomach. Ever since Matt had found out that Margaret intended to give her money away to an arts foundation, Asha had wished fervently for nature to do a quicker job on the ill woman. She had even looked up articles on the rate at which cancer spread, but there was no agreement among the specialists. Margaret could live for a month, or for years. Asha had to do something. The question was, what?

She buzzed Linda.

'Can you come in for a moment?'

'Yes, Miss Chan.'

'Can you find out where Margaret Drummond is? I know she was in London earlier today, but I want to know if she is still in town. Ask Matt's office, but don't let them know who you are.'

'Understood, Miss Chan.'

Asha was determined to get her hands on that money even if it meant doing something drastic. Nothing illegal like taking out a contract on Margaret—just something to hasten her along to her end. But what, and how?

4.45 p.m. London/Central Lobby, Houses of Parliament, Westminster

That was Eric's problem. How was he to get rid of Harry? He and his group had come back empty-handed from their meeting with Harry. He had challenged them openly to defy him at the party meeting. How were they going to organize their numbers? The Libya issue was bubbling, but had not yet come to a boil. There were rumours flying around of an Anglo-American stitch up, which was about to start unilateral bombing. Could Eric and his group somehow stop this carnage?

'Hello Eric, you look worried. What is the matter?'

It was Ian who had drifted, out of habit, into the Central Lobby of Parliament. His lunch had been soaked in booze apart from which, a haunch of venison with all the trimmings followed by a summer pudding soaked in double cream was hardly health food. So he had decided to walk down from the Garrick. He had got on to Charing Cross Road, and strolled past Trafalgar Square and Whitehall to the Palace of Westminster. Along the way, he had been tempted by the bookshops and the antique shops. He had dawdled a while, but stopped himself from buying anything. Even a good first edition of

Geoffrey Boycott's autobiography. He was sorely tempted though, as the Yorkshire batsman was one of his heroes.

Now, after a hot day out walking, he appreciated the coolness of James Barry's lovely construction. Ian loved the splendid high dome of the Central Lobby from which hung a large chandelier. On the four ends were four arches, and above them were the likenesses of the four patron saints of the United Kingdom. There was St George for England above the arch leading off towards the House of Lords, St Patrick of Ireland on the door to St Stephen's, through which he had come in. St Andrew reigned above the door leading off to the dining rooms and the terrace below, and St David above the arch leading to the House of Commons Chamber. In between the arches, there were marble statues in the classical style, of prominent politicians of the nineteenth century. There was Gladstone and Lord John Russell, both Liberal prime ministers. There was the now forgotten George Gower, the Earl of Granville and Stafford Northcote, who had been a foreign secretary under the Tories. He'd had a heart attack when Salisbury took over his portfolio for himself without warning him. With the obituary still on his mind, Ian thought about the role of sudden death in wrecking and launching political careers. Looking at the MPs strutting around busily in the Central Lobby, he wondered how many had thought of sudden death as a possibility.

The Central Lobby was the place that gave lobbying its original meaning, for this was where citizens could come and ask to meet their Member of Parliament. All they had to do was write the name of their MP down, and off would go the attendant in search of the quarry. Hence the number of MPs here, lingering to meet the groups of voters who had asked to meet them. It was also the place for aspiring researchers and eager political anoraks to hang out. There was always a buzz with people passing through on urgent errands from and to the Chamber.

This was old hunting ground for Ian. The attendants knew him and his pass was still valid, so he was free to wander through the arch under St David and towards the corridor just outside the Commons Chamber. He nodded to the policeman on duty, said a cheery hello to the attendant, and passed into the inner sanctum. There was a statue of an aggressive looking Lloyd George and a bulldog like one of Churchill. Few would recall the glory of Anthony Eden who also somehow rated a statue here. He had started full of promise as the successor to Winston Churchill, but led the disastrous Suez expedition and came to grief. Would they honour Harry White as equal to Lloyd George, or would he end in ignominy like Eden? Ian had walked on, speculating idly, and found himself face to face with Eric Thor.

Ian had known Eric since their university days. They had been close once, but had fallen out over Vietnam. Eric was a minister then, and pro-US policy, while Ian, a journalist even then, was against it. But they had made their peace in the long years Eric had spent in opposition, getting farther and farther to the fringes of his own party. For a man who was once thought to be a likely leader, it was a long way down and out. Of course, there were still some who wished for Eric's return. The People's Party was incorrigible.

'Have you heard any news about Libya, Ian?'

Eric did the usual thing of answering a question by asking one in return. He didn't really want to let Ian into his plans, but it wouldn't hurt if news got out that a rebellion was brewing.

'I know no more than you, Eric. Even less, perhaps. I don't, as you know, labour in the vineyards of the print medium any more. But rumour has it that Harry and the president are thinking of bombing Libya.'

'Does it now? Don't you think the country will rise up in revolt if that happened? Shouldn't we stop him?'

'No, to both questions. The country doesn't have any love for

Gaddafi, or Libya, or for anyone who supports them. And you couldn't stop Harry even if you wanted to, because he would crush you.'

'He will have to seek the approval of the party, or at least of the Cabinet, surely?'

'Since when has Harry given a fig for either the party or the Cabinet? He will do what he likes, Oliver will tell you all what to think, and the sheep will dutifully jump over the cliff.'

'You are too cynical. I am sure if we started now, by Wednesday's party meeting we could build up the momentum for a challenge.'

'Well, that's news, Eric.'

'But you are not to tell anyone. This is strictly off the record.'

'As I told you, I am no longer an active journalist. All I do is write obituaries. Now, what can you tell me about Harry White that I can use for the juicy bits of the obituary?'

'You've come to the wrong man for that, Ian, as surely you must know.'

'Well, thanks anyway, and good luck.'

Ian knew he was on the scent of a story. Even after all these years, the excitement of a news story never diminished. He would have to ferret out bits and pieces. It was too early to go to Annie's, it wasn't even five o'clock yet. But he thought the terrace on the river might provide some willing talkers. What an item it would make for the obituary, if it blew up.

2

4.45 p.m. En Route to Glasgow

Sarah had never been in a private jet before. This one was not private, but it was the prime minister's personal jet for priority use. There had been no checking in, no waiting, no long walk to the boarding gate. They had been driven straight on to the tarmac. Gideon Crawford and his Scottish entourage were already there. When Sarah hesitated, Harry took her arm and led her to the steps. Her bags were carried in by the crew, and before she could think about it, they were airborne.

Sarah sat by herself. She wanted to gather her thoughts. Harry and Oliver were deep in discussion a few rows in front. Gideon's crowd were noisily drinking and chatting at the back. They had carried their beer cans with them. Sarah felt acutely self-conscious. What would the day bring? What was expected of her? Christine had asked her to buy things to wear, and she had done that. But when was she going to change and where?

A middle-aged stewardess walked up to where Harry and Oliver were sitting.

'Prime Minister, your Martini, just as you like it, with an olive, and Mr Knight, your whisky.'

'Thanks, Maria.'

'A pleasure, Prime Minister.'

It actually did give Maria pleasure merely to be able to mouth the words 'prime minister'. She had said them many times and to several prime ministers and yet they always gave her a thrill. She saw Sarah sitting by herself and could see she wasn't used to travelling VIP class.

'What would you like, madam? Can I get you a drink, a cup of tea, or coffee perhaps?'

'Just a cup of tea, please.'

'And how do you take it? India or China, milk or lemon?'

'China please, with lemon. Thanks. Oh, and sugar, if that's alright.'

'No problem at all, madam.'

Maria took her time serving her guests up front because she knew that the Scottish contingent at the back were going to be odious and demanding.

'What sort of trouble do you think Matt has in mind?' Harry asked Oliver.

'Difficult to say. He has been gunning for Terence ever since Terence sued *The Herald*. I can't see what he has. Terence is squeaky clean about money. He is happily married, with three lovely daughters. They may have found something from his past, long before he became a minister. I'll make inquiries.'

'Do. And what about this evening?'

'Gideon has organized a meeting of party activists, on a university campus of all places. Our security people will be there, so we'll keep the Trots out, but our own members up here are pretty loony.'

'The usual—taxation, nurses, pensions?'

'Yes, more money, more redistribution. No tuition fees. Oh, and Libya.'

'You reckon?'

'Sure. Foreign matters always attract nutters. The farther away and the more exotic the country, the nuttier the support. So you will have to do yet again what you did to Eric and the brothers.'

'Ok. And then the game.'

'That's a dawdle. It should be a good game, so even you may not find it too boring. It's not often that these two teams have a fixture this late, but what with the other competitions they have been in—the European Cup, the Scottish FA cup—it's become the season's last game. And it's crucial for them both. They are on the same overall number of points, but Rangers are ahead on goal difference. Celtic have to win outright. If they draw, then Rangers are champions in the Scottish League. Of course, if Rangers win, they are clear champions.'

'I hope I am not expected to understand the subtleties of all this,' Harry said.

'Don't worry. They will tell you themselves, several times. I am just warning you. And remember, it's not just football. It's also, as you know, tribal warfare. In Northern Ireland, they fight with guns and bombs; in Glasgow, they do it with footballs. Both teams command fiercely loyal sectarian support. You have to be careful not to be seen to be supporting either side during the game. Your hosts are the Rangers bosses but even if they goad you, stay neutral.'

'As I don't know much about the teams and care even less about football, that should be easy.'

'You are not to admit ignorance under any circumstance. But no one could know as much as they do, so they will keep telling you really obscure stuff. You just have to keep smiling.'

'So these are Protestants?'

'Thank God you know that much. Though it's more relaxed now. They hired Graeme Souness as manager a while ago, despite him being a Liverpool player, rather than Everton.'

'So what?'

'Oh God. Liverpool is a Catholic team, right? So they are like Celtic. Everton are like Rangers—Protestants.'

'They can't still be taking all that seriously.'

'They do in Ulster, don't they, and Glasgow is just a large suburb of Ulster. Or maybe it's the other way around. They fly the Irish Republican flag on Celtic roof tops.'

'Is that allowed?'

'Who is to stop them? Do you want riots in Glasgow as well as trouble in Belfast? They tried once in the 1930s. Celtic said they would rather get thrown out of the Scottish Football Association than take the flag down, so the flag flies.'

'Will there be trouble at the match?'

'Nah, it's all under control now. It used to be bad in the old days. They once had a game more than a hundred years ago, in 1887 as a matter of fact, which had to be abandoned after seventy minutes. The match was oversubscribed, and the crowd spilled over on to the pitch. Mind you, Rangers were trailing Preston North End by eight goals to one, so the fans may have just sabotaged the game. But nowadays things are much easier. The football stadiums are all refurbished, and no one has to stand on the terraces any more. It's an all-seating stadium like everywhere else. The fans may fight later on, of course, in the course of their pub crawls.'

'How long will all this last?'

'Kick-off is at seven forty-five. It's an unusual fixture, being on a Monday, but Matt's Rainbow TV has a tie-up with the Scottish FA, and he insists on some big games being scheduled on days other than Saturdays.'

'Not Matt again.'

'He's everywhere. Anyway, the match should finish at about quarter to ten and then there will be a reception and dinner in your honour.'

'Do I have to?'

'Well, you promised Calum Kennedy that you would come and be chief guest. He is very keen.'

'He is a strange creature. What drives him? Why does he keep funding these moronic football clubs?'

'He is a docker's son and was a docker himself. Then he did a grand tour of the revolutionary left. He was a Stalinist, then became a Trot, and had a go at being a Maoist in the heyday of the Vietnam war. But then he dropped it all and went into selling advertising space. Some say he was disgusted by the Cambodian dictator Pol Pot, who managed to murder a sixth of the population of his country, others say it was his marriage falling apart that did it. He needed money for alimony, and had to quit agitation. So advertising it was, and his bullying manners made him a great success. Now he owns a TV station or two, and gives the party a lot of money.'

'What's his game?'

'He wants to be Lord Kennedy of the Gorbals.'

'Can I skip the dinner, if I promise that?'

'No, come on. You'll enjoy it. All the business leaders of Glasgow will be there as well as a lot of political types from all parties, I should add. Prime ministers don't often come to Scotland, and when they do, they go to Edinburgh and not Glasgow. So this is a big event, and you will get a lot of kudos for it.'

'As long as I don't cheer halfway into the game, if Celtic score.'

'That's about it.'

6.00 p.m. Vienna/The Hofburg

That, Terence thought, was that. The Cyprus olives were sorted out. As usual, Alan had been brilliant. He had waited till the moment when he knew the French and Italian delegations were beginning to think of their flights home. Then he produced one of those classic European Community solutions. It solved nothing, but gave everyone the chance to go home and live to fight another day. Eighty per cent of the Cyprus olives were to be covered by the scheme immediately, and twenty per cent absorbed within five years of Cyprus's entry. France and Italy were to lose twenty per cent of their quota, but this was suspended until the date of entry. They could exceed their quota (i.e., cheat), if they paid an excess charge. But this excess was to be calculated in present prices, not future prices, unless the price of olives fell. Every other country was to agree to not import olives from anywhere else except in bottled form. No one could calculate what any of this would eventually cost, but no money was required upfront. And by the time Cyprus entered the European Community, the ministers would be different, and it could be argued all over again.

A good day's work done, and it was time now for the fun to begin. Fond farewells had to be said all around, but Alan quickly rejoined Jo. This being Europe, he could hug him and kiss him lightly as well. In the meantime, hands had to be shaken with all the various ministers and officials, double kisses on the cheeks for the closer colleagues and the few women. Briefcases were snapped shut, little mounds of paper left behind for recycling, also half-filled water glasses and bottles of Evian now looking stale and forlorn.

Terence did the farewell bit superbly. He was in no hurry. He was staying over. His pleasures were to come later and they were not to be hurried. He could be gracious and effusive to the ministers and officials. He remembered their wives' names and sent his compliments unfailingly, asked after their children, bantered knowingly about local gossip. He was happy to be in Vienna. Anywhere but Glasgow, where Harry would face the mob. No doubt Chris would call him later, to fill him in on the news. Normally Chris would have been with Terence, but they had thought he should keep an eye on Harry, the excuse being that he could help out if Harry needed someone to assist Oliver. They both knew that Oliver would rather die than ask Chris for help.

The boys were impatient, so Terence swept them along. He had never liked the posh hotels near the Opera. He knew of a decent four-star place near the Schotten Ring. As a Scotsman, he had gravitated there long ago and now kept up the connection. Hotel Franz Joseph was comfortable, easy to get to, and more intimate than the posh ones.

As they squeezed into the car, Terence graciously sat in the front with the chauffeur, leaving the love birds to get on with it. He knew the answer he would get, but still he asked for form's sake.

'I reckon you lads won't want to join me at the Ambassador's house for dinner? I can make excuses on your behalf.'

'Thanks, Terence, that's very considerate of you. Do give my most sincere apologies to Sir Clive and Lady Olds.'

'Done. Remember, we have to leave early tomorrow morning. You will have to be down in reception by six thirty.'

'Oh, I hate these early morning flights. Can't we take a later one?'

'There are two flights leaving almost simultaneously in the early morning, and then nothing until after lunch when again two flights take off.'

'That's airline competition for you. Do we have a busy day tomorrow?'

'Aye. Harry is in Glasgow tonight and goes to Belfast for an early meeting tomorrow morning. I'd better be in London in case the Libya thing blows up. We can't rely on Frank Thompson now, can we?'

Frank Thompson was deputy prime minister, but was for ever being made the butt of jokes. 'Yes FT, no comment' was the least rude thing people said about him. Frank was loyal, Frank was solid. He had deep roots in the party, and in his own unaffected way, attracted fierce loyalty. He was like a frayed old shirt, once fashionable, which you wore for comfort and nostalgia, not style, and were faintly embarrassed about keeping in your wardrobe. But Frank was Harry's battering ram if the party misbehaved. He was so grateful that Harry had chosen him as his deputy on the leadership ticket, and then kept faith by making him deputy PM, that he was ready to kill for him.

'Ok, you win. Six thirty in the morning it will be. But don't expect us to be awake.'

'Would I ever?'

The car swept up to the entrance of the hotel. Terence turned around and smiled at the boys.

'Franz Joseph, here we come!'

5.15 p.m. London/Lyttelton Theatre

'So, are we all set?' Lisa asked. The cast had gathered in a huddle on the stage. There had been hugs and kisses and congratulations. Everything had gone according to plan. Lisa had only to sort out a few things with the lighting. And Annie needed a more directed focus in the funny bits; people had to be able to see that lovely face, even though she was playing a stupid man.

'What's the plan?' Annie asked.

'There's a pub-cum-restaurant at the National Film Theatre, which is just next door. We can sit outside and get pissed. Then a short walk, no road to cross, to The Archduke. We eat there, and as long as we clear off before midnight, the owners won't mind.'

'And you want us to act tomorrow after this?' Kath groaned.

'You don't have to be here until half past four in the afternoon. Anyway, hangovers improve concentration.'

'The butterflies in my stomach before the performance will be more than enough,' said Annie.

'The bus will take you back home, or to the hotel, as you like. So you don't have to hold back. No driving, just lots of drinks.'

Lisa didn't like cars, nor driving. She went everywhere, if she could, by public transport. Sometimes the security men worried about this, but Lisa was adamant. By herself, she would not get into a car, but if necessary, she took a taxi. As the prime minister's wife, she would do as she had to, but she did not hide her hatred of cars or the pollution they caused. She disliked, even more, the political discussions about the voter preferences of the Mondeo man and the Sierra woman. Harry was much taken by these images, but Lisa thought it was criminal to glamourize cars and their owners.

So the motley looking group of fifteen women set off. Even before they were out of the door of the Royal National, they attracted attention and even some wolf whistles. A crowd was gathering in time for the evening performance. A quartet was playing soothing, harmless music. Even the short walk from the Royal National to the National Film Theatre took a longish while. Several people went into the bookshop inside the theatre, while others spilled out on to the South Bank and stood by the river. There was an open market with many stalls of second-hand books which absorbed Annie and Lisa.

'There will be several gossip items in the papers tomorrow, Annie,' Lisa said.

'What about? We've hardly done anything yet. I could, if you want some publicity.'

'No, thanks. The British journalist finds the most trivial acts of people in the news fascinating. We are a nation of snobs, you know. When they read tomorrow about us carousing noisily, they will feel like they almost know us. Anyway, it sells papers.'

'You are pretty relaxed about this constant pressure, Lisa. How do you cope?'

'Well, I know that they think I am a bit crazy. As long as I fulfil their expectations and shock them, they don't probe too deep.'

'And what would they find if they did?' Annie asked, clearly trying to provoke Lisa.

'Let me get the drinks orders, and then I'll fill you in.'

There were wooden benches at the NFT, with tables set up like a campsite picnic area. They were lucky to find enough empty tables, and Lisa went inside to get the drinks.

5.45 p.m. Glasgow/The King and the Spider

Two hours before the start of the game, the Spider was chock-a-block with Rangers fans. There was noisy singing and many were already drunk, though Kenny could not imagine how. He had arrived at the airport with the rest of the gang about two hours ago and had been catching up with those who had come by coach and ferry. Their own group was fifty strong and they were all in the same stand so Kenny knew that whatever happened, he would be among friends. Red had already told them they were not to take any weapons into the stadium and had to leave the rucksack with him. He knew the publican and could safely put things behind the bar until he needed them. He, of course, would not be at the game. He didn't tell them anything more, just reminded them to be at the airport in time for the return flight.

Ritchie took charge now. The most essential task was, of course, to buy the drinks. He turned to Kenny and said, 'So what will it be, Kenny? Are you old enough for a pint of the best or will it be diet coke?'

'What are you having?' Kenny asked, just to have some time to think.

'Well, I'll have my pint of Guinness with a chaser of double malt, Lagavulin. But I wouldn't advise you to try that. It will kill you.'

'Let me have a pint of bitter. You choose whatever you think will be good for me.'

'Aye, lad. That's wise. Your mam will kill me if you go home sick. Ok, lads, what will it be for you? The usual?' Without waiting for an answer, he marched off to the bar.

6.00 p.m. Glasgow

Red was far away from all this. He had to keep his head clear and refrain from doing anything foolish that could lead to the Glasgow police coming after him. He had been in trouble in Glasgow before, though not as often as in Belfast. Glasgow was, after all, a home away from home for him and his people. But Red had to concentrate. He had already checked that the rucksack contained the ingredients he needed, the mercury, the small sandwich box and the timer. He had read up about bomb making and got himself the smallest bomb, which he hoped would do the trick. It was based on the simple notion that the movement of the car itself would trigger the bomb. You could hardly call it murder; it was almost a suicide. In just another couple of hours, Harry White would be fitted up. The game would get over too, and then he would have a proper drink with the lads.

6.15 p.m. Glasgow

Drinks were on Roger's mind as well. He had looked up his book of cuttings on recipes for cocktails. There would be the usual beer and Guinness drinkers, and those who would not let anything but a Highland malt touch their lips. But once the game was over and they had had their first thirst quencher, some of the guests were sure to get fancy. Getting invited by the directors of Rangers for an Old Firm game would go to their heads. They would look at the free booze and start muttering Chartreuse, and demand an Armadillo or a Negroni. You had to be prepared and quick, of course, because there would always be five others banging on.

But at this moment, it was a simple cocktail that occupied Roger—an American style Martini. It required gin and vermouth in any combination you liked as long as it was dry. Gin in a large measure, a multiple of the amount of vermouth, ideally chilled with some crushed ice, though some preferred ice cubes. Americans liked crushed ice and some Glasgow types went that way. The English from down south liked theirs with ice cubes. Not that they came to Glasgow often, and even if they did, they were unlikely to come to the Ibrox.

But the Englishman coming tonight wasn't just anybody. It was Harry White, prime minister to everyone else, but as far as Roger was concerned, a warped and evil man. Not because Roger was left wing, which he was. He had spent his wilder days on the extreme left in Glasgow, though Calum Kennedy, his old mate, was probably the only one who still remembered him from then.

They had been comrades once, Calum and he. Roger shuddered as the thought of how far they had come from their past. From two young agitators for the Communist Party selling *The Morning Star* to the shipbuilders on cold wet mornings and fighting the Trots at public meetings, they had ended up miles apart. Calum was a millionaire and Roger was just about alright. He had the dole, or rather the Jobseeker's Allowance as it was called nowadays, and he also found casual jobs for cash as a bartender. In fact, it was Calum who used to find him such jobs in the old days, when they first went their separate ways. Now he got them through his own contacts. He was careful not to be greedy, though. He did the odd job, now and then, for big companies. They could pay good wages and lose a large wad of cash in their accounts, and no one was any wiser. Often, there would be five hundred quid at the end of the evening. But that was only the half of it. Less than half. Maybe only one per cent.

This was an evening Roger had been waiting for since that fateful morning twenty-five years ago, when he had been summoned to the Bursar's office. It was early for Cambridge undergraduates to be out of bed, especially since he, like many others, had been up till three the night before. Yet the summons was peremptory, the porter banged hard and long on the door to make sure Roger woke up. As he staggered to his door, muttering and cursing, he was told to dress quickly and come to the Bursar's office. Roger could not recall what he had done the previous evening. As he splashed cold water on his face, he tried hard to remember. He had gone to a union meeting where they had debated the legalization of drugs. Roger had spoken in favour of course, but the religious societies had backed the union and the motion lost. He had then come back and drifted into Mill Lane and gone to the pub on the river. At the pub, he had met Melissa.

When Roger got to the Bursar's office, he saw immediately that something was seriously wrong. There were five police officers and the mood was deeply sombre.

'Birch, thank you for coming. May I introduce Detective Superintendent Atkinson? He wishes to ask you some questions.'

Roger was frightened now.

'What is the matter? What have I done?'

'That remains to be seen, Mr Birch.'

Roger was tall, just under six feet, but he was hunched up that morning and the policemen seemed big and burly next to him. Roger felt a chill going down his spine as Atkinson produced a photograph of Melissa.

'Do you know this person?'

'Yes, of course, it's Melissa.'

'When did you last see her?'

'I haven't seen Melissa for months. We quarrelled. We were friends last year. What has happened?'

'Are you sure you did not see her last night?'

'Only from a distance at the bar. We did not speak.'

'Think carefully, sir. This is very important. You are not under oath but it would be in your interest to co-operate with us.'

'Is Melissa hurt? Has she had an accident?'

'Birch, Miss Musson is dead.'

It was the Bursar who spoke. Atkinson looked unhappy that this vital piece of evidence had been revealed. Roger went numb. He had to sit down. Atkinson waited patiently for a while, then repeated his question, 'Are you sure you didn't speak to her?'

'I talked to her, but not for long. We quarrelled a few months back and were not really close after that. Then suddenly seeing her last night...oh God...' Roger began to sob.

'Go on.' Atkinson didn't have much sympathy for such dramatics.

'I said hello, and then something sarcastic about her looking pale like a princess. She smiled, but she was looking tired and sad. All she said was, It's nice to meet like this, because I may not come to the bar again. I thought she meant this being the final year, she had to get

serious about her work. So I asked her if she would come to the final
May Ball with me. She didn't say anything, just turned away and
went out. I thought she had tears in her eyes, but I couldn't be sure.'

'What time would this be, sir?'

'About half past ten. They were still serving drinks at the bar.'

'How do you know?'

'Because I was so gutted by her walking away like that, I decided to
get totally pissed. I went up to the bar and bought a triple brandy for
myself with a double whisky chaser. I'd already had several beers earlier
in the evening. Excuse me, may I go to the toilet? I feel sick.'

The Bursar took Roger firmly by the shoulder and sped him to the
rather elegant toilet attached to his office. It didn't get easier after
that. Atkinson informed Roger that Melissa had committed suicide
by taking sleeping tablets. Her next-door neighbour Christine Brown
had gone to borrow some milk and found her limp on the floor. There
was a note to Roger. It said: *I am sorry I couldn't explain, Roger. I meant
goodbye.*

No one knew what it was about, except Roger.

It was at the end of term the previous May that he had taken
Melissa to a party given by Harry White. Roger had come to know
Harry in the union. Harry was a very good speaker, and everyone
thought he would get to the top some day. Roger was a poor speaker,
but he was very well read despite being a student of science—
chemistry, in fact. He read widely and discussed things with Harry,
and was always chuffed when he found echoes of his ideas in Harry's
speeches. Harry would never forget to acknowledge him afterwards,
and they became good friends. Roger could see that Harry was
ambitious and cunning, and yet he felt that Harry was straight. At
least, with him.

And then Harry stole Melissa from him. As soon as they got to the
party at his flat, Harry gave Roger a glass of punch he had made himself.
Then he asked Melissa what she would like. Melissa was a non-drinker.

She usually stuck to juice and coke. She said, 'Oh, anything. Even water is fine.' So Harry led her into an inner room where the drinks were. Roger didn't remember much else from that evening. The punch had been spiked by Harry. He talked to some people for a while, but then he had to sit down. The next day, he woke up with a hangover. Even in his dreadful state, through hazy eyes and thumping head, he saw Harry and Melissa entwined in another corner. Melissa had little on, but she was blissfully asleep in Harry's arms.

Roger tiptoed out of the room. He could have killed Melissa, but then maybe it was Harry's fault. He tried later to contact Melissa to have it out with her. Why had she kept him away all these months, saying she was not ready for the full thing? Roger was in love with her, yet she had slept with a man she had just met.

But Melissa wasn't in the mood for explanations or even a simple meeting. She refused to see him. In any case, the holidays were round the corner. When they came back to Cambridge, he lost touch with her completely. Harry acted as if nothing had happened, and never mentioned the party or Melissa. It was their final year and Roger was less active in the union. Harry was reading economics, which was easy compared to chemistry. He never saw Harry with Melissa again, and he thought it best not to be nosy.

'Can you tell me, Mr Birch, when was the last time you met Melissa before last night? Can you recall? Try.'

Roger didn't have to think.

'We went to a party at the end of last term. That was when our friendship ended.'

'Can you tell me why?'

'I got drunk and passed out. She became friendly with someone else.'

'I am sorry to have to ask you this. Did you and Miss Musson have a physical relationship?'

'No, of course not. She wasn't that sort of girl.'

Atkinson smiled. The Bursar looked away.

'Can you be available for the rest of the day if we need you?'

'Yes, of course. I'll see to it.' This was the Bursar taking over.

It was some days before Roger found out. Melissa was pregnant when she took the sleeping pills. It had to be Harry who was responsible. Roger tried to confront him, but Harry laughed it off.

'Don't be daft, Roger. People sleep around these days. Who knows who else she had in her thrall? Just because she fooled you with her act of innocence, it doesn't mean she fooled me. Anyway, if she didn't want the baby, she knew what to do. Mind you, she was an easy lay. It took only a small amount of vodka in her second glass of orange juice to get her going. Fine body, though.'

Roger lunged at Harry but Harry was too quick. Tall though Roger was, he was not nimble. Harry landed a punch on him and then remarked quite casually, 'Grow up Roger. You will meet a lot more of them in your life. Lay them, don't love them.'

Roger felt humiliated. He talked to Melissa's girlfriends and managed to piece together the whole story. Melissa had told no one about Harry. She had gone back to her parents after the party. They always went camping for their holidays. She sent Harry postcards, but received nothing from him. When term started, she had thought they would resume their tryst. But Harry was cold and aloof. He showed no interest in her. She was a conquest, another trophy notched up. Melissa began to find out about other women he had seduced. Her next-door neighbour Christine Brown was one such. Christine told Melissa that Harry was a one-night-stand man. Charming, seductive and swearing love when he needed to, but cold and withdrawn the morning after. Christine did not seem to care; she was still friendly with him.

Melissa was destroyed. She had always thought that everyone was nice and trustworthy and loving like her parents. Like Roger, who had stuck by her and never breached the barriers. She planned her suicide carefully. She went to the college health officer and complained about her inability to sleep. This allowed her to stock up on sleeping pills. Then that night, she went to the bar and ran into Roger. When he asked her out after all she had done to him, she could not bear it. She ran back to her room. But she felt she had to say something to Roger, so she left him a brief note. If she did leave a note for Harry, the police did not find it.

Roger never finished his degree at Cambridge. He became ill and had to drop out. He took up temporary jobs as and when he needed the money. He couldn't face his parents, who were disconsolate about their son's failure and could find no explanation for it. Now, finally, after years of wandering, he was to come across Harry White in person. This was his chance to serve Harry a drink, and there was no way he was going to miss it.

Roger had thought long and hard about how he would take his revenge on Harry. He had thought he would go to Parliament and confront him and perhaps beat him up. But when he went to London and to the Central Lobby of the House of Commons, he found the atmosphere too intimidating. There were too many people and policemen and attendants. He did fill in the slip to summon Harry from the Chamber, but then lost his nerve and left before Harry arrived. As Harry rose in public esteem, Roger found it more difficult to plot his revenge. He could have approached some tabloid for a kiss-and-tell story, but he had no proof and he did not want to hurt Melissa's parents or her memory. The only way out was to kill Harry.

How does one kill a prime minister? Britain was not like the US where anyone could own a gun, and people took potshots at presidents.

Political violence was much more an Irish thing. The Irish Republican movement routinely used violence as a weapon. There was a constant battle between the loyalists and the IRA in Ulster, which occasionally spilled over to the mainland. The IRA managed to bomb the Grand Hotel in Brighton where the Conservative Party leadership was staying during the conference in 1984. They may have planned to kill Margaret Thatcher, but did not succeed. Two minutes before the bomb went off, she had been in the bathroom of her hotel suite, which was completely destroyed. But she escaped. They killed some other people instead. Now, with ceasefire in place in Northern Ireland, the assassination of Harry White was not on the cards. Roger had to think of a way of killing Harry himself.

The idea of poisoning Harry came to him gradually. The odd jobs Roger picked up included bartending and catering for small parties at private functions. He began to educate himself in the art of cooking and cocktail making. He soon learned how food poisoning can occur if one is careless and mixes the wrong ingredients. His chemistry education came in useful, since he could understand the chemical composition of the ingredients, and which chemical could be combined with which other, to what effect. He knew he could poison Harry's food if he got the catering contract some day. What held him back was the risk of killing more than just one person. But drinks, he figured, were personal, and cocktails were made to order for each person. So his fantasy moved on to poisoning Harry with a drink. As Harry became prominent in public life, articles about him began to appear, and Roger took a keen interest in them. He occasionally got a job as a library assistant, and read up old newspaper files to look for details on Harry's habits.

It was then that he discovered Harry's favourite drink, an American style, very dry Martini with an olive in it. It was the olive that could become Roger's weapon.

So Roger began his study of poisons. After all, even in fairy tales, there were stories of princesses being poisoned by wicked stepmothers. They were usually fed some berries which, though dipped in poison, still tasted sweet. Would an olive retain its flavour after being rendered poisonous, he wondered.

Roger knew from his studies that the human body contains many poisonous elements, but in such modest amounts that they help rather than hurt. Poisonous elements like mercury, arsenic, lead and antimony exist in small amounts, as do metals such as cobalt, iron and tin. Also iodine, sulphur, nickel and molybdenum. Even silicon exists, though in a small quantity. There were two things Roger would have to keep in mind when working with poison: the injected dose would have to be lethal, more than the body could use. And the body would have to absorb it, not reject it immediately. Harry would have to swallow the poison, and it would have to reach deep into his gut.

The death would have to be quick, but not instantaneous. Roger would have to administer the poison hidden in a drink and make his getaway before Harry died, and before an autopsy could be done. Nowadays, with forensic sciences being so advanced, the poison would be traced to the olive soon enough. Roger would have to rely on the shock and confusion caused by the sudden death of a prime minister. It would be some time before anyone made a clinical examination, at least an hour, or maybe two. So Roger saw himself leaving town and country as quickly as possible. He could get to Ireland without anyone examining his passport. Once there, he could flee to some obscure South American region, perhaps the Amazon jungles of Brazil.

All this planning had been done while Roger drifted around Glasgow on his own, consumed by his hatred for Harry. He had tried getting into a relationship many times, but every time he had ended up back on his own. Melissa's memory haunted him to such an extent that he had even lost his capacity for loving. He had tried counselling, but did not want to let anyone into his secret. He learned from the sessions though, that there was a big obstacle at the back of his mind which had crippled him emotionally, and concluded that only by taking his revenge on Harry could he become whole again.

What he had not counted on was meeting Deirdre and Samantha. He had not thought of Deirdre as a person he could have a relationship with. She was so different from anyone else he had been with. He was used to middle-class women, professionals. She was working class, and not at all his type. Perhaps that was why he dropped his guard. With his parents now dead, Deirdre and Samantha were the only family he could claim, and he had grown fond of them. They did not know much about his past. He kept his Cambridge days well hidden. He told Deirdre he came from Cornwall, which sounded far enough away to her. But once Harry was dead, the police would trace him back to her home address, and she and Sam would have to answer for him. He wished he could avoid that or tip them off in some way. Perhaps he should leave a long note.

In the course of his research, Roger learned that mercury could kill but only a very large dose of it, and indeed may not kill immediately. It could take as long as a week. Harry would have the best medical care if he was found to be poisoned; they would empty out his insides and frustrate any effects. Arsenic was in some ways a better bet, but the art lay in the precision of the dose. In its mineral state, arsenic is solid and does not dissolve. But if he could get hold of arsenic trioxide, he would have better luck. It was soluble and colourless, as well as tasteless. He could dissolve it in water and then soak the olive in the solution. Hopefully, the arsenic would transfer itself to the olive. But he had to be sure. He had read about too many cases of abortive attempts at murder through arsenic where the culprit was punished though he had only succeeded in making the victim violently ill. He had to be sure. It was time to put his scientific training to some practical use.

Roger needed to mix his poisons and experiment a little before he could be sure. Luckily for him, Glasgow had a number of institutions of higher education. The old university of Glasgow, Strathclyde University and the Poly, though it had now upped itself to a university called Glasgow Caledonian, all had chemistry departments. There were also hospitals with medical research divisions that hired assistants. Students did not like to take science options nowadays, so chemistry departments were running low on teaching work. Some survived by getting funds from research grants to carry on work. But Scottish universities had not suffered the severe cuts that English universities had and so there was still a bit of fat to employ occasional research assistants, like Roger, to help out in the laboratories.

So Roger had his locker in the Uni and though he did not have a permanent job, they never took his locker away. He could go in and out and access the ample supply of chemicals stored in the department. He got his mixtures made, and then tried them out on hamsters he bought in the pet shops. This was before he moved in with Deirdre. Samantha loved little creatures, and would have scratched his eyes out if she knew what he had done.

It was only a fortnight ago that Roger had learned about Harry White's visit to Glasgow. Calum had sent word that he could fix him up with a big job at the Ibrox for that evening as he was hosting the dinner afterwards. So Roger got to work. He bought some olives, fat and dark green, and two jars. One jar was for pickling, and he kept a few of the olives in it, in his locker, soaking in his favourite solution. In the other jar, he saved the clean olives. He knew someone else would ask for a dry Martini, once they heard Harry asking for it. There were always toadies when a prime minister was around. Roger did not want anyone else killed by accident. He was squeamish that way.

When he reached the gates of the university, he saw there was something afoot. Young men and women were thrusting leaflets in people's hands. They were political leaflets. with Harry Shite! prominently printed on them. Roger could see that this was one of his old Trotskyist factions. They would no doubt go on about imperialism and bloated capitalists and poverty in the Third World, and blame it all on Harry White and his pusillanimous party which had sold out the cause of socialism.

Roger saw that people were steadily drifting in, no doubt heading for the hall where Harry would be speaking. He quickly slipped past them and found his way to the chemistry building.

He was surprised that even at this late hour there were people working in the department. As he reached the entrance, he ran straight into Ken MacIntosh. Dr MacIntosh was a senior lecturer in chemistry and had been with the department for some twenty-five years. He was active in the teachers' union and in the local Labour Party, but not very much in chemistry.

'Kenneth, I thought you never worked after lunch. What has happened to you? Mandy not talking to you?' Roger thought it best to put Ken on the defensive so that he would not probe too deep into what he was doing in the building so late.

'Don't you go on as well. It is diabolical, what they expect nowadays. We have research assessments every four years, and we are supposed to submit four published papers for judgment by our peers, which means outsiders, unknown snoopers. It is slavery working in higher education, not fun.' Kenneth was ready with his tale of woe.

'Doesn't sound bad to me—one piece of work per year. Not like what we have to do at the coal face in the outside world.' Roger wanted to appear relaxed and to keep him talking; it would help his alibi later.

'How can you say that? We don't just do research, after all. It's not even our main job. We have teaching assessments and tutorials, we have to mark continuous assessments, there are departmental and university meetings to go to, and we have to mentor junior staff. Then someone evaluates us every two years to see if we have met our targets and whether we have any problems. I would say I have plenty. How can one get any research work done with a work load like that?'

'But I thought you were active in the staff union. Why don't you go on strike?' Roger knew what Ken really spent his time on.

'You must be joking. Those days are gone, lad. It is worse than in the days of Thatcher's cuts. We thought the new lot would give us some respite, but no way. Students have options, and we have to deliver. And you should see some of the new staff recruits. Everyone has his head down and eyes firmly fixed on the greasy pole of promotion. They are apolitical, the lot of them. Anyway, what brings you to the slave ship?'

'Oh, I was passing by on my way to Ibrox so I thought it was as good a time as any to clear my locker. It has been sometime since I looked in and I reckoned I should collect my things before they start smelling and get thrown out.'

'What are you doing at Ibrox then? Got a ticket for the game?'

'No, I can't afford a ticket, not with my income. I got a job to mix the drinks in the directors' box as the PM is coming tonight.'

'That bastard Harry Shite? Oh my God. He is everywhere. Why don't you poison him while you are at it? I could give you a few tips if you want.'

Roger went cold with fright, but only for a second.

'No, thanks. I am not political any more. I just want the wad of dosh at the end of the evening. Poisoning Harry White may make it difficult for me to get paid, especially if he were to drop dead at my feet, thanks to one of your lethal recipes.' Roger was skating on dangerously thin ice now, but the irony was delicious.

'Well, he is coming to the campus in a few minutes, and I am off to barrack him. You may be apolitical, I am not. I want to teach him a lesson that will make him stay away from Glasgow for ever. See you.'

Roger heaved a sigh of relief. He was running out of time and Ken could talk for ever. He wanted to get out quickly to avoid any chance of Harry seeing him. He did not think Harry would recognize him after all these years, but then politicians have long memories when it comes to faces and names. And if he saw Harry before carrying out his plot, his own resolution might weaken.

6.25 p.m. London/South Bank

It took some time, but Lisa came staggering out with a large tray loaded with everyone's favourite drink. It was difficult to get Pernod, but not impossible. The bartender had had to look through the stocks at the back for a spare bottle; the sherry and bitters and vodka tonics were easy to get. Shouts of joy and applause greeted her. They were determined to make every gossip column the next morning. No such thing as bad publicity, Lisa always said.

'So tell me Lisa, what is it that you get away with?' Annie was still curious.

'You know, the odd escapade, just to keep one's ego intact.'

'Like who?'

'Well, since you don't know anyone, and are not likely to meet them...'

'Or remember their names, even if you told me...' Annie was egging her friend on now.

'There was a nice Tory once. Man called Roscoe Hartley. Tories are ever so polite with women. They are chauvinist bastards, of course, but then so are Harry's lot, except that Tories have manners. They also have the dosh so you can meet in posh places, very safe.'

'Sounds alright to me. But what was Harry doing at this time?'

'Well, he was in the opposition, and I am afraid he was working hard to make a fool of Roscoe in Parliament.'

'Did he succeed?'

'He had to. It was the least Roscoe could do for me. Though mind you, I never asked. He had given me enough to be happy as it was.'

'Do you still see him?'

'Occasionally. He is in the House of Lords now, and also on the board of the Royal National.'

'So will he be there tomorrow?'

'I hope so, but so will Harry.'

'You must introduce me. I'd love to meet the gallant Lord.'

'But you wouldn't fancy him. You are not into *les garcons* in any case.'

'Well, it's always fun to, how did you put it, keep the ego intact. I don't want to be typecast, you know, chin chin.' Annie winked and raised her glass.

'Down the hatch and long live liberation.'

6.30 p.m. London/The Bell Yard

Linda knocked and came in.

'She is on her way to Glasgow on the shuttle and they expect her there by seven forty-five. She will be at the Meridien. I gather the office car will pick her up at the airport.'

Linda knew the score. No names mentioned. She handed the flight details to Asha on a piece of paper; you couldn't trust email.

'Thanks, Linda.'

'Shall I get our friend in Glasgow for you?'

'Please, Linda. Thanks.'

Asha knew that Linda could read her mind a couple of steps ahead, but would never say the words, just in case she had to answer any queries in the future.

6.30 p.m. Glasgow/Ibrox

One of the hundreds making their way to the game was David Byrne. He held on tightly to the hands of his twin sons Robbie and Alistair. Although there was still an hour and a bit to go, the stadium was filling up quickly. He had chosen the tickets in a somewhat expensive range, thinking this would keep the crowds down. Sophie had been unsure whether taking the twins to the game was a good idea, given the reputation of the fans on both sides. So David had called the Rangers ticket office and said he wanted to bring his eight-year-old twins to the Old Firm game and asked whether there was any problem, any risk of violence. A polite, soft-spoken woman at the other end of the phone assured him that Rangers had a strict stewarding policy nowadays. They wanted families to come and enjoy good football. When David said it was the boys' birthday treat, the woman said she would give him a good price for the seats. She also gave them seats near the bottom so the boys could see the game without people blocking their view. Still, David took the precaution to arrive early.

David was an ex-marine who now worked on various security assignments. They had a lovely house in Ayr, from where David and the boys had driven down at ten in the morning. Sophie thought it best to be at home with Nicola. She was six and very cross that she was not included in the party, but Sophie promised to take her to Glasgow on her birthday, just the two of them. And that did the trick.

Now father and sons were in the stadium.

'Dad, this is so big, isn't it?' Robbie's eyes were popping out.

'Dad, how old is this place? Is it very old?' Alistair asked.

'Dad, when will the match start?' Robbie wanted to know.

'You know it starts at a quarter to eight, Robbie. Dad has already told us that.'

David intervened. 'Ok. We have plenty of time, so let me tell you. Rangers started way back in 1872. But they moved here about a hundred years ago.'

'Is that older than you are, Dad?' It was Alistair again.

'That's older than your mum and me put together. If you add Grandpa's age and mine, it comes to just over a hundred.'

'Dad, who will win today? Rangers or Celtic?' Robbie asked.

'I want Rangers to win,' Alistair said.

'Why, Alistair?' David asked.

'Because this is their ground.'

'I want Celtic to win.' Robbie had to choose the other side.

'Who do you think will score first? Rangers or Celtic?' David asked.

'Rangers. Numan will score first.' Alistair had read about the match.

'I think Larsson is the best,' Robbie said.

'Well, let us see which of you is right.'

The stadium was filling up on all sides. There was already a lot of singing and shouting. Looking around, David Byrne was not reassured that this was a family-friendly gathering. Many displayed tattoos and clean-shaven heads, bare arms and knuckle dusters at the ready. Their dress was an odd mixture of T-shirts, torn trousers and kilts, funny hats and earrings, and even some wrist bands which were more like steel bangles. There were not many women but those present were akin to the men, with faces painted the colours of their team and garish make-up and yes, tattoos and various degrees of underdressing. There was music playing on the PA system and the overhead TV was showing clips from previous Rangers matches. The boys, at least, were fascinated.

David carefully noted the various exit signs. You never knew what might happen.

6.35 p.m. London/House of Commons

Frank Thompson hated it when Harry was away and he had to be in charge. One would have thought and indeed, many hoped, that he would be itching to take over and give the party its old heritage back. But Frank knew he had reached the peak of his career. A coal miner's son from Barnsley, he had escaped the fate of going down the mines like his father and grandfather, but only by running away from home. It happened after one of those nights when his father had come home more drunk than usual and taken the strap to his mother. Frank had intervened and was beaten to within an inch of his life. He had staggered out the very next day, intending to run away to the sea, but got only as far as Grimsby. He joined the fishing fraternity, but they soon found out that he was only fourteen, and so Social Services took him in. He was then sent to a technical school. When they noted his ability to read and write, they taught him the printing trade.

By the time he was eighteen, Frank had a job in Leeds in the newspaper printing business. Those were the days of the hot metallic press, and printing unions were rough and powerful. Frank learned his revolutionary economics in the trade union branch. Soon he was a delegate, and before he was forty he was on the Executive Committee and an alternate delegate to the Trades Union Congress. He could attend the annual conference of the TUC and vote if the main delegate was absent for some reason.

He kept up his studies, following courses with the Open University. Being a union official gave him the chance to do evening courses at Leeds Polytechnic. He enjoyed them and argued the backs off his teachers. They all fancied themselves as Marxists or whatever, but they had never been near a lathe. Frank kept haranguing them, as they subtly taught him the ways of winning an argument. It was they who made Frank into a well-read, patient persuader. He was extremely proud of his B.A. in political economy and did not mind that it was only an Ordinary, not an Honours degree.

There was a knock at the door, and the chief whip, Austin Mills, came in without waiting for an invitation.

'What's up, Austin?'

'Have you heard anything about Libya? What is Harry planning?'

'Haven't the faintest. Ask Nick Davies.'

'Can't after lunch, as you know. He is too pissed to talk to. He will sober up at about seven for half an hour.'

'Isn't that soon enough?'

'It's just that I have a feeling Eric and the idle boys are up to something. Jimmy would not come with me to Annie's for a pint.'

'Well, that is pretty serious. What's up?' Frank came back to his favourite conversational gambit.

'Eric and Alex and Jimmy will probably table a motion on our Libya policy for Wednesday's party meeting.'

'Let them. They will get ten votes.'

'Harry would take that as a serious revolt, and my job would be on the line.'

'I wish our leader had lived through the days when we had no majority to speak of. Two lads down with the flu, and we were on tenterhooks. In those days, you expected a revolt every afternoon and thanked your stars it had not happened by division bell time at ten. He now has four hundred MPs and freaks out at a revolt of ten.'

'He was still learning his knives and forks at Cambridge in those days.'

'Oh no. Harry knew that in his kindergarten. They don't let you into those posh public schools with coal in your bathtub. No, he was learning his economics, which helped him make a lot of money at that fancy foreign bank.'

'Which is why he can speak German in Bonn and French in Paris. He is not one of us, is he now?'

'He is our leader, and that is good enough for me. I have been here longer than he has, but it makes me nervous to stand at the despatch box. And look at him. The way he slaughters Peter Portugal every week.'

Frank had found that all his education did not measure up to a tenth of what Harry had. He was not fluent in any foreign language. He could harangue the conference, but in the cut and thrust of the House of Commons, he usually lost. In the earlier days, the new MPs were trade unionists or teachers, or maybe the odd old barrister. But the new lot were all fresh university graduates with doctorates and the like. They spoke posh and used long words that threw Frank. But while the others patronized him, Harry had made friends. He had asked him about the lore of the party—the myths and the legends, the hoary old disputes and the alphabet soup of initials of the many sectarian formations. Harry never said what his opinion was on any issue or person. He always listened attentively, and thanked Frank enthusiastically at the end. Previous leaders had not forgiven Frank for one or other quarrel of the 1970s but Harry was innocent of all that, or wished to be.

In befriending Frank, Harry was buying into the party's past. In numerous subtle ways, he won Frank over to his side. He wielded the scalpel and used Frank as a battering ram when necessary. The more he got to know him, the more Frank was convinced that he himself was not cut out to be a leader. He was a deputy, and a faithful one at that. Harry was the works as far as Frank was concerned. Anyway, he loathed Terence and the Scottish mafia.

'Listen, I'll send my spies out. Can you do a stint in the Chamber?'

Frank looked at the House of Commons Annunciator and groaned. On the TV screen it said the subject being discussed had to do with the Department of Culture. They were debating the Arts Council grant, a right load of waste if there ever was one.

6.40 p.m. Glasgow

Sarah was pleasantly squashed in the car between Harry and Oliver. The inspector sat in front, next to the driver. Harry had seen to it that Sarah was at his side. It was something Sarah had not even dreamt of the previous weekend. But here she was, thigh to thigh (with layers of fabric in between, of course) with Harry. He smelt nice.

'Why don't we drop Sarah off at the hotel before we go for the meeting? Someone can bring her to the game, Oliver.'

'No problem. It's on our way anyway, since the university is downtown as well. But we'll have to be quick.' Oliver did not want Harry to linger too long with his new conquest.

It would have been much more sensible to send Sarah off in one of the local cars but Harry would have none of it. So a detour had to be made to drop her off at the Meridien. She would have an hour to change. Sarah thanked her stars she did not have time to dither about what to wear. Her lunchtime expedition had fixed her choice. It had better work, she thought. But work at what?

Oliver's pager buzzed. It was Christine.

'Expect a call from DC.'

It soon came. It was the president.

Harry was suddenly very serious. Everyone else in the car knew they were not supposed to listen.

'Hi, Rob. What can I do for you?'

'Harry, glad we can talk. We are about to go on Operation Rosa. It should happen by 5 p.m. Eastern, ok?'

'Sure, Rob. No problem. That would be ten o'clock our time. We'll handle it at our end. I'll tell Mary Duggan to liaise with your guys. Our chaps are eager to go.'

'You're a pal, mate. We'll go public five minutes before zero hour.'

Operation Rosa was the code name for the US bombing of Libya. It had been under consideration for some time, but the precise date and time had been left to the Pentagon to decide. Harry had won a small role for the RAF as support team in the operation. The American bombers were to take off from Fakenham in Norfolk, so there were bound to be questions in Parliament. He would have to warn Mary Duggan right away.

Mary was Harry's unorthodox choice for defence secretary. She had been on the left of the party, but was not a pacifist. With her Irish Catholic background, she had always regarded force as necessary for achieving a united Ireland. In her student days, she had associated with IRA front organizations. But over the years, she had steadily drifted away. She realized that a sectarian movement can easily turn intolerant; there is a huge distance between sectarianism and socialism. Mary was a socialist, first and last.

Now she was in Harry's Cabinet. She had shadowed defence very successfully, and they liked her immensely in the armed forces. She could swear like a trooper and never fussed about going anywhere, no matter how risky or inconvenient. She wore no make-up, and her clothes were jumble sale stuff. Mary had become one of the boys, a true success story of Harry's cabinet.

'What about Nick Davies?' Oliver asked.

'If we keep the news from him past his wakeful hour, he will never complain. Tell Christine to get Frank ready for questions in the Commons. It should be a prime ministerial statement, read out by Frank. That way, neither Mary nor Nick can complain. Where will we be at ten o'clock?'

'The game finishes at around quarter to ten, so you will be at the dinner in the director's room at the Ibrox.'

'I'd rather be in the air on my way to Belfast. That way, the reptiles won't get to me.' Harry's first concern was to avoid the media at this juncture.

'I can keep them away if I have to. And we can always claim urgent business.'

'If the bombing starts at ten, they will want a spokesman on *Newsnight*. Get Mary Duggan to cover that. Frank can schedule his statement after division, say around ten fifteen. They can carry that live on late news. Ask Christine to send over the draft statement I left with her, and while I am speaking at the party rally, you revise it. I'll give it a final read when we are on our way to the game. Can we get it across before the game starts?'

'If we get out of the rally soon enough, we may just make that deadline. If not, I'll do it while you are watching your least favourite sport. Don't worry. We have all the stuff necessary to set up a mobile communications centre.'

'Can I be of any help?' Sarah asked hesitantly.

'Thanks Sarah, but it's not really necessary. You will be reached at your hotel by Christine if she wants to pass something on. We've cleared the hotel for security. You can then bring it over to the match.'

Oliver was businesslike as usual, but he didn't really want Sarah to see a top secret statement. Harry turned to her and fixed her with his blue eyes.

'You haven't come here to work, Sarah. Christine said you had to enjoy your trip.'

He threw his arm around her shoulders, and drew her a fraction of an inch closer. Sarah was happy to be squeezed by the prime ministerial fingers. Things can only get better, she thought.

'I intend to enjoy myself. If I don't, Christine will kill me.'

Harry caught the mischief in her eyes.

'Oh, no. It's me she'll blame. So I have to see to it that you have a good time.'

Oliver busied himself with his mobile. Harry's hand was now travelling up and down Sarah's bare arm. Oliver shifted a little to the left. Sarah let her hand rest on Harry's thigh. Then, very easily, she found herself stroking it.

'Could you tell Gordon's people to go straight to the meeting? Tell them we will stop at the hotel for a few minutes when we drop Sarah. Ok, Barney?'

'Yes, sir.' Inspector Barney Jones got on his mobile.

How many minutes would that be, Sarah wondered. She knew she had to be ready for whatever it was that Harry had in mind. It was only eight hours since Christine had broached the subject of her going to Glasgow, and here she was already panting for… for what?

They were at the hotel in George Square. Gideon had connections, so all the big visits ended up at this location. Rooms had been booked for the PM's party, though everyone knew he would not be there for long. But an office had to be set up, and Harry preferred it away from the usual party bureaucracy or the Scottish office.

They stopped just off the square, and got out swiftly. There was no crowd but Sarah could hear some people shouting, 'Hey, Harry! How are you?' The Harry in question gently detached himself from her, and once again became prime minister. The manager had come out with all his staff to welcome the prime minister. He made a little speech welcoming Harry to Glasgow and to his hotel. Sarah wished he would shut up and get out of the way.

Harry thanked him graciously and introduced Sarah and Oliver, his manner urgent without being hurried. The manager offered to show them to their room, but Harry signalled that they had to rush. He took the keys from the manager's hand and got into the lift with Oliver and Sarah.

Not a word said, but Oliver went on to the big suite, and Sarah was led by Harry to her room. It was a large room overlooking the square and dominated by a large bed. There were two sofa chairs by the window, and a table. Sarah threw her jacket over one of the chairs as she heard the door click shut behind her. It was Harry, right behind her, holding her. She sighed, and leaned back into him. She took his hands and put them where she knew Harry was headed. He had to see that she had a superb pair of breasts.

He was kissing her now, with passion and power. She was with him all the way, meeting his tongue with her tongue, laughing and murmuring his name. He was fantastic, cupping her breasts in his hands, nuzzling her neck, sliding his hand down her back and grabbing her firm buttocks to arch her closer.

Sarah was amazed to see how strong and taut Harry's body was. His jacket was off and he had loosened his tie, so all she had to get on to was his belt. But he seized her busy hand, and took it further down so she could feel how stiff he was. And impatient, Sarah thought.

Her dress had slipped off and fallen to the floor, and now Harry expertly unhooked her bra at the back. A man of experience, to be sure. He gently nudged her towards the bed. Her feet were still on the floor but there she was, drawing Harry's mouth to her nipples. He yanked off her—oh my God, what colour were they, were they decent?—underpants. No time to think. The man wanted her and

Sarah welcomed him. Harry was half standing, his mouth now exploring her belly and venturing further down. She suddenly had a thought.

'Harry?'

'What?'

'Can I have a…?'

Harry looked surprised, and thrilled. She slid down and crouched, taking his throbbing cock in her mouth. She licked it, stroked it with the tip of her tongue and then, just for a quick second, put her mouth around it. He gasped.

'Ok, all yours.'

She was back on the bed, spreadeagled, welcoming Harry inside her. His first hard thrust made her gasp. He was unstoppable as he came in and out, all the while telling her how fabulous she was, kissing her, biting her, as she tried not to dig her nails into him.

It seemed like ages before he exploded inside her. She hadn't even thought about it, but here they were practising unsafe sex. The more unsafe the better, she reflected with a smile. By the time he got a condom, the division bells would ring in London.

Harry reached for a box of tissues by the bedside table and ever so gently withdrew, kissing her yet again on her hard nipples. He handed her a tissue and started carefully wiping himself. Sarah drew the bedsheet over her, suddenly shy. She had not been so aroused for ages and her orgasm had left her serene and floating, savouring the moment.

Harry was in and out of the bathroom in no time. He looked immaculate, his tie back on, hair in place, not a smudge of lipstick or anything worse. He leaned over her, gently pecked her nipples, and then kissed her full and long.

'It will be slower next time, I promise you.'

'If I allow you to be slow, that is. Sprinters do more laps than marathon runners, Prime Minister.'

'Yes, Miss Disney.'

'See you at the match.' And he was gone.

She looked at her watch. It was not yet seven. He had plenty of time to get to his meeting. They had taken only five minutes after all.

Sarah stretched lazily, only half awake. Then she ran a hot bath for herself. The hotel had thoughtfully provided aromatic bath salts and gels. As she lay there in a heat induced torpor, she wondered what Alan would think if he saw her now. And there was more to come. She had to be at the game. There was so little time, now that her life was in the fast lane.

8.00 p.m. Vienna/Hotel Franz Joseph

Alan was too astonished at how smooth, white and fragrant Jo's body was to think of anything else, much less of Sarah. This was the first time he had been with Jo with absolute privacy and acres of room to play in. In London, Jo shared a flat with three others, and the few times they had been at his place, the flatmates were forever going in and out of each other's rooms as if it was some BBC sitcom. They had had to rush everything; it was almost like teenage sex in the backseat of a car. Now, there was this large double room in the Franz Joseph with a Do Not Disturb sign in four languages outside. The drinks had been ordered, along with enough sausages and chips to keep room service out of their way. And then there was Jo.

Jo was almost as tall as Alan, but younger and thinner. His attraction had been his appearance of vulnerability, and his eagerness to please. Alan had watched him at work, and on the football pitch. One day, while they were in the shower together, he realized that he was smitten. But there were eight other raucous men in the showers after a hard game of five-a-side soccer. Thus it was that Alan began to make excuses to Sarah. He was exhausted, or worried, and would come very late to bed. He had realized his true passion.

Now, as Alan drooled over Jo, he also began to thrill to the discovery that young as he was, Jo was no novice. A nibble here and a bite there, some amazing deep throated kisses, a skilful hand directing Alan to where he wanted to be caressed. He teased Alan as much as he could in the confines of their room, escaping and then getting caught. As he impatiently pushed himself inside Jo, Alan knew he had found heaven.

8.02 p.m. Vienna/Hotel Franz Joseph

Terence Harcourt felt much the same way. Not that he was engaged in any carnal pursuits. Not yet, anyway. Terence's style was to prepare carefully and then take his pleasure in a leisurely way. He believed that making love was like committing a murder. However passionate the act, you had to be cool-headed about it before and after. You had to plan every move to get your quarry. Then, after the deed, you had to make sure that no clues would be found. Clear away all the smudges and stains. Wipe off every telltale sign. Change the sheets, dump the towels in the laundry basket, flush the biodegradable bits down the loo. The point of pleasure, especially of the illicit variety, was to be able to enjoy its afterglow. For that, you had to take the worrying out of it, the thought that someone somewhere might find out what you were up to. This was why he preferred inside to outside, home to hotels, and younger to older girls. They tended not to complain or tell tales. Even when one was having adult consensual sex, a politician could not be careful enough. Journalists do not judge politicians by their own moral standards, and even young and innocent looking volunteer researchers keep diaries for that future newspaper exclusive.

So Terence did a lot of his pleasure seeking abroad, and he restricted himself to towns where there was a culture of tolerance. Vienna was his favourite city for that reason. Brothels were legal there, as was soliciting in the city centre. He had made this discovery thirty years ago, while walking in the Kohlmarkt after a good dinner. He was surprised at first when the tall blonde approached him. She could not have been as old as she claimed to be. She was obviously dressed for a purpose, and her matter-of-fact manner took him aback. But he had enjoyed this first encounter in a large bedroom in a hotel nearby that seemed to be furnished for pleasure. It turned out that the hotel was owned by an Italian woman who had a stable full of young girls. Rosa Giulia was a kindly lady who seemed to be a kind of universal mother whore.

There was no fuss, no worry at Rosa's place. She provided all her girls with condoms and health care. Terence took some time to get used to a condom, but he had no other complaint. The girls knew how to please him, and got up to all sorts of tricks once he had conveyed his desire in sign language. The money was reasonable— the pound was strong in those days. It didn't take long for Terence to discover his El Dorado.

Tonight, Terence was looking forward to visiting his old haunts. He preferred to be away from Stephanplatz and Kohlmarkt, and along the Gurtel where there were other nightclubs and houses, and women soliciting the cars speeding past. What with the Balkan wars and Eastern European immigration, young Slav and Hungarian and Polish women had flooded Vienna. The choice was fantastic. Soon, he would make a beeline for Rosa Giulia's. But first, he had to have dinner with the Ambassador. He needed a stiff drink or two to endure that.

7.05 p.m. London/House of Commons

'Cheers,' Frank said as he raised his pint of John Smith. 'So what's up, Ian?'

Ian was looking for stories, he wasn't about to provide any. He had been hanging around the House of Commons terrace hoping to catch some minister, even of a lowly variety, to find out more about the revolt brewing. But he'd had no luck. The old practice of MPs hanging around Annie's Bar and the terrace or the Pugin Room had waned. They all had halfway decent offices now, but outside

the Westminster Palace and a short walk away on the other side of
the street. They were young snots, sitting at their computers,
emailing their constituents. They came into the palace only when
asked by their pagers to do so. As for the rest, the whips had to make
sure that enough bodies were in the Chamber to keep track of the
business, but not too many as they might start caucusing. That way
lay trouble. Only the old hands, the unreconstructed reprobates,
still behaved like independent, free thinking adults. But Ian knew
their stories anyway. It was to avoid them that he had wandered
past the library.

As he walked down the long corridor behind the Speaker's Chair,
who should come out of the Chamber but Frank. Ian had never known
Frank to be so pleased to see him.

Frank had been bored out of his mind listening to the Arts Council
debate. He was getting angry, and could have shouted 'Bollocks' at
more than one speaker as they went on about the good things the
Arts Council did. He had done his time, and Austin should be
content with that.

Ian took a sip of his whisky. He said, 'Nothing very much, Frank.
You know I am retired, so I am hardly the person to ask.'

'If you are retired, what are you doing in this den of iniquity?'

'To tell you the truth, I was hoping to pick up a few stories about
Harry White that I could use in the obituary I am writing. No, don't
panic. Nothing has happened to him.'

Ian had to add the last bit quickly, because he saw Frank was about
to spew his beer all over him.

'Well, it's not as if there aren't a few people who wish he was dead.
And they are in his own party as well, even here.'

'You are not getting paranoid, are you now, Frank?'

'No, it is the ingratitude of the human race that gets me. Especially
in this party that I dearly love. They don't remember any longer that
we were crushed flat till Harry came along and added two hundred

seats. Now they have found their old religion again, and it's Tolpuddle Martyrs time all of a sudden.'

'Surely that is a healthy sign. The party is back to its bad old ways because it is no longer scared of losing the next election.'

'You've been around long enough, Ian. We behaved like that when we had a negative majority, remember? Harry is innocent of all that. I had to tell him the stories of those long nights when we had comrades in wheelchairs and ambulance beds arriving to vote. Now we have a rota to keep them off the premises in case idle hands turn to mischief.'

'How can you keep Eric off this place? It's his home.'

'His kennel, more like.'

'You are in a foul mood today, Frank.'

'Aye, I always am when Harry is not around. And I suspect that gang is up to no good, but don't quote me on that.'

'Promise. But what are they up to?'

'The usual. Motion before the party meeting on Libya. What else?'

'But that would get them ten votes. Why bother?'

'Just what I said to Austin. But he's afraid Harry will be cut up.'

'Even at such a small revolt?'

'Harry is the only Stalinist I know who wins elections with an opposition that is not in jail.'

'Can I quote you on that?'

'Don't you dare.'

7.10 p.m. Glasgow/Ibrox

Daring was what Roger had decided to be. Daring and discreet. He knew Harry wouldn't recognize him, not in the middle of a crowd of sycophants, all jostling to get the prime ministerial ear. All he had to do was get his drink ready.

Roger was sure Harry had not changed his drinking habits. But there were still tricky issues ahead. He guessed Harry would not arrive in time to have a drink before the game. So it would be either in the half-time break, or after the final whistle, that he would want a drink. Roger had to be careful, since he did not want to be around when Harry was sinking. His experiments had only been on hamsters, and the rest was based on his extensive reading of cases of death as a result of poisoning. He reckoned he would have to give Harry his lethal drink sometime during the dinner after the game, say at about ten o'clock. Harry was bound to get away quickly after dinner, and so Roger could safely leave as well.

'Roger, nice to see you. Didn't know you were on today.'

It was Alex. He always greeted people at the Ibrox. Alex had been there for decades, and knew all about the club. He bored Roger stiff since he had heard the stories a hundred times.

'So Alex, what are you all dressed up for then? Not for the papists, surely?'

'Now, now, lad. We don't talk like that any more, do we? It is the prime minister himself that I put my finery on for. You know something, Roger, in all the years I have been here, let us say fifty-three years man and boy, not a single prime minister has come to the Ibrox, not even for the Old Firm game.'

'You wait all these years, and all you get is Harry White, eh?'

'Don't be cheeky now. We have to give him a welcome he will remember for the rest of his days. I take it you will be dishing out everyone's favourite poison as usual? Let Harry White have the best of whatever he wants.'

'Will do, Alex, as you say.'

'Did you know, Roger, that the Rangers are still ahead on the score since the first fixture in 1888? Guess how far ahead?'

'Tell me, Alex,' Roger said, his voice resigned.

'We are three ahead, thirty-five to thirty-two, the rest having ended in a draw. And you know what, they have not had a win since...'

'Must go, Alex. Have loads of work to do, preparing for the big event. Cheers.'

'I should say. We are going to have the biggest crowd tonight in a long time. Do you know when we had the largest crowd ever?'

'No, tell me, Alex.' Roger started climbing the stairs and Alex followed right behind.

'January 1939. It was an Old Firm game and there were 118,567 in the crowd and you know what? There has never been a larger crowd anywhere in league level football, not in Scotland and not in England. Not anywhere. Tonight may compare with it, though.'

'Well, I hope they all behave themselves. It is such a crucial game, I hope nothing bad happens,' Roger said, more in hope than anticipation.

'Don't worry, lad. We have not had that sort of trouble here for ages. I tell you, Scotland is a new country since we got this Parliament promised to us. People know the eyes of the world are on them.'

Alex would have detained Roger for some more time, but he saw someone coming towards him, and stopped.

'Hello, Uncle Alex,' said Red.

Alex was very surprised to see his new visitor. The invitees with seats in the top rows were coming in, and he did not wish to be seen with this new arrival.

'What on earth brings you here, McGann? I hope you are not looking for tickets because there aren't any, and even if there were, you are not welcome.' Alex was firm.

'Is that any way to speak to your own nephew? Don't worry. I don't want any tickets and I am not here to embarrass you.' Red was unusually emollient.

'So why are you here? I have work to do. Tell me quick.'

'I just wanted a glimpse of our prime minister. I thought you could let me stand here somewhere so I can see him arriving in his snazzy car. I thought I could take a photo. You know, for my mam. She would love it.' Red showed Alex his digital camera as proof of his intentions.

'I don't believe a word of that. But seeing as you are my sister's only son... Stand in that corner under that awning and don't attract anyone's attention. If you get caught, I don't know you.' Saying this, Alex turned away from Red.

'Tell me, Uncle Alex, are you going to be standing outside all evening and not get to see the great game?'

'Don't you fear, son. I shall be watching it on Rainbow, in my office down here where I can keep an eye on the comings and goings. It isn't just me, you know. I have to look after all the drivers who don't want to miss out either. So we have set up some nice entertainment facilities down here. But don't go around getting any ideas of troublemaking. There will be police presence through the evening. It is not every day the prime minister comes to Ibrox.' Alex knew his nephew was up to no good.

'Why should I make trouble, and that too at Ibrox? I just thought I could relieve you of looking out so you could watch the game.'

'No, thank you. Now get going.'

Red got to his spot, which was perfect because it was to the front of the main entrance, where the VIP cars would be parked. He saw various painted signs for the chairman and the vice-chairman. There was even one for the manager. Reserved car parking space, real posh. So Harry White's car was bound to be parked here. That was all Red needed to know. Now he just had to wait. Most of the policemen, he knew, would get complacent after a while and drift in to watch the match. He just had to be prepared for the moment.

After leaving Alex, Roger bounded up the stairs to the directors' dining room. It was by no means a big room, nor even very luxuriously furnished. Roger had once been at the Oval, when Cambridge played Surrey. The Oval lunch room was prodigiously large when compared to this. The walls here were covered with Rangers trophies, with the pride of place belonging to the European Cup Winners' Cup of 1972. That was the memorable game in Barcelona when Rangers beat Moscow Dynamo 3–2, with Willie Waddell as the manager. The moment was captured in a photograph of Waddell with the winning team. Even more prominent was the photograph of Bill Struth, who had been manager in the twenties. To soothe his nerves, Bill used to play the piano, which used to be kept in a separate room for him, called the Blue Room. Roger thought Waddell was the greater manager, though he had stayed only three years. He had been a player for the Rangers but had come back to manage. Once Jock Stein had won the European Cup for Celtics in 1967, it had been agony for the Rangers to be taunted by their arch enemy that they had been only runners-up at best, never winners. So 1972 was the most memorable victory in the annals of the club. Waddell quit after having brought the Cup to Ibrox.

There were lots of other trophies and memorabilia in the room: Scottish FA cups, Scottish League cups, including the racing bicycle that the St Etienne football team had presented to the Rangers team when they played in the European Cup together in 1975.

To the left of the room, there was a smaller office for the really important guests, and on the right was an anteroom where preparations had to be made for the half-time drinks. They would have to re-arrange the rooms for dinner. Roger had been told to set up his bar in the corner to the right, next to the windows.

7.15 p.m. London/The Bell Yard

Asha was busy planning her long-distance gig. She had to be careful and hope that Willie, her mate in the transport unit of LDNC's Glasgow office, understood her.

Willie had had to leave Singapore on account of his radical politics; Asha's father had been his mentor. Once he got to Britain, Willie lost his politics but he also found it very difficult to get any job that used his education. They could not quite understand his accent here, so he was hopeless as a tutor. He started doing odd jobs. Then he got a job in the newspaper industry, arranging delivery. This was high pressure work as a lot of lorries had to be galvanized in a short span of time to deliver the new print run late at night across Glasgow and the rest of Scotland. Some bundles had to be put on trains so they got to London and Manchester and Birmingham. Willie soon became an expert since he had the mathematical skills for scheduling such transport runs.

Willie met Asha soon after she arrived in London and helped her settle in. He was now quite a well paid manager in Matt Drummond's Scottish newspaper offices. When Asha wanted something done that she could not trust anyone else with, it was Willie she turned to. He was her Chinese cousin.

Asha had taken care to go to a public telephone outside the Temple to call Willie. It was her favourite red telephone box at a time when they were becoming a rarity. But the noise was awful on the Strand, and she had to shout.

'Just a brush, not more. All we want are scars, and hospitalization. Take great care. I expect she does not use seat belts.'

'I hear you, loud and clear. Over and out.' Willie had also taken care to go to a public telephone in Glasgow. He had at his disposal many delivery vans as well as drivers on a casual contract, and driving at an insane speed was their speciality. If one of them drove a limousine off the road in a crash, so what?

7.18 p.m. Glasgow

'So what if the Scot Nats win, you say? I'll tell you what is at stake. All that the Scottish Labour Party has built up here in Glasgow and all over Scotland, all that the Labour Party in the country has built up—the schools, the hospitals, the benefits…'

Harry had spoken for five minutes and could sense that there was going to be a lot of heckling. So he swiftly moved into question-answer mode. That way the heat would go out of the meeting.

'Bullshit. Who cut the single mothers' benefits?' Ken MacIntosh was first off the mark.

'We did not *cut* them, as you say. We have radically restructured them so that single mothers have opportunities to work, to get out of the poverty trap, to have better life chances.' Harry had to shout in the crowded hall of hundreds of angry men and women. There were banners everywhere: 'No War with Libya', 'Raise the Minimum Wage to £ 5', 'Nationalize ScotRail'.

'Call that socialism, do you?' Ken persisted.

'I'll tell you what. Which country do you think has the same single mothers' benefit system as us?'

'Bantustan,' someone shouted, and there was laughter and loud applause.

'No, it is Sweden, socialist Sweden, which has the same policy that we do. And so do Norway and Denmark. We don't live in Clement Attlee's Britain any longer. There is a big revolution out there, called globalization. If we don't prepare to compete with the world, it will be the Chinese workers and the Korean bosses who will dominate world trade. We need to reskill our workers. Even single mothers will need a proper job some day, when their babies grow up. They need education, as do the long-term unemployed. They should be in further education institutes getting a diploma, not hanging about in despair because they are on the dole. We need to invest in our people, not dream about Scotland's oil as the Nats do. They will just spend all the taxpayers' money and crash the economy, and then who will bail Scotland out?'

'Scotland's oil for Scotland,' someone shouted.

'Shouting slogans is easy. But who will pay, if the oil is nationalized? Are you willing to take on a debt of seventy-five billion pounds? And for what? So that the oil companies who are at present taking risks of profit and loss, sleep happily at peace with our money, while our grandchildren end up paying off the interest on that debt? Is that what you want? Because that is what the Scot Nats are offering you. Dreams and delusions of spend now, pay tomorrow and the day after and for a century more. Is that what we want?'

There was applause, albeit signalled from the platform by Gideon's claque. Harry White appreciated the pause.

'What about Libya? Are we going to be America's poodle and bomb Libya?'

'I am proud of our special relationship with America. Every Labour prime minister has cherished that special…'

'Except Ramsay MacDonald,' someone shouted. There was more applause and laughter.

Harry needed this.

'Well, I am sorry, but I have never thought of Ramsay MacDonald as a Labour prime minister. If you think he was, you are in the wrong party, mate.'

There was thunderous applause. Harry had touched the oldest raw nerve in the party's collective psyche. A cliché, yes, bashing Ramsay MacDonald, but it worked, especially in Scotland. Go to any Labour meeting and you only had to say 'Ramsay MacDonald' to know that your audience was with you.

Ramsay MacDonald had betrayed the Labour Party in the midst of the Depression and got into a cosy coalition with the Tories. In fact, he was the only Scottish leader who became prime minister and then he blotted his record. Scotland never forgave its son.

'And not just every Labour prime minister. Even Stan Davies, our dear departed leader, and how I wish he was standing here in front of you as a Labour prime minister…' The rest of Harry's sentence was drowned in applause.

'Yes, and it is for Stan who promised Scotland its own Parliament that we must win the election. Don't let the Scot Nats steal our clothes and pretend that they did anything to bring this about. It is our party and our party alone, with the able leadership of Gideon Crawford—where is Gideon? Come up here—Gideon Crawford, my friends, who will lead the party to victory in the coming elections. Thank you, and goodbye because, as you know, I must go now to a genteel tea party at the Ibrox.'

More laughter and applause, but also boos and shouts of 'No War for American Oil Barons' followed Harry and Oliver as they made their way to the door. Gideon Crawford had the unenviable task of closing the meeting and seeing the rabble off. But he too wanted to be at the game. So he took the gavel.

'All right?' Harry asked.

'Brilliant. I like the way you managed to say nothing about Libya. Honour saved.' Oliver was clearly relieved.

'Of all the crowds, the radical hotheads are the easiest to manipulate. They are sentimental and unthinking. Now, if this had been a meeting of City brokers or the Women's Institute, I would have been unable to get away with that kind of bullshit. But then, that's our great party for you.'

7.30 p.m. London/House of Commons

'The party will be in turmoil, I am afraid, when this gets out,' Austin said.

'That will come later, and maybe not until Wednesday, when Harry gets back. What we now need to sort out is the rest of today and who is going to which news programme,' Frank replied.

They were gathered together in his office at the House of Commons—Austin, Christine, Mary Duggan and Nick Davies, surprisingly awake and coherent.

'Harry's message is that Mary should go to *Newsnight* as soon as they request someone. But we need someone urgently for Channel 4.

I have promised Jon Snow someone will get there before the end. But whoever goes is to say nothing about the American announcement, and nothing at all about us.'

'Shall I go?' Nick suddenly perked up.

'Are you sure you can cope?' Christine asked bluntly.

'Well, darling, as you know, this is my lucid half hour. And what is more, if I say I know nothing, I will mean it.'

'Ok, there is no time to lose. Off you go to London Television Centre. Don't drive. Take the pool car, won't you?' Christine was solicitous as ever. Nick Davies left immediately.

'So, Nick to Channel 4 and Mary for *Newsnight*. What else?' Frank asked.

'There is a prime ministerial statement which you will have to read, Frank. Austin, will you clear it with the opposition chief whips? Has someone told the speaker's office yet?' Christine had to make sure that proper courtesies were observed. A statement made by any minister in the House of Commons required that the appropriate shadow minister from the two main opposition parties be present to respond. It was the job of the chief whip to sort out such details to make the flow of business smooth. This would all take place behind the scene, through the *usual channels*, as the whips were called.

'I have already tipped off the opposition whip's office that a statement could be made. I'll confirm that and let you know if they have got John Altrincham ready. I've also told the speaker's office. I reckon the division should take about twelve minutes in all, so we can schedule the statement at 10.15 p.m.' John Altrincham was the deputy to Peter Portugal and he was the appropriate person to respond to Frank when the statement was made.

'That would be good, since it will be the lead story on *Newsnight*. Do we know who it is tonight?' Mary wanted to know.

'Jeremy,' Christine said. 'Don't let him bite you; go on the attack immediately.'

'Don't worry. I'll sort him out.' Mary had sparred with Jeremy Paxman on *Newsnight* on many occasions.

'How soon can I have the statement, Christine?' Frank was anxious.

'Oliver says once the game starts, he will have time to finalize it. They must now be finished with the rally and on the way over, Oliver was to let Harry make the final corrections. He will then dictate it over the phone to the secure office in the hotel and we should have it by eight o'clock at the latest. Will that be all right, Frank?'

'Yes, of course. I just need a couple of reads before I get to the despatch box. But I also need a full briefing from the FO and your lot for any questions that may come up. The Tories won't create any problems, but we've got to watch the LibDems. You can never trust them.'

'And Eric from our back benches, don't forget.' Austin had had Eric on his mind all day.

'Aye, but then I know almost word for word what he will say, and since he will take his own sweet time to say it, I can always prepare my answer. Even I can think faster than he speaks.' Frank resented Eric's education and his patronizing attitude.

'Fine, then. I'll see to it that you have a full briefing. And I'll coordinate with our beautiful friend, the Baroness, about the FO,' Christine said.

Letitia (Letty) Brighton was the foreign office minister in the House of Lords, where they said the opposition benches were always packed whenever she had to answer a starred question or make a statement. They came not to listen but to gawp at her. Letty used to be a model before she went on stage. Now, to the regret of hundreds of theatre fans and the delight of the noble Lords, she had taken up her perch on the government front bench. She doubled as leader of the House, so she would be reading the statement there.

7.40 p.m. London/Drew House

The front page had just one word in large red type: FILTH. Above it, next to the masthead, the first sentence of Vera's piece said, 'Children are God's tears on Earth.'

There was no page three, no nipples, no talk of nooky. This was the hard version of *The Herald*. Vera's piece occupied all of page three. The one photograph with the girl's face blacked out and the tattoo showing MUM with a heart pierced with an arrow, was spread across pages four and five. Stuart's back was shown, as was a part of his hip with the black mole. That mole had been the crucial factor in Roddy's acceptance of Andrew's claim that the pictures were authentic.

Lex had been staring at it for nearly five minutes now. He had gone over the design with great care, camouflaging anything that would identify the young girl. For the first time in his life, he felt sorry for Terence. This would hound him not just out of politics, but out of the country as well. It was the nuclear option. Left to himself, he would have tipped off Terence, given a hint of what was to come. Terence could then have resigned quietly, making the standard excuses—to spend more time with the family, seek new challenges, hang up ye old boots, or whatever. That would have settled the matter. Even now he was tempted to call Chris and give him a hint of what was coming. Where was Chris? He dialled his number.

'Chris?'

'Yes. Hi Lex, how's tricks?' Wherever Chris was, there was a lot of noise.

'Where are you?'

'In Glasgow, with Gideon Crawford, and at the greatest game in town. What's up?'

'I need a few minutes. Very important. Can you talk in confidence?'

'Not now. Maybe later. Tell you what. Can I call you at half-time? Can it wait that long?'

'Sure. There's no hurry. But do call me at half-time. And don't tell me the score when you do, ok?'

'Done.'

So, that gave Lex just about fifty minutes to agonize about how much to tell Chris. If he messed up and Terence escaped, Lex knew Matt would kill him before firing him. There was half a mil on this one, and if carried in tomorrow's *Herald*, an expected sale of five and a half million. He had to get the timing absolutely right.

7.45 p.m. London/The Bell Yard

Asha calculated that the event in Glasgow would take place sometime before eight o'clock. Before, that is, she had to join Matt and the ten largest institutional shareholders of LDNC in a private dining room at the Ritz. She did not want her mobile to go off in the middle of dinner. She was hoping Willie would call while she was on her way to the Ritz. It was to be a wrong number signal if everything had gone right. Otherwise, a text message saying, 'Miss You'.

It was not often that Asha felt stressed out.

7.47 p.m. The London-Glasgow Shuttle

The stewardess cleared away Margaret's half-drunk glass of Chardonnay. This was the sign that they were preparing to land at Glasgow. She looked at her watch. The flight was on time and she looked forward to being in her hotel by eight thirty, traffic permitting.

'Tell me,' she asked the stewardess, 'what will traffic be like at this time in Glasgow?'

'Whereabouts are you headed, madam?'

'George Square.'

'Normally, on a weekday, it should not take more than half an hour from the airport. But there is a football game tonight at the Ibrox. The prime minister is coming for it, so traffic could be bad. But the game starts at seven forty-five, so everyone going to it should be off the roads by then. Shouldn't be a problem, I reckon.'

'Thanks.'

'Not at all. You're welcome.'

These Americanisms were everywhere now, Margaret thought. She wanted Britain to be different from America, to keep the old charm and not become like a shopping mall. She had to try her best to help preserve the difference. Tomorrow, she would see the lawyers who had drawn up the deeds for the trust under Scottish law, which was better than English law in this regard. Now that culture was a devolved subject, she could also be sure that her plan to spend the money on culture would not be subject to a challenge by Matt after her death. The Scottish Parliament would not change the law just to suit Matt, as she was sure Harry White would gladly do.

7.55 p.m. Glasgow/Ibrox

Sarah was looking forward to whatever it was that Harry would do. There was a wait, an agonizing two hours at least, before she could get close enough to touch him, forget being alone with him. When would they get some time together? On the way to the airport? On the flight to Belfast? Or later still? She had a lot of time to think, now that she had arrived at the stadium and was sitting down.

Sarah was trying to be calm. Her luxury bath had refreshed her and she was glad about the dress she had chosen. It was simple, but the halter neck showed off her shoulders and just a hint of cleavage, and a lot of bare back. She had chosen sheer purple tights, which she thought showed her legs off better. She was preparing carefully for her adventure. She had sprayed herself generously with the Samsara that she had bought as long as five hours ago at Harvey Nick's, just to remind Harry of the joys to come.

When she arrived at the stadium, she had been greeted by a young man whom she had seen earlier on the plane with Gideon's party.

'Hello. I am Jamie, Jamie Hencke. Gideon Crawford told me I had to make sure you were well looked after.'

'Thank you very much, Mr Hencke. How kind of you. And how nice of Mr Crawford.'

'It is nothing, really. Except Gideon will be very cross with me if something goes wrong. And if it gets as far as Terence Harcourt, I am a dead duck in Scotland.'

'Would that matter?' Sarah was just trying to make polite conversation while climbing the interminable stairs to their seats.

'Yes, if I want to make my way in Scottish politics, maybe even British politics. I am hoping Gideon will help me, maybe have Terence take me on in his office in some capacity or another. That will do for a start. Then, who knows how far I can go?'

'So how far would you like to go? To where Harry White is?' Sarah was trying to provoke a response.

'Well, hardly. That would be too far up and what is more, the prime minister is quite a young man. He will be there for twenty, maybe twenty-five years more. I would be happy if I ended up in the Scottish Executive or maybe even in the Cabinet.'

'What interests you, sports and culture?'

'No, it's health really. I am a medical doctor, and I would like to stay with that. But I have to pick up some economics and stuff like that. I am doing a Masters in health economics at the Uni here. How to pay for the NHS is something I worry about. Maybe I can help Terence think about how the European experience in financing health services can help tackle the NHS's problems.'

Sarah was seriously impressed. She had not met many men who could bear to hide their light under a bushel. Here was a man who was a doctor and just about Alan's age, but modest. She looked at him properly for the first time. Not bad looking either, she concluded.

Sarah looked around as she settled into her seat. There was still some daylight, though it was already half past seven. But the ground was floodlit and there were bright lights in all the stands. The noise was deafening. Even five minutes ago, when she arrived at the gates, she had not registered the commotion.

The directors' box had about hundred seats, but wooden ones. She presumed that everywhere else, the seating must be spartan.

The public address system sputtered to life.

We welcome today the Right Honourable Harry White, Prime Minister of the United Kingdom. Welcome to the Old Firm fixture, Prime Minister. Have an unforgettable experience.

There was scattered applause, mainly from where Sarah was sitting. From the crowd on her left came a chant:

Harry Harry Harry. Out Out Out.

There was general laughter and catcalls. Not to be outdone, the stand on her right shouted, *Harry White Total Shite.*

There was a sea of people singing, shouting and waving banners. On her left, the stand was full of green-coloured shirts.

'Those are Celtic supporters. Across there are the home side, the Rangers,' Jamie said helpfully.

'I am told this is real sectarian warfare.'

'Used to be much worse than it is now. Now they have players who are from the other sect, or not Christian at all.'

'Like what? Muslims?'

'No, Jews like me,' Jamie replied.

Sarah remembered the joke Alan had once told her.

'Yes, but are you a Catholic Jew or a Protestant one?'

'I see you know all about us in Glasgow.'

'Not really. I once had a boyfriend who was a football fan, so I picked up a few of the myths.'

As against my current boyfriend, she thought, who hates football and can't wait to get away from here. Nor can I. She looked around. Behind her, right at the top of the directors' stand where she was, the prime ministerial welcome group had gathered. Harry was surrounded by the chairmen of the two clubs and many suited middle-aged white men. There was Gideon, of course, in the same row of seats. Oliver was there, and waved at her. Harry looked in her direction and flashed his lovely smile. She waved back at both of them.

'You know this is one of the great fixtures of Scottish football. These two have been rivals for over a hundred years and have been at the top of the Scottish League all that time.' Jamie thought he should impress upon Sarah the importance of the occasion. He was about to go on, when a roar erupted.

'Oh my God,' Jamie shouted. 'They have scored.'

Celtic had scored. There was an explosion on the green stand. The two big TV screens atop opposite stands were showing the goal in slow motion. The public address system announced, *Hendrik Larsson scored that goal.*

There was another outburst of applause from the Greens. Sarah wondered who the announcement was for, since everyone there must know who had scored. Even she had read the information on the replay on the large TV screen.

'Why do they do that? Surely we all know,' she said.

'Well, yes, but there are some blind spectators here.'

'Seriously?'

'Yes, of course. Both clubs have special facilities for disabled spectators. There are some partially sighted, and one or two blind fans. They come regularly and just love the atmosphere. Families with small children are also being encouraged to come and watch so that football becomes everyone's game, not just that of the fanatics. It is a real community here.' Jamie glowed with pride.

8.00 p.m. Glasgow/The Stands, Ibrox

'Did you see that, Robbie? Wasn't that what you wanted?' David asked.

The boys had to strain to see; they were pretty much at ground level but people kept passing in front or jumping up in front of them. David had told them to look at the TV screen just to make sure.

'I saw it on the replay, Dad. It came too quick to see the first time,' Robbie said.

'I want Rangers to score now, quick.' Alistair was still hoping.

8.02 p.m. Glasgow

There was a screech and a thump.

'Fucking blind, are you? Watch where you are going.'

Margaret was jolted from her newspaper. Her chauffeur had just narrowly missed a motorcyclist, who had come up on the wrong side.

'Sorry, madam. Are you alright?' the chauffeur asked.

'Yessss…'

Even as she started to respond, Margaret was thrown to one side of the car, and that was the last thing she remembered. She found out later that a large delivery van had come up behind the car and rammed into it. They had just come off the M8, past the Ibrox ground, and got on to Paisley Road. This was always a tricky junction and the light had just begun to fade moments ago. Cars screeched to a halt behind the van and a crowd gathered, but the back of the car was badly damaged and both the driver and the passenger were slumped in their seats, unconscious. The delivery van driver was Chinese and knew just a few words of English. He was close to tears. Ten minutes later, when the police arrived, he had gone missing.

8.05 p.m. Glasgow/Ibrox

Oliver was trying to concentrate. He had come away from the directors' box and was down in the dining room. He had to speak softly so that the person standing there, polishing glasses, would not hear. Roger indicated that there was an inner sanctum where Oliver could be alone. Oliver, still on his mobile, waved a thank you and moved into the inner office on the left, and shut the door behind him. He had to let Christine have the text of the statement. He got a safe line via the unit they had set up at the hotel. He heard an ambulance go by and wondered what it was all about. Maybe someone too drunk to make it to the match but ill enough to need attention. Old Firm games were an excuse for drunken orgies among other things.

8.10 p.m. London/Pall Mall

Asha's taxi was just turning into St James's off Pall Mall when her mobile rang. Thank heavens, she muttered. There were only minutes to go before she arrived at the Ritz. She looked at the number and said, 'Hello.'

'Sorry, wrong number,' a voice replied.

Now all Asha had to do was to look surprised when Matt was told about Margaret's accident. She hoped it was only a few bruises and nothing more serious.

She got out of the car at the Ritz, and said to the driver, 'Thanks. I'll call you later to collect me.'

'Yes, Miss Chan.' Asha was a valued customer of the City Cab agency. She took cabs everywhere as it was more tax efficient.

'Good evening, Miss Chan.' The welcome at the Ritz was warm as usual.

9.10 p.m. Vienna/British Ambassador's Residence

'How nice to see you again, Secretary of State.' Lady Olds gave Terence a peck on his cheek. Sir Clive was standing right beside her. The two men shook hands.

'Welcome to our humble abode.'

'I like that, a humble abode indeed. What beautiful surroundings you have here in the nineteenth, or is it the seventeenth district, Ambassador. It must be lovely in the summer, to sit in those wineries and wander about in the woods.'

Terence was showing off his knowledge of Vienna. The Ambassador's house was near Wienerwald, the woods at the edge of the city. Terence had visited some hostelries there, where the vineyards sold their latest vintage. Sitting out in the open in the rustic outskirts of the city was a special pleasure.

'Well, yes, it certainly is. Some day you must come for a longer visit in the summer.' Sir Clive was warming to Terence.

'And you must bring your wife and daughters too. You shouldn't be the only one having all the fun,' Lady Olds added.

'If you think talking shop about olives for a whole day is fun, I will gladly let you do my job. Thank heavens for Alan Carling, who sorted it all out finally. I don't know what I would do without him. Incidentally, he was too exhausted after that marathon negotiation to come for dinner. He went straight to bed. He asked me to convey his most sincere apologies.' Terence smiled to himself at the thought that he was as close to the truth as he could be about Alan's whereabouts.

'What a shame. But then we have you all to ourselves. Jolly nice.'

Terence almost expected Katharine Olds to say 'Tally Ho' any second. The FO was characterized by these horsey wives of public school men. When would the old culture change? Who would dare change it? Not Nick Davies, surely.

8.10 p.m. London/Channel 4

Nick had done well. He had survived the Channel 4 News ordeal. Jon Snow had tried to get the truth out of him about the government's Libya policy, but he had held on to a diplomatic answer.

'I have myself had no conversation with Washington. I have also not spoken to the prime minister today. We have to wait and see how soon Libya is ready to comply with its UN obligations. What the future will bring, who can tell?'

Having said that, he tried every variation on it. Jon Snow was quite frustrated. He could see that Nick was lying, or at least not telling the whole truth. As the news ended, Jon asked, 'Now tell me, Nick. Just off the record. What the hell is happening?'

'You know me, Jon. I am only in the Cabinet because of Wales. Since my dear darling wife Val died eighteen months ago, I have not been any good at my job. They carry me kindly, but come the next reshuffle, I will be glad to go. Harry is his own foreign secretary. He is happy with me because I don't bother him. But I'll tell you this, I smell trouble ahead.'

'Really, Nick? Tell me more.' The journalist in Jon was curious.

'Trouble on the back benches. Expect rumblings by mid-week. I wouldn't be surprised if we had a revolt.'

Jon realized he was being soft-soaped. This was hardly news. What was Nick hiding?

'But if nothing has happened on the Libyan front, why should there be trouble?'

'Did I say nothing would have happened? It all depends on Harry. He would love to bomb Libya if only to rub Eric's nose in the dirt. He is a vindictive bastard, is our Harry.'

'So you expect Libya to be bombed before mid-week?'

'I say neither yea nor nay. Good night, Jon. It's getting past my bedtime.'

'Good night, Nick. Take care how you go.'

8.12 p.m. Glasgow/Directors' Box, Ibrox

Sarah kept glancing back at Harry. He was being introduced to people who were leaving their seats and walking up to the top to shake his hand. A good thing too, Sarah thought. At least he won't get to watch much.

Suddenly there was a howl from the crowd. A Rangers player was writhing in agony on the ground while a Celtic player was waving his arms and asking him to get up. The referee blew his whistle and walked over to the injured man. He then ran over to the linesman and back in a second or two. He blew his whistle again and pointed towards the Celtic goal. It was a penalty. There were shouts from the crowd and the referee was surrounded by players in the Celtic green, remonstrating and pleading with him.

'I am afraid Giovanni was fouled by Raphael. It's a penalty. If Rangers score now and hold the match to a draw, they will have won the league.' Jamie was being helpful again.

On the pitch the two teams were at each other's throats. Someone, it looked like the man who had scored the goal—Larsson, Sarah remembered—was pulling a player away. The referee was waving his hand, clutching a piece of paper. He was about to flash a card at someone. There was shoving and punching. The referee picked up the ball and someone from the Celtic side behind him tried to knock it out of his hand. The referee turned around and waved a red card. There was a huge howl.

'Oh, my God. He has sent Riseth off. This is awful. It's not like Peter Houston. He is normally a mild referee.' Jamie looked shocked.

'Why did he do it?'

'I think Riseth must have argued the penalty, or maybe he just swore at him. This is bad news for Celtic. Oh no!'

Somebody had thrown an object at the referee, and hit him full on the head. The stadium exploded. Everyone was up and shouting and hurling abuses. The missile had come from the Celtic stand, or so it was presumed. Police began to gather at the bottom of the stand where the Celtic fans were. Some of the stewards made their way into the stand and their colleagues on the ground indicated the places where they thought the culprit was likely to be. One fan jumped over the barrier and started running towards the referee. A policeman ran after him and tackled him. More policemen converged on the man and took him away. Some fans still inside their stand engaged in fisticuffs with the stewards who had climbed in to find the person who had hurled the object.

'I think the referee was hit by something sharp and hard, maybe a metal key or a sharp coin. Or a two-pound piece—that would do it.' Jamie was not a doctor for nothing.

The referee was sitting on the ground, being seen to by the Rangers' physio, who had run on to the pitch. Blood spurted from his head. The players were still arguing with each other but at least they were not fighting. The PA system was vying for the attention of the crowd.

Please sit down. Please sit down. Order must be maintained. There will be arrests if missiles are thrown at the players. Please comply with the police orders.

And on and on. But it was hard to hear. Even in the directors' box many were standing up. Sarah could see that the rival chairmen were gesticulating and shouting at each other. No one quite knew what would happen next.

8.15 p.m. Glasgow/The Stands, Ibrox

'What's happened, Dad? Why has the game stopped?' Robbie asked.

'Is the referee hurt, Dad?' Alistair wanted to know.

David was himself trying to figure out what had happened. He could sense the danger level rising.

'Wait for a bit. It will all be clear in a minute.' That was the best David could manage.

The referee blew his whistle. His bandaged brow was red and the blood was still oozing out. With a determination Sarah had to admire, he marched to the penalty stop outside the Celtic goal and pointed at a Rangers player.

8.18 p.m. Glasgow/Directors' Box, Ibrox

'That is Numan. He is brilliant.' Jamie was obviously a home side fan. Sarah had decided that as a person from the deep south, she had better stay neutral.

There was a moment of absolute pin-drop silence and then, as Arthur Numan scored the penalty, there wan an explosion of noise and banner waving from the opposite stand as the Rangers fans screamed their joy. There were boos and shouts from the Celtic fans, and more things were thrown on to the pitch. The referee pointed to the centre again, and asked the two teams to come to order. Everyone was standing up now. Two players, one from either side, who looked to Sarah like they could be the captains, were walking towards the middle. Elsewhere, the players had still not calmed down and there were scuffles among them. One appeared to be punching another. The referee's back had been turned but he soon saw what was happening. He blew his whistle and stopped the game from resuming. He walked over to the scuffling players.

8.20 p.m. Glasgow/The Stands, Ibrox

'Did you see that goal, Alistair?' David asked.

'Yes. What a super penalty kick.' Alistair was happy.

The referee held up a red card at two more players. They were Celtic players. Sarah could see Larsson again, the only one she could identify, pleading with the referee but being pulled away by another player. Suddenly the Celtic stand erupted and dozens of fans jumped onto the pitch. This proved to be a signal to the Rangers fans and they poured down from their stand. The Belfast boys were keen to prove they were no slouches when it came to a fight.

That was when Carson's Irregulars got to work. Kenny was

astonished to find himself lifted over the barrier by Ritchie. As he landed on the pitch, he heard the others hit the ground behind him. Ritchie was shouting himself hoarse, and he was not alone by any means. It was as if a trained army had got its orders to charge the enemy.

The players and the referee were bewildered by this new assault. The whistle blew again and the referee indicated he had stopped the game. Soon the players and the referee were fighting their way back to the tunnel. The police waded in, trying to separate the fans, but to no avail. There were fisticuffs and blows and kicks. The noise was incredible now. The PA system seemed to have given up. Loud pop music was being played instead of appeals. If they thought it would distract the fans, they were wrong. Firecrackers were being set off, and soon enough, one was hurled at the directors' box.

8.22 p.m. Glasgow/Directors' Box, Ibrox

Jamie and Sarah stood up.

Barney Jones was quickly at their side.

'Miss Disney, the prime minister says you better get out of here and meet us in the directors' dining room.'

The entire mass of suited men and the few women in their heavy fur coats (in May at that) were rushing out. Sarah looked around for Harry. He looked quite clam, while the two chairmen were behaving much like the fans. Sarah had no choice but to follow Jamie as Barney had indicated. He was hurrying back to be at Harry's side. The stairs which had been mildly uncomfortable earlier in the day were now full of people pushing and shoving, some almost slipping and falling. There was loud, raucous singing coming from the ground.

'What is that?' Sarah asked Jamie.

'More trouble, I am afraid. Each side has its songs, mainly to hurl abuse at the other side.'

'Such as?'

'The Rangers fans are singing "Billy Boys". I can't possibly tell you all the words but it goes something like, "We are up to our knees in Fenian Blood". You can imagine the rest.'

'Oh, how horrible. Why are they like that?'

'The other side are no better, but I won't get into their song. Let me assure you though, this is not at all normal.' Jamie was angry and apologetic at the same time. He was embarrassed for Rangers and for Scotland. Perhaps a bit for himself as well, as he had wanted to make a good impression on this good-looking woman.

'We have had accidents like when the stand collapsed during an Old Firm game, killing sixty-six people. But that was nearly thirty years ago and there has been a lot of rebuilding since. They don't allow any bottles to be brought into the ground, and that usually keeps the violence down.

'We thought we had gone past such sectarianism. But in a game like this, because the league championship is at stake, every goal counts. You see, Celtic needed to win outright and being a goal ahead, they were onto a winner. A draw favours Rangers. So the Celtic players are angry. A penalty decision is bad enough, but three Celtic players were sent off and there was no telling where it would end. I do hope the police can restore order and we can resume play. After all, the second half is still to be played. It would be terrible for Scotland if the game results in the wrong kind of headlines when the prime minister is here for the first time.'

The prime minister could not care less, if you only knew, Sarah thought, but Jamie was so nice, so gauche, that she decided not to shock him. An Old Firm game was a great treat for him but for Sarah, the only concern was when it would end.

8.23 p.m. Glasgow/The Stands, Ibrox

David stood up, grabbed his two boys, one by each hand, and said, 'Hold fast to me. Don't let go. We are getting out of here.' From where they were seated, they had to go up halfway before they could get to an exit. People were rushing down to the bottom to scale the barrier so they could jump onto the ground. David fought his way up, making sure the boys were alright. Robbie and Alistair did not say a word. They were scared but they knew their dad would take care of them. They knew he had been in the Marines. They had seen pictures of him in uniform and heard stories about his adventures. Slowly, with great difficulty, they pushed their way through the jostling crowds. All around them were people trying to get out. Someone had let off fireworks and there was smoke everywhere. Somehow, David managed to reach the exit without falling or letting go of the boys' hands.

8.25 p.m. Glasgow/Outside Ibrox Stadium

The noise inside finally had the policeman on duty running in to help out. Red saw his chance. He figured he had about ten minutes before reinforcements arrived. He opened his rucksack and got to work.

Meanwhile, Chris Mott decided that he had better return the call from Lex. He had spent many years in public relations and had been friends with Lex for even longer, but he sensed that this time, it was more than a friendly call, there was something big afoot. He would not normally rush off in the middle of a good story unfolding in front of his eyes but something told him he had better get hold of Lex.

He had difficulty getting down but his experience as a bouncer came in handy. Various people cursed him but he was down and out in the open before anyone else. He walked into the car park where there was relative quiet. There was only one person lurking under an awning, on his knees. Maybe he was looking for his car keys, Chris thought, so he kept away from him. Red was equally happy not to be disturbed.

Chris was out of breath from rushing down. But he got through to Lex immediately.

'Lex, you must watch this on the box. There is a superb front page for you in the punch up going on here. Penalty, a red card, the ref hit by a coin, and then two more red cards. Fucking incredible it is.'

'Chris, are you alone?'

'Yes, what is it, Lex?'

'I have a front page already and it is very different. I was going to keep it a surprise but I thought I had better warn you.' Lex was still uncertain how much to tell. It was nearly eight thirty. The time to order the print run was fast approaching.

'What are you talking about? Is it to do with Terence? Is he alright? He was in Vienna earlier today, coming back tomorrow.' Chris could feel the fear rising within him.

'Listen carefully. We have now got solid evidence—authentic photos of Terence. Devastating stuff.'

'You filthy bastards. That shit Matt Drummond. I hate him. I'll get him someday.'

'Don't lose your cool, Chris. Concentrate. This is mega. When this hits the streets, Terence is dead.'

'Is it that bad? What is it? Floozies? Boys?'

'It's much worse. Let us say a female relation, underage.'

'Oh my God, my God. So, what do you want? We can buy the pictures off you. Terence has money. How much?'

'Whatever else Matt Drummond may lack, it's not money. We are not talking blackmail here. The nation's morals are our concern.'

'You filthy hypocrite. What are you asking for? His resignation?'

'That's a promising start. But I must warn you, when this gets out, Terence will be unable to live freely in this country. He is finished. He will have to disappear.'

'You are joking.'

'Well, the police would be interested in these pictures. It's not just paedophilia. It's incest. The British people do not take kindly to that sort of thing. I can show you if you wish.'

The last time Chris had felt so sick was when, as a child, he had tried to empty his dad's brandy bottle in one go. His head was spinning.

'Listen, I need to call Terence. How long have I got?'

'You know the newspaper business as well as I do, mate. We are printing a million extra, so I would like an answer soon. Don't tell him to call me or Matt Drummond. This is between you and me. Matt will kill me, if he finds out I told you. This is for old times' sake.'

'Thanks, I guess. I'll call you back.'

Chris looked around. The man on his knees was no longer there. But even so, he could not be sure. He had to have absolute privacy. He had to locate his car and call Terence.

8.35 p.m. Glasgow

'Is there anyone you would like to call, madam?'

Margaret had just opened her eyes. There was a big wad of cotton wool across her left eye, and a young man in some kind of uniform was bandaging her wrist.

'Where am I? What happened?'

'You are in an ambulance, madam, in Glasgow. Your car was involved in a crash with another vehicle. Luckily, you are not badly hurt.'

'What about Paul? The chauffeur?'

'I am afraid we had to take him to emergency. He was badly cut, and lost a lot of blood.'

'Can I go to my hotel? It's in George Square.'

'Don't you have relatives here, or friends?'

'No, I just came from London and must fly back tomorrow. I have some important work in the morning. I am Margaret Drummond. The LDNC office here can look after me, I am sure.'

The paramedic looked puzzled.

'Oh, I meant *The Glasgow Times* people.'

'Would you like us to call them?'

Margaret was about to say she could call herself. But she realized her handbag must be somewhere else. And her hand was hurting. Her legs were covered with a blanket, they felt numb.

'Yes, please. Ask for Willie.'

'Yes, madam.'

Within seconds, the connection had been made, and Willie came on the line. The paramedic held the mobile so Margaret could talk hands free.

'Listen, Willie. There is nothing to worry about, but I've had a bit of an accident. Paul has been taken to hospital with severe cuts. But I am alright. Tell everyone not to worry. Tell the hotel I will need special attention when I get there. I don't think I'll be able to walk easily. I may need a wheelchair.'

The paramedic was impressed. She was old, perhaps his granny's age. Well-dressed and posh. But so calm after such a serious accident.

'Oh, Mrs Drummond, I am sorry to hear that. Let me come and collect you. Do you want me to tell the boss? I can find him, wherever he is.' Willie was relieved that Margaret was not seriously hurt. He was eager to please, and wipe out any evidence of his role in this. He said a silent prayer that his chosen way—hiring a Chinese driver who was in the country without a visa and driving a delivery van without signs—had paid off.

'Well, he is in London, and I doubt he is thinking about me. But tell him, just in case it gets into the news before he hears about it.' Margaret had a hazy recollection of cameras flashing as she was carried into the ambulance near the scene of the accident.

'Will do, madam.'

Margaret shut her eyes with a sigh, as Reggie turned off the phone.

'Please, can you tell me if the other driver was hurt? Is he alright?' Margaret was solicitous as always.

'We think he ran away. Someone told the police that he seemed to be of Chinese origin.'

'Oh, poor man. I do hope he is alright. Do you think I can go now?'

'One moment, madam. Let me see about the traffic.' Reggie got out and walked over to the police car flashing its lights nearby.

8.55 p.m. London/The Archduke, South Bank

The drunken party of fifteen women had found a table large enough for them. Lisa had wanted a round table, or at least an oblong one. At a rectangular table, you couldn't see everyone properly. Knowing their favourite client's preferences, the restaurant had found just what Lisa wanted.

'Would you care for an aperitif, madam, before you order?'

'I am not sure, Melvin. We've been at it solidly since the late afternoon. Oh, what the heck. I will have a Pernod, as would my friend Miss Annie here. You can ask everyone else what they would like.'

Lisa was determined to make this an occasion. Just then, her mobile rang. She looked at the unfamiliar number. Was it a newspaper hack?

'Hello, who is it?'

'Lisa, this is Margaret.'

'Darling, how are you? Have you reached Glasgow? Where are you calling from?'

'Listen, I've had a minor accident. It is nothing, just that my car was hit by a delivery van. I am bruised, but otherwise alright.'

'Oh, Margaret. So where are you? In a hospital?'

'No, darling, just in an ambulance where a very nice young man has been taking care of me. I've told our office here to tell Matt, so he doesn't worry. If I find the energy for a long argument, I may call him myself. Don't you worry either. I am sure I'll be alright. I'll make the first night if I have to crawl.'

'Margaret, do take care. I'll say a special prayer for you. Do you want me to ask Harry to come and see you wherever you are?'

'That's very sweet of you, but I am sure Harry has other things on his mind. Apparently, there's some trouble near my hotel as well.

They are trying to find me another one. But I am well looked after, so don't worry.'

9.00 p.m. Glasgow/Directors' Dining Room, Ibrox

Harry wished he had other things to do. He was being talked at by several people. The Rangers chairman had just quit haranguing his Celtic counterpart. He still thought the penalty was legitimate as was the first red card and the next two, and while he did not say so, it just proved what animals Celtic fans were. Calum Kennedy was trying to fence Harry off from the others. He had planned to talk to Harry at some length, mainly about himself and his claim to proper honours. But his plan had gone awry.

'Prime Minister, let me sincerely assure you that this is not typical nor normal. We are all shocked at such behaviour on the pitch, and in the stands. I am on the Scottish FA Executive and let me say, we shall take a most serious view of this. This sort of thing cannot be tolerated. I hope both teams are fined a large sum.' Calum could at least afford to show he was neutral.

'How can you say that, Calum? It wasn't the fault of the home team.' The chairman, who Harry thought was called Sir Archibald something, interjected.

'What you have to do is suspend the other side for five games at least, or take away ten points next season.'

'I heard that. You can be sure we shall fight it in the highest courts if that happens. It was the fault of both sides. Don't you agree, Prime Minister? You saw the game.' It was the turn of the Celtic chairman.

'Gentlemen, I may be foolhardy in many things I do, but intervening between your two clubs on such a sensitive matter is not one of them. I say a word and my party will be in wilderness for a generation. No, thanks.'

They laughed politely. Harry was still holding a pint of bitter someone had thrust in his hand when they arrived. The directors' dining room was heaving with people. Many were there without invitation. Harry had been taken into the inner room and, before he could say anything, someone had said, 'This should calm your shattered nerves, sir.'

Since then, Harry had taken one sip, no more. He could see why he had to watch this rabble kick a ball about in a frenzied fashion, but not why he had to drink this muck. He was hoping Oliver would come and rescue him. Or Sarah.

'So when will the game resume? I am told football is a game of two halves.' Harry thought he had better keep the conversation on an even keel before the two chairmen fell out again.

'Well said, sir. We can find out for you. Normally there is a twenty-minute break, but given the circumstances, we cannot be sure. We haven't even finished the first half yet. Let's hope we can resume quickly.' Sir Archibald got on his mobile.

Harry was relieved to see Oliver had made it to the inner sanctum. He smiled when Oliver flashed him a thumbs up: the statement had gone safely. Harry raised his glass and made a face. Oliver laughed and mouthed softly, 'See what I can do.' He went out again to where the bar was.

10.15 p.m. Vienna/The Gurtel

Terence had abandoned his taxi near the Gurtel. Being a peripheral road that circled inner Vienna, it was constantly carrying traffic along its four lanes. Terence felt at home in the noisy surroundings. The dinner with Sir Clive and his Lady had been suffocating enough; he had not stayed a moment longer than what might have been considered polite. He wanted to walk a bit, and have another drink before he got to Rosa Giulia's, which was only fifteen minutes away.

The bar he came to was called Casanova's. There were the usual strobe lights, and women were performing in a variety of outfits that looked more like lingerie, while scouting for punters to take them into the curtained rooms. Terence watched in an uninterested fashion. On the way here, he had been propositioned by women in feathers and fishnet stockings, but he had shrugged them off. His treat would be special, and he was prepared to wait.

Terence liked Casanova's with its mixture of Italian and French artefacts and women from every central European country you could wish for. Bertolt at the bar greeted him, but was too busy handing out drinks and keeping an eye on the girls to come and talk to him. Terence ordered a large brandy.

His mobile rang.

'Terence, can you talk?' It was Chris.

'Sure, what's up? Did Harry fuck up then?'

'No. This is very important. It is too noisy where you are, I can't hear you clearly. I need to talk to you in confidence. It's vital.'

'Ok, hang on while I find a quiet corner in this bar. Just wait. Or, tell you what—call me in five minutes, I'll find some place.'

It was too far to go to Rosa Giulia's. The pavement outside was noisy with the constant traffic. Terence looked at the performing women. The best solution was a room at the back. So he summoned the freshest looking among them, more girl than woman. She smiled and said, 'Would you like to take me to a separee? It will be three hundred euros.'

Terence was not about to bargain. He said yes, and off they went with a wave to Bertolt. Terence was led to a narrow passage behind the door that said 'Amore' with hearts and arrows. When they got in, he found a very narrow room with a bed, but also a tiny space with a bidet and a hose for washing oneself.

'I am Natalie. I speak English. You like fuck?' Saying this, she began to undress and fondle Terence.

Terence's mobile rang again.

'Sorry,' he said as Natalie made a face. He continued, very slowly,

'This is important but not long. I will be with you shortly. Why don't you do a show for me?'

That will keep her busy, he thought, and she will think she is earning her keep. Terence had no intention of staying beyond the time it took to answer the call.

Natalie turned on the TV in the room, but with the sound off. A porn film was being shown. She began gyrating and taking her scanty clothes off in some sort of a dance.

'Ok, tell me, what is so important?'

'Terence, it's all over. They've got pictures this time. Very explicit. You with your...' Chris spluttered over the words.

'What?' Terence felt his body go cold. 'Who has?'

'*The Herald*. There is no doubt, and I tried to offer to buy them back but they won't play. They want your scalp.'

"I'll show them, the bastards! I'll kill Matt Drummond.'

Terence was shouting now. Natalie cowered in a corner, her skimpy dress crushed between her hands.

'It's no good, Terence. I've seen the spread in tomorrow's edition. You will be done for child molesting and worse. Do you even know what they hand out for incest with children?'

As he listened to the implacable voice at the other end, Terence's face flushed bright red, and the next moment, he collapsed. Natalie let out a scream. Bertolt rushed in, fearing she was being beaten. When he saw Terence lying on the floor, he wrapped a big towel around Natalie and rushed her into a separee which was not in use. He told her to lie down and came back to Terence. He bent down to check his heartbeat. Nothing. Yet he could hear a sound, as of someone shouting. He picked up Terence's mobile from the floor.

'Hello, who is this? Listen, your friend has had a very serious accident.'

'What? Who is speaking?'

'The barman at Casanova's. It's a night club. Your friend is dead. Heart attack, it looks like. He came here alone. I will have to call the police and...'

'Oh God, oh God. Listen, do you know who he is?'

'No, but he comes once a year or so. Buys good drinks. Sometimes spends money with girls. But his favourite is another place near here. He is rich, yes? Does he have friends I can call here?'

'No, it is more than that, you don't understand. He is a minister in Britain; very important. Can you get the British embassy on the phone and tell them? His name is Terence Harcourt. Thank you. If he owes any money, the embassy will pay. Oh, and can you take my number and call me later, and tell me what happened? Thanks again, and I am sorry. I cannot help as I am in Scotland right now. Can you manage?'

'That is ok. We have all kinds of mensch here. We are used to this. The British often come to Vienna. Sometimes the excitement gets too much for them.'

9.20 p.m. Glasgow/Directors' Dining Room, Ibrox

Oliver found Roger at the bar. Roger smiled and said, 'What can I get for you, Mr Knight?'

'How do you know my name?'

'Everybody knows your name. You are the prime minister's press officer. It says so in the programme. Anyway, what would you like?'

'It's not for me. Can you make a Martini for the prime minister? An American style Martini with gin?'

'Say no more, Mr Knight. I have read he likes a lot of gin and a touch of vermouth with an olive and some ice.'

'Well, I am impressed.'

Roger had to take a gamble on the number of drinks Harry would end up having. He calculated that even if the game was cancelled, his hosts would not let Harry get away without dinner. It would have to be brought forward, but the haggis was easy to do even for a posh dinner. So, at least two more drinks. Roger decided to wait and gave Oliver a clean Martini with an innocent olive.

9.25 p.m. Glasgow/Outside Ibrox Stadium

'Lex, stop the press.' Devastated as he was, Chris had to stop *The Herald* from coming out, even though Terence was beyond any mudslinging. He had to protect poor Catriona, her father's pet.

'What's happened? What did Terence say?'

'Terence is dead, Lex. He had a heart attack in Vienna.'

'When?'

'A few minutes ago. When I told him.'

'Where was he? What was he doing?'

'Enough, Lex. Let him be; he is dead. You and Matt Drummond have got what you wanted. Now leave him alone, and protect that girl's future. She is innocent.'

'How do I know you are not lying?' Lex could see his first edition going down the drain after half a mil and all that hard work.

'Because you know I would not lie about such a thing. I called to save your reputation, which would have been worse than mud if you had maligned a dead man. If you want, the British embassy in Vienna can confirm the news. Do you want their number?'

'No. Leave it. Do me a favour. Give me a thousand words on Terence, pronto. I'll pay you five quid per word. I'd better find out about the game and start a fresh front page.' Lex was never less than professional.

9.30 p.m. London/House of Lords

Lettie Brighton was enjoying herself in the peers' dining room. She and her partner Matthew had invited some friends for dinner, and they were on the last course of pudding and brandy. The meal had been excellent, as she had expected.

Lettie's guests were American friends of her partner. They were special because it was at their house that Matthew and she had met. She had been touring New York with the Royal Shakespeare Company and Mathew, who was then working on Wall Street, had taken his friends to see the stunning English actress who was playing Rosalind in *As You Like It*. Norman and Hattie had invited Lettie home for a post-theatre party and Lettie had been impressed by Matthew and his cultured American friends. They came to London regularly to take in the theatre and who better than Lettie to direct them to the best plays in town? Along the way, Matthew and Lettie became fond of each other. Matthew relocated to London to be with her. That was nearly fifteen years ago.

Hattie was curious about Lettie's new job.

'How did you get into this? Was it worth it, giving up your lovely stage career?'

Lettie was used to the question. She tried to vary the answer slightly each time she had to tell people her story.

'Oh, I didn't plan to end up here. But you know how it is. Political parties have to raise money. We did not do it in the old days but now we are all Americans. The party found me useful for fund raising and hosting dinners. That is how I met Elisabet. Do you know her? She is Harry White's wife and a brilliant theatre director. Maybe I could wangle a couple of tickets for you for her new play at the National.'

'Don't worry, we already got them. It's hot news in New York and tickets are selling fast. So did she get you the job?'

'Not quite. But through her I was put on the group which was writing the arts and culture part of the manifesto. No one ever reads the manifesto except the nerds who quote it to accuse the party leaders of having betrayed it. But we have to do it at every election. After three defeats and three manifestos, I was a veteran. So when we won, and they needed bodies in the House of Lords, I said, what the hell, I can always get back to the stage when we are out.'

'You are not supposed to say that, Lettie. They will hear you,' Matthew interjected.

'I don't give a fig. I enjoy this job, but they only come to gawp at me and when the charm wears off, I will be dumped like the rest of them.'

'Then you can write your memoirs and make a killing.'

'Who knows? Memoirs of politicians only sell if they've been sacked or found flagrante by some paparazzi. Now, who wants a liqueur?'

The boys had enjoyed their Angus beef steak and the girls their Dover sole. For dessert, the girls had gone for cheesecake and apple tart while the men settled for fresh fruit salad and strawberries and cream. After black coffee and liqueurs, brandy for the boys and Chartreuse for the girls, Lettie was feeling quite pleased that she had given Norman and Hettie a good dinner. They would linger a bit longer and really savour the charms of the place, she decided. They had plenty of time.

Lettie was waiting to see if the opposition front bench wanted to hear the statement on Libya. In such cases, the House of Lords had the choice whether to take the statement being made in the Commons. The *usual channels* were sorting it out. Usually, not many noble Lords lingered till late at night. Not after dinner in any case. But all those who were there would saunter into the Chamber if they took the statement.

As the prime minister's equivalent in the House of Lords, Lettie would have to read out the statement. That would guarantee a near full house even late at night. But few people knew about it as yet. The Annunciator for the Commons was trailing the statement as being read after the division at 10.00 p.m. But nothing was said as to what it was about and there was no indication of what the House of Lords would do. In any case, she could only read the statement after Frank Thompson got up in the Commons. So there was at least an hour and a bit before she had to be at the despatch box. No panic. She was going to enjoy her second helping of Chatreuse.

Her mobile rang.

The other noble Lords in the dining room looked mockingly aghast at such bad behaviour by the leader. Mobiles were not allowed in the peers' dining room, and Lettie had to rush out to take the call. It was from the sweet young duty officer at the FO.

'Baroness Brighton, I am sorry to call you at this hour.'

'Never mind. Tell me, what is it, Malcolm?'

'Bad news, I am afraid. The Vienna embassy just called. The secretary of state is dead.'

'Who, Stein, the Austrian secretary? Oh dear…'

'No, madam. Our secretary of state for Europe, Terence Harcourt.'

'What? Oh my God! How?'

'Heart attack, it seems. In a bar. Rather suddenly. They are trying to contact his wife.'

'Oh. I'd better go and tell them at the other end. Look, thanks, Malcolm.'

Bloody hell. Terence Harcourt dead. How and why was he in a bar in Vienna? She would have to find out later. She went back in and called Matthew out, unaware of the tears running down her cheeks. Her American guests were disconcerted while the noble Lords looked at her curiously.

'What is it? Why are you crying?' Matthew put an arm around her.

'Terence Harcourt. He died of a heart attack in Vienna tonight. I had better go and tell Frank and Christine. Will you hold the fort for me, love? Take them in for extra coffee in the guest room if you like. I must run.'

9.35 p.m. London/10 Downing Street

Christine was trying to get hold of Lettie as well. She wanted to know if she had got the opposition to agree to not take the statement in the Lords. There were so many ex-foreign secretaries and ex-FO people there that there would be a serious mauling of the government policy. Lettie could handle it, of course, but even then the Hansard would tell a sorry tale tomorrow. The policy community out there read the Lords Hansard before the Commons one.

9.37 p.m. London/House of Lords

Lettie ran across the red carpets of the House of Lords, and past the Pugin Room. She was soon on the green carpets of the House of Commons as she tried to reach Frank Thompson's office. Her mobile rang again. Another breach of protocol.

'Yes,' she said somewhat peremptorily, her tone indicating that whoever it was should get off the phone, pronto.

'It's me, Christine. How did the negotiations go at your end? Are you taking the statement?'

'Christine, it's Terence. He is dead. Of a heart attack. In Vienna.' Lettie was sobbing now. 'He died in a bloody bar, for God's sake.'

'What? How did you find out? Let me look at the wires.'

'Our embassy told the FO just minutes ago. I am off to tell Frank. I must rush. Bye.'

Christine could not believe what she had just heard. She loathed Terence, of course, but never wished him dead. Poor Dorothy. Had anyone told her yet? And those three sweet, pretty girls. Oh, how sad. I must tell Harry, she thought.

9.40 p.m. Glasgow/Directors' Dining Room, Ibrox

Harry drained his glass. They had heard that the match was off. The SFA had decided that the referee could not carry on with a bandage over his left eye, and they were not going to provide a substitute referee. They would also have to announce a fine for the clubs soon. In the meantime, there was still a battle raging on the ground between the two sets of fans and the police. Stabbings were reported. Harry was relieved. The story would dominate tomorrow's papers in

Scotland at least, and displace Libya to the back pages. That was one good thing. Now, how soon could he get away?

'No, Prime Minister. We would hate to see you go without dinner. We have prepared sumptuous Scottish fare for you.' Calum was most insistent.

'Aye, it is haggis, the best there can be, with all the trimmings, and lashings of whisky to wash it down with. We have to live up to our reputation for hospitality at Ibrox, Prime Minister.' Sir Archibald something wanted some credit for this event.

'What time will that be? We have to get to Belfast tonight.'

'I don't think that will be a problem. We can get you to the airport in no time at all.'

Oliver came in with a second glass of Harry's favourite.

'Thanks,' Harry said. 'What is the news?'

'I believe there are riots all over Glasgow. I was just talking to the Commissioner and he reckons there must have been planeloads from Belfast, both loyalists and republicans, prepared for a punch up. They are looking at the flight records. It has never been this serious in the last thirty years. The match was being shown live in every bar downtown and people watching it have gone on a rampage. We will have to see how we can get out of here.'

9.45 p.m. London/The Ritz

They had just been served the dessert. Matt Drummond was hoping to soften up the major shareholders before he told them of his expansion plans for which he needed to raise more money. Just then, the head waiter came up and spoke to him discreetly. He was sorry, but he had another call from Glasgow. He had fielded the previous ones but this time it was his wife. Did he want to take it?

Matt knew that Margaret would not call him for any trivial reason. Something must have happened. Had she got a new prognosis?

'Hello, Margaret,' he said.

'Sorry to get you like this, Matt. I just wanted to say, if you hear about my car accident, it's nothing serious. I am bruised, and must use a wheelchair for a couple of days, that's all.'

'What on earth! When did this happen and where are you?'

'Don't panic. I am in Glasgow for one night, and will return to London tomorrow for Lisa White's play at the National. I just thought you might worry if you heard it on the news or something.'

'Why should it be on the news?'

'Well, my chauffeur Paul died in hospital, and the van that hit us had the markings of *The Glasgow Times*, which someone had attempted to paint over. So the police are anxious to question Willie. I am sure there is nothing to it. Have a nice evening, whatever you are doing.'

'I am having a working dinner, dear. As usual. Get well.'

He walked back to his dinner but his fertile brain was working on the jigsaw puzzle of Willie, a delivery van belonging to his company, and the accident. Who was behind this, he wondered.

As he joined the group again, he saw Asha trying to catch his eye as if to ask if all was well. He decided to ignore her. His creditors were more important. He called a waiter and asked him to clear away his plate. He was no longer in the mood to eat. Once all the plates had been cleared, they could start the discussion.

The head waiter came back and whispered that there was a call from Mr Pritchard, who said it was most urgent. Matt was angry now. He was not used to his business dinners being interrupted.

'I am terribly sorry. I have to leave you again, but I shan't be long.' He bowed to the assembled company and left.

'What is it, Lex?'

'Sorry to get you like this from your dinner. But I just heard that Terence Harcourt died of a heart attack in Vienna, half an hour ago.'

'What? How? Did someone tip him off? Did you?'

'No, of course not. I just wanted to ask, if it's all right with you, I could pull the planned edition with the pictures. We'll throw together something else.'

'Ok, do as you like. But I want a full account of what happened.'

Matt went back in. Here were two unexpected events. Lex, he was sure, had warned Terence and caused his death. His mobile record would have to be examined. But Margaret's accident puzzled him even more. Who would want to hurt her and from within his—and her own—company at that? He put it out of his mind for a moment and addressed the curious faces looking up at him.

'Gentlemen and Miss Chan, I have just heard that the secretary of state for Europe, Terence Harcourt, died earlier this evening in Vienna.' He did not make eye contact with Asha as he spoke.

The dinner broke up. All the institutional investors had to rush back and work out the impact of the news on the bond markets. Tokyo would open soon.

They were left alone.

'What was the first call about, Matt?' Asha asked.

'Tell me frankly now. Did you ask Willie to bump Margaret off?'

'What are you talking about, Matt? Why would I want to do that? How could I?'

'You are the only one I know who has the sort of devious mind to do such a thing. Willie used a delivery van from the office but he had *The Glasgow Times* sign painted over. Unfortunately, not completely. The police will want to know who did it. I will be asked, and I am going to have to tell.'

'Is Margaret all right? Is she…?'

'She is bruised and concussed and in a wheelchair.'

'Thank God for that.'

'But her chauffeur, you know him. He works for our Glasgow office. Paul. He is dead.'

'But what has that to do with me?'

'My dear, Willie does not have the brains to stage an accident all by himself. Someone told him to have Margaret hit. Just hit; maybe not killed. Just to speed up her death, to debilitate her. It has to be you.'

'Nonsense. You have no reason to say that. You have no proof.'

'Ah, so you did it, but don't think I have the proof. You underestimate me. If you don't talk, Linda will.'

'Rubbish.'

'I pay her a second salary, twice what you pay her, to keep an eye on all your movements. I am not such an old fool that I would be besotted by your lovely dark eyes, Miss Chan. We are through. Goodbye.'

'I'll sue you. I know all your tax fiddles. You will regret this.'

'You will be in jail, my dear. And what is more, every one of my tax fiddles was arranged by you. Against your professional code of ethics. The Bar Council will not like what you do, Miss Chan. As I said, goodbye. I have work to do.'

9.55 p.m. London/House of Commons

Frank Thompson was aghast. Terence Harcourt dead. He had better tell Austin, who could spread the news. This meant he had to draft a tribute to Terence, as well as make the statement. Hell! Gideon was away, otherwise he could have helped. He had better ask the library. He now wished he had not sent his parliamentary secretary back to his constituency. But Rupert had a Scottish seat and was worried about his majority. So Frank had agreed to let him have the Monday off, twice a month.

He dialled Austin's number. As expected, he wasn't there. So Frank left a message. He could not handle a pager, and would just have to wait till Austin got the message. In desperation, he did what he always did. He called Josephine, his wife.

'Josie, what's up?'

'Nothing much, darling. Had a hectic day as usual. I had to buy something to wear for Elisabet's play tomorrow night. I hope you haven't forgotten that we are going. Then I had to make sure I had a slot with Jacques to come and do my hair. I have to look my best for you, for the big night at the National tomorrow. I've had a nice bath and will wait for you to come home. What's up with you?' It was the simple pleasures of life that Josie liked, now that they had left the working-class penury of the early years of their married life far behind.

'Oh, don't ask. I wish I could have a nice bath and curl up in bed.'

'What is it, darling? Why are you fretting?'

'You know I never like it when Harry is gone and I have to stand in his place at the despatch box.'

'But my sweet, you have done it before, and you know you are very good at it.'

Josie had met Frank when they were both children in Barnsley. She came from a miner's family as well, and had tried her best to keep up with Frank's rise to eminence. She had come a long way, but she remained a simple soul even if she took her privileges in her stride. Above all, she remained close to Frank and calmed him each time he was stressed.

Frank continued his tale of woe. 'Now Terence has just dropped dead and in Vienna of all places.'

'Who? Terence Harcourt? Oh, poor Dorothy. When did you find out?'

'Lettie Brighton just told me. Her foreign office got a message from our embassy. Heart attack. I have to read out a tribute to him. How am I going to do that?'

'Sweet man, you knew him, and you two have been in the same movement for some twenty-five years together. You quarrelled a lot, but you were fighting for the same things. He started a poor man like you. Only he married a rich woman, and you got stuck with me, penniless as I am. Just speak from your heart. Don't be pompous or sarky like Harry. Just say what a great guy he was. Leave the long obituary to someone else.'

9.58 p.m. London

Ian was happy. He was walking up from Pond Street to his home in Frognal. He varied his path depending on his mood. He had had a long day with a lot of drinks. So a longer route was to be preferred. It was a lovely evening, warm and pleasant. The twilight had gone, but on the heights of Hampstead you could see a glow in the far distance. He had crossed Haverstock Hill and walked along Lyndhurst Road. That way took him on to Fitzjohn's Avenue. Then, to make it interesting, he had strolled downhill along Arkwright Road. He was just turning into his front garden when the door opened and Hilda came out.

'There was a call from Marcus, love. They want you as soon as possible. I am sorry. Would you like a quick cup of tea?'

It was not like Hilda to be concerned about calls from Marcus. Normally she regarded all of Ian's friends and employers as bad news. They always led him into unhealthy habits, she felt. She did not see why he had to work so late, now that he was in his seventies. Her own practice gave them enough to live on and more.

'Why does Marcus want me? I have just been there all day.' Ian fibbed a bit.

'Terence Harcourt dropped dead of a heart attack in Vienna, no doubt boozing and overeating. When will they ever learn?'

'What on earth is happening? Terence at such a young age? I saw him last month, and he was fine. Anyway, let me have a cup of tea and call them. I want a taxi. I am not going back to the bus stop.'

'They offered to send a taxi. Knowing you, I agreed that while you would not be best pleased, you would go if they sent a car. There should be one in five minutes, so you better have your cuppa.'

Ian crossed to his favourite chair in the living room while Hilda went into the kitchen. He could hear the hiss of the kettle being put on. The phone rang.

'Hello, who is it?' Ian asked.

'Ian, I am glad I found you. This is Frank Thompson.'

'Well, this is a surprise. The deputy prime minister himself! What's up?' Ian used Frank's gambit.

'I guess you have already heard about Terence. Have you?'

'I just heard as I came home. Hilda told me.'

'Well, I need you to help me with my tribute to Terence. I have a statement to make on Libya, as I mentioned to you. But I should start by saying something about Terence. I wish Harry was here.'

'Listen, Frank. Young Marcus is sending me a taxi to go to *The News* office. I will ask them to take me via the House and en route I'll scribble something for you. Hopefully, I'll get there on time. After that I'll need to rush to Marcus. You may need to provide me with police outriders so I can get there quick, ok?'

'You are a pal. Anything you ask for is yours. Another day like this and you can have my job, I tell you.'

9.59 p.m. Glasgow/Directors' Dining Room, Ibrox

Oliver's mobile rang. It was Christine.

'Have you heard? Terence died of a heart attack in Vienna. The news came just a while ago via our embassy. He was in a shady bar with some woman. The embassy is trying its best to keep the reptiles off. Tell Harry. He will have to make a statement. He had better sound sorry.'

Bloody Matt Drummond, Oliver thought. He was sure he knew what had caused Terence's death. He sidled up to Harry, and whispered in his ear. Harry was genuinely shocked. He immediately clapped his hands, demanding silence.

'Listen, please. I have a very sad announcement to make. It is sad for Scotland and it is sad for the whole country. We have just heard from our embassy in Austria that the secretary of state for Europe,

Terence Harcourt, who was in Vienna in connection with an EU ministerial meeting, has died of a heart attack.'

A sense of shock swept the gathering. One of the fur clad women began sobbing into her drink.

'Terence was a brilliant Cabinet minister, a consummate politician at the British and European level, a doughty fighter for justice and the rights of ordinary people. I have lost a good friend, Scotland has lost a great son, and our country has lost an outstanding political leader. Our sympathies go to Dorothy and their three lovely daughters. I request you to observe a minute's silence in his memory.'

In that one minute's silence, Oliver savoured what a fantastic politician and impromptu speaker Harry was. Sarah was crying, she did not know why. She hardly knew Terence, but Alan had told her a lot about him, not all flattering either. But she felt as if she had lost a close friend. She wished the day would end. She wanted to get out of this place.

As did Harry, of course. He needed space to think clearly about the political implications of Terence's death. Who would he pick to replace Terence? He needed to talk to Oliver and Christine. He had to get out of here.

The silence continued beyond the minute. There was a palpable sense of incredulity mingled with grief. The more senior people who had known Terence were thinking, There but for the grace of God go I. Then suddenly, Jamie who was in tears, began to sing 'Flowers of Scotland'. Soon the entire crowded room was singing with him. Harry had to keep still and appear to be mouthing the words of this song he did not know. Sarah didn't know it either, but Oliver did. Sarah looked admiringly at the distraught Jamie and held his hand. She was deeply moved by his gesture.

The song ended. There were murmurs of appreciation for Jamie. Then Harry spoke again.

'There is no question of us sitting down to dinner now. Let us go, all of us, to our tasks. Terence would want us to. He had a sense of duty to the last day of his life. When something like this happens, you realize how lucky you are to be alive. We all need to meditate on this sad event, each on our own. I hope you don't mind if we leave now. Let me thank you for the hospitality you extended to me and my staff, Oliver Knight and Miss Disney.'

'Thank you for coming to Ibrox, Prime Minister.' Calum had decided to take over. 'We are very sorry that the game was interrupted, and then comes this sad news of our comrade's death. But I am sure I speak on behalf of all of us here when I say that we hope you will come back on another occasion, and grace us with your company.'

'Well said.' Sir Archibald wanted to have the last word.

'Ok, let's go. Where's Barney?' Harry asked.

'I am here, Prime Minister.'

'Can we go?'

'Let me contact our police escort. They are somewhat overwhelmed as fights have broken out all over the city.' He took out his mobile.

Harry gestured to Sarah to join him. She came, followed by Jamie. She tried to appear casual yet professional.

'Prime Minister, this is Dr Jamie Hencke. He is a medical doctor and has been kindly looking after me all evening.'

'Thank you for that, Jamie. What do you do?'

'Sir, I work for Mr Crawford in his Glasgow office. I was hoping to come to London to work for Mr Harcourt. But sadly, that will not happen now.'

'Why not? Come. What were you going to do for Terence?'

'Sir, he had asked me to come and look at the European experience of health insurance to help ease the financing problems of the NHS. I am just finishing a Master's degree in health economics for that reason.'

'Listen, do come. Just give my office a call. You know Sarah now, so you are on the inside track. If she asks me, I have no choice but to say yes. You can work on the same problem in my office, ok?'

If nothing else, he will take Sarah off my hands when I am fed up with her, Harry thought. Barney was off his phone.

'Sir, can we talk by ourselves?'

'Come into this anteroom, Prime Minister,' Calum said graciously. Oliver followed. Harry asked Sarah to join them. She came quickly. Harry ever so lightly brushed himself against her. Sarah was thrilled. Harry whispered in her ears, 'Stay close. I have dropped my contacts. Can't see a thing.' Sarah laughed.

Harry called Oliver over. He said, 'That and this riot will at least take the heat off Libya. Tell Christine, whoever is on *Newsnight* must put Terence before Libya. Poor Terence. Mind you, that is the best way to go if you have to. Quickly.'

'And just in time for *Newsnight*.'

They all gathered in the inner office where Oliver had been before. Calum asked Barney whether he should stay or go.

'I don't mind you staying, sir. I just didn't want everyone to listen to what I have to say.'

'What's the problem, Barney?' Harry knew it must be something serious.

'Sir, the chief constable sends his apologies. He was going to be here for the dinner but he has been called away. He says the situation is much more serious than we thought. They have now come across evidence that the riot was possibly pre-planned. Two planeloads came from Belfast, one a loyalist group and the other a republican group. These were chartered flights. Also, buses came over on the ferry from Ulster. Strathclyde police have intercepted some mobile phone traffic too. There is a possibility, no more, but still it is there, that there was also a plot to attack your car, even perhaps to kill you. I am sorry to be so blunt, sir. But the chief constable says he cannot provide you with full security transfer to the airport. There is a lot of trouble at the airport as some of these gangs have headed there. He is sorry, but these are the worst riots he has known.'

'So, what does he advise?'

Harry was cool and factual. Sarah was numb with fear. Oliver was incandescent about the bloody Northern Irish.

'Sir, he hopes that a police helicopter will be available within an hour when he expects the trouble to have calmed down. Then they can take you to the airport.'

'Well, it is ten now. At this rate, we won't get to Belfast till midnight. I wish it could be sooner. Where is the nearest RAF base?'

'Prime Minister, can I suggest a quicker way? My helicopter can be summoned immediately, and it can take you wherever you wish to go. It is a six-seater Eurocopter twin squirrel aircraft. Fast and comfortable. Why not go to Belfast directly and avoid the airport?' Calum Kennedy saw his chance of doing a favour to the PM and reclaim some goodwill despite a completely disastrous evening.

Harry turned to Oliver and Barney.

'What do you reckon?'

'Sounds fine to me. It will get us out of here and we can avoid the ride from the airport in Belfast as well. Barney?' Oliver was impatient.

'If it is fine with you, sir, I am happy to come along. Or, if you like, I can see about the RAF facilities.'

'Ok, let's take Calum's offer. Thanks a lot. That will sort out our problem.'

'I am delighted, Prime Minister. I can get the 'copter here in ten minutes.'

'Fine. While we are waiting, we had better get back in there and join our shattered colleagues.' Harry was feeling generous towards his Scottish hosts. He also wanted to see how they were taking Terence's death. Would it help in the elections to the Scottish Parliament?

They moved out, leaving Calum to bark orders to his personal assistant. Harry decided now was the time to be effusive to Sir Archibald something who had lost his game, his reception, and even the dinner.

'Now, Sir Archibald, we are all set. Hopefully, Calum Kennedy will get his helicopter to land here. But I am afraid that means you have to suffer our presence for ten minutes more. I hope you don't mind.'

'Prime Minister, how can you say that? We are sorry to send you off without a taste of our Scottish hospitality. It has been a difficult and sad day. But may I ask you and your party to join me in a farewell drink? How about a large malt whisky, the nectar of Scotland?'

'May I be very rude and say no to the whisky? I will however have another glass of the excellent Martini that I had earlier. It was perfect.'

At the bar, Roger stood deep in thought. There had been much less drinking than he had expected. The waiters they had hired to help him were carrying the usual beers and whiskies, leaving Roger to do the fancy stuff. Now the dinner was cancelled and the evening was about to end. Would Harry have another drink? Suddenly he saw Sir Archibald approach.

'My dear fellow, can you make one last Martini for the prime minister? He loved your last effort. Tell you what, if it is so good, make me one as well. I will wait here so you don't need to carry them.'

Roger saw the complication at once. He would have to hand the specially made martini to Harry himself. He could not possibly rely on this old fool to do the job right.

'No need for that, sir. I will bring them to you in a trice. The prime minister needs your company, I am sure.'

Sir Archibald had realized by now that Calum had stolen a march on him. He had better get his share of the PM's time. He hurried back. Roger was quick. He had to manipulate his two bottles of olives and remember which was which. The special olives were a shade darker than the clean ones. His deft hands moved fast, and within minutes he had the two Martinis ready. Calum walked up to him.

'Jesus, Roger, I had forgotten you were here tonight. Give me a large malt, will you? My favourite, please.'

'Te Bheag, isn't it? Sure.' Roger pulled out a bottle of Te Bheag, which only the true aficionados drank. 'There you are. Calum, can I ask you to do me a favour? This Martini is for Sir Archibald and this one for the prime minister. Can you take them in please? But keep them separate. They are different recipes. The prime minister is very particular.'

'Ok, you old rascal. Just for old times' sake. Now, tell me again, which is which.'

Roger realized that Calum was beyond the driving limit, and would fail a breath test by a mile. The risk was too great. He would rather be recognized by Harry than kill Sir Archibald. Anyway, Calum could not carry three drinks.

'Don't worry, you old Stalinist. I'll do it.'

Roger went towards the large group surrounding Harry. A path was cleared for him. He gave the clean drink to Sir Archibald, and almost simultaneously the special one to Harry. Sir Archibald was feeling expansive.

'Prime Minister, this is the man who made you your perfect Martini. Indeed, he has converted me to it now. It's Roger, isn't it?'

'Yes, sir.' Roger wanted to be away as soon as possible. But he had not reckoned with Harry. For a politician, every new person is a hand to be shaken, a potential vote to be bid for. He took Roger's hand and the familiar blue eyes looked into his. Roger cursed to himself, Shit, this is it. He knows who I am.

'Nice to meet you, Roger. Thanks for a finely made Martini. Let me say, if I do come again, I want you to be here to make me another one.'

Harry looked intently at Roger as he spoke. Roger was not to know that Harry could not see him well. His myopia was such that Roger was just a blur.

'Thank you, Prime Minister.' Roger withdrew with alacrity.

Calum gulped his drink down. His mobile was ringing. He answered it and said, 'Ok. We are ready. The copter will land in just a minute. It's all clear but watch your steps, there are broken bottles about.'

Harry looked at his drink. Should he abandon it? He hesitated. Then he drank it down in a single gulp and as a result swallowed the olive whole. He hated that. Oliver, Sarah and Barney were already on their way down. Calum stayed with Harry and continued to plug his case.

'It is a state-of-the-art machine, Prime Minister, and Angus Stewart is an experienced pilot who has done fifty thousand miles. You are in good hands. You should be in Belfast in no time whatsoever.'

'This way if you want to avoid the press, Prime Minister.' Oliver was anxious to get away. They went down a long dark tunnel and emerged on the pitch, where just an hour ago fights had raged. It looked like an abandoned battlefield. The Rangers' cleaning staff were picking up the broken glass, with the floodlights as their only help. Angus Stewart was standing at the foot of the helicopter. He held one door open and shook hands with Harry.

'Welcome to the *Queen of the Clyde*, Prime Minister. I am Angus Stewart, your pilot.'

'Thank you, Angus. This is Sarah and this here is Oliver Knight. Barney Jones will also be travelling with us for security.' As he spoke, Harry put his arm around Sarah and helped her up, making sure that they would be together at the back. Oliver and Barney knew their place and got in the front, leaving a row of two seats between the boss and themselves. Harry waved to Calum and mouthed thank you, but the noise was too great for anyone to hear. Even before they were off, Harry's hand had slid under Sarah's dress. Sarah sidled closer to him and whispered, 'Don't be shocked, but no panties, clean forgot.' Harry laughed.

10.00 p.m. London/House of Commons

This is the ten o'clock news on the BBC.

First the headlines.

Terence Harcourt, the secretary of state for Europe, has died of a heart attack. We look at the implications for the government.

Riots in Glasgow at the match between Rangers and Celtic. Two dead and dozens injured.

Is America about to bomb Libya? Is Britain's RAF going along?

First, Terence Harcourt. Our correspondent Nyta Roberts reports...

Watching the BBC in his room, Frank was relieved. Nothing about Libya. This meant that the news would be known only when the Americans made their announcement at five o'clock their time. So far the BBC had not picked anything up. So, even if CNN picked it up and reported it as breaking news, and then the BBC's Washington correspondent called London, the BBC would not report it until, say, ten past. So, by the time Mary got to *Newsnight*, they would have only the tiniest bit of information. Even better if *Newsnight* started with Terence or the punch up at Ibrox, and Libya got squeezed out. If Frank had been the praying sort, he would have done so now.

Eric came to him in the division lobby.

'Frank, can I have a word with you?'

'Eric, nice to see you in our lobby. What's up?'

'Are you announcing a US attack on Libya? Is HMG going along? If so, I am bound to ask you some searching questions following your statement. I thought it best to warn you.'

'Fair enough. Eric. As you know, it would be a breach of privilege if

I was to tell you what was in my statement before I told the House. But ask me what you wish. It's a free country.'

10.05 p.m. Glasgow/Glencoe Hotel

Margaret was watching BBC news in her hotel room. The hotel was up on a hill, in the university area, across the river from where she'd had the accident. It was very comfortable and her suite was the best they had.

Margaret had been taken up in her wheelchair. She had some soup and bread, and was now ready for bed. But she could not sleep yet. Much had happened today, and tomorrow was going to be crowded. She had to sort it all out. Watching the news was the best way to settle her mind. She did not want to watch Rainbow, the channel that LDNC owned, since she hated commercials during news. So BBC it was.

They were still on Terence Harcourt's sudden death. Margaret had never met him, but knew vaguely that Matt hated his guts, though not why. Matt had his own collection of loves and hates. The boyish looking BBC political editor was saying that this could increase Harry's control over the party, and drive the rebels further into isolation. Then they moved on to the Glasgow scene with the riots. Margaret started browsing through the recent issue of *The New Yorker* she had carried with her. She hated to see the ugliness of such violence.

10.02 p.m. Glasgow/Directors' Dining Room, Ibrox

Roger started clearing away and packing his things. He had been relieved when Harry failed to recognize him. But if Harry had eaten the olive, as he liked to do in his last drink, Roger had no more than an hour to get out of town. Harry himself seemed to have left early, Roger did not know where or how. The noise he had heard of the helicopter could have been the police or it could have been Harry. Roger did not care any more.

'That was a very fine drink, young man, and the prime minister appreciated it as well. Can you make me one more for the road?' It was Sir Archibald.

Roger had no choice. He nearly picked the jar with the poisonous olives, but refrained. He was in enough trouble as it was. He had to avoid doing anything that might raise suspicion. The place was crawling with policemen.

'Would that be for yourself or for the PM as well?' Roger thought it best to feign ignorance.

'No. The prime minister has rushed off. Mr Kennedy kindly made his private helicopter available. He hopes to be in Belfast in an hour or so. I do hope he pays us a visit again. We need to show him some real hospitality. And I hope you will be available then to mix our drinks. Pity about the haggis, though.' Sir Archibald was still sore about the wasted food.

Roger handed him the drink. At least for an hour or so, the news about Harry would not be known, and if he died on the way to Belfast or in Belfast, it would make for an even longer delay before the law came chasing Roger. He had to get out. He called over Billy, one of the waiters at the bar, and told him to hold the fort while he went to the toilet. Billy agreed, but was puzzled to see Roger walk off clutching a jar of olives. How was he to know that Roger was just destroying evidence?

10.15 p.m. London/House of Commons

Frank was relieved. Ian had given him a beautiful short text to read out. It mentioned Terence's Northern Irish background and his progress through Glasgow University, his battle to wrest power from the old guard, his early promotion during the Wilson–Callaghan years, his role as deputy leader under Stan, and finally his marriage with Dorothy. Frank knew all this but he could not have written it as well as Ian. He must tell Josie to invite Ian and Hilda for dinner at

Chevening, their weekend residence. The lovely old house belonged to the foreign office but Nick Davies wanted to be in Wales as much as he could, so he had given it up to Frank.

'Tell you what, Ian. You must never retire. The world and I need you to be around,' Frank said. The clock was at quarter past ten and the division would end soon. Frank had come out quickly to meet up with Ian. Now he debated if he should risk a drink before his statement. Habit proved superior to reason.

'Let me buy you a pint. I owe you a big dinner, but that will have to be arranged between Josie and Hilda. Come, lad.'

It was pleasant on the terrace but the gloom was palpable. Austin joined them with a Scotch in his hand.

'In the memory of a great Scotsman. What a tragedy. How will the party cope?'

'The party will have to learn to cope. Harry has the more immediate problem of finding a successor.'

'Have you spoken to Dorothy?' Austin asked.

'Oh yes. She was very badly cut up. All she kept saying was, "my poor lambkins". And that he was such a lovely father. After a few minutes of her crying, I had to politely say I would get in touch with her about the funeral. She said to get in touch with Terence's secretary, Adrian Andrew. I can't get hold of him on his mobile. So I've asked the switchboard to track him down.'

'Just how did he die? What was he doing in Vienna?' Ian asked.

'He was attending a European ministerial meeting on the costs of enlargement. Boring, hard work if you ask me, but someone has to do it. He had dinner with our Ambassador and then suddenly, phut. Off he goes.'

'I hear he was in some bar or the other.'

'You don't want to listen to the reptiles. They are sniffing around for a scandal.' Frank wanted to put a lid on this line of inquiry.

'Frank, I almost forgot.' Austin was on Frank's wavelength and changed the subject. 'The Tories say that they would like to do the tribute to Terence first as a separate item so their tributes don't get mixed up with some argy-bargy over Libya. The LibDems are happy to go along with that, given that they think they are going to win big in Scotland. Is that alright with you?'

'To tell you frankly, I prefer it all in one go. If they like, they can pause for breath between their tribute to Terence and their comment on Libya. I don't want the media accusing us of bringing up Libya so late in the night that it doesn't make the papers tomorrow. What with the punch up in Glasgow and the news about Terence, if we get Libya also in, it would get less space on the front pages. Anyway, that is how Harry would play it, I am sure. So can you unwind it?'

'All right, if you say so. And oh, how did Harry cope with the punch up in Glasgow?'

10.20 p.m. *Queen of the Clyde*

Harry was all over Sarah. It had taken all of his restraint to stop from nuzzling her bare back and lovely white shoulders when they were in the big room with everyone looking. When they got into the helicopter, he couldn't wait even for the take-off. Nor for that matter could Sarah. She eased the straps off. She took his mouth to hers and then to her nipples. His fingers worked their way deep into her, where she wanted him. They both slid further down so they could not be seen from the front. The noise was so loud that Sarah's moaning was inaudible to the others. Sarah removed Harry's belt and pulled down his zip. Harry nuzzled Sarah's neck and kissed her full on the mouth, and stroked her breasts. Then, suddenly, he slumped and slid along the seat and onto her lap, his hands limp and hanging loosely.

Sarah first thought he was playing at something, then she grew alarmed. She tried to stand up, adjusting her dress, to attract the pilot's attention, but she was thrown back as the helicopter suddenly lurched. She shook Harry, shouting his name. But still no one at the front looked back. The helicopter lurched again, and Sarah screamed. She hadn't looked out at all since they got in. Now, suddenly, she saw a big white shape looming in front of the helicopter. The pilot was shouting and swearing. The helicopter lost height again, then started to come down at a sickening pace. Oliver and Barney were thrown out of their seats.

Angus Stewart was trying to get his vehicle to rise higher. It was dark and he could not see clearly. Earlier in the evening, he had been watching the Old Firm game on TV with his mates. He knew Calum Kennedy was staying in town, and assumed there was no chance of his being called for duty. So, a few beers had been had among friends. When the call came from Calum's assistant that he had to go quickly, he could not possibly plead an excuse. He was supposed to be on duty 24/7, and drinking was not allowed on the job. But it was a big game, and he so loathed Celtic that he wished to see them thrashed. He quickly washed his mouth with Listerine and set out. The air was foul as it always was in Ibrox so Calum did not notice his breath, not that Calum's was any sweeter.

The woman at the back was screaming.

Oh shit, oh shit, he had hit something.

10.25 p.m. London/Heathrow Hilton

Adrian was enjoying the room service at the Heathrow Hilton. He had come away as soon as he got his cash. He needed time to work out how to convert his money in ways he could use it. He reckoned airport hotels would not be surprised to be paid cash for rooms, especially if he took a big suite. He also had to figure out if it was best for him to leave the country. He would have to see what Lex did with his photographs, and how Terence reacted. He had to hide somewhere safe and what better place than the Heathrow Hilton?

He had spent the day lazing. He lingered in the jacuzzi, sipping champagne, and then snoozed for a while. It was years since he had felt so relaxed about money. He had given up such luxuries as a five-star hotel. Now, at least for a bit, he could indulge. For a short time, he would allow himself to drink some decent stuff.

He woke up hungry. It was nearly ten in the evening. He had been asleep for six or seven hours. He ordered room service to bring him their best grilled salmon with salad and another bottle of Bollinger. He then settled down to watch the news.

When he heard the news on BBC, his first instinct was to call Dorothy. He was one of the few who had her mobile number. Adrian reactivated his own mobile which he had switched off once he left LDNC.

'Dorothy, I am so sorry to hear…'

There were sobs at the other end. Adrian waited patiently. Then Dorothy spoke.

'Where are you, Adrian? I need you to be here. We all need you. Terence is gone, and I have no friend but you. Can you get here soon?'

Adrian was taken aback. Of course, Dorothy had no idea what part he had played in Terence's death. Unless Roddy talked, no one would ever know. And here was Dorothy, desperate for his company. He had thought she would be with her relations or friends. But in many subtle ways, he had made her dependent on him. He would have to go to her. Perhaps he could break it gently to her that he was not gay. What was more, he could be there and destroy the evidence by removing the cameras.

'Dorothy, I am in London. I'll get to Heathrow first thing and find a flight to Edinburgh. I'll call you as soon as I get a flight reservation. Don't worry. I'll be there.'

'Oh thank you, thank you, Adrian. I always said to Terence I could rely on you. You come from such a solid, good family. These things matter when the time comes. Thank you, thank you, Adrian. Come as soon as you can.'

Adrian called the reception.

'Hello, Mr Andrew. What can we do for you?'

'Can you tell me if there are any airline taxis that can fly me to Edinburgh now?'

'Sure, sir. Just give me a couple of minutes.'

Adrian was pleased that he had not done anything in haste.

10.25 p.m. London/The Archduke

Kath slid down in her chair, and onto the marble floor with a clatter. As a fashion model, she was used to a strict diet regime. This long bout of drinking and eating and talking and singing had finally gone to her head. Everyone broke into hysterical laughter.

'I guess it's curtains for us, sisters. We'd better get on our broomsticks and fly back home.' Lisa was pissed, but perfectly in control of the situation. It was only half past ten, but The Archduke was quite empty as Monday was always a slow day. The staff was waiting patiently for this drunken rabble to wrap up their dinner. Lisa stood up and raised her glass.

'To Ubu, and to stupid men and husbands everywhere. Until tomorrow.'

'Down with kings and presidents and leaders everywhere. Up with Lisa,' Annie responded.

Lisa summoned the waiter and asked for the bill.

10.25 p.m. London/House of Commons

Frank Thompson stood up at the despatch box and began.

'With permission, Mr Deputy Speaker, I wish to make a statement on behalf of my right honourable friend, the Prime Minister, on Her Majesty's Government's policy on North Africa. But before I do that, it is my sad duty to inform the House of the sudden death of the right honourable member for Renfrew, and Secretary of State for Europe, Terence Harcourt.'

Ian was shaping his obituary in *The News* office but, just in case, he had the Parliamentary channel on. He wanted to see how Frank fared, and also how the Libya statement went down with the Commons, especially on the government back benches. He was also looking up the cuttings file on Terence that he had helpfully been provided with. He had his previous draft in front of him, but that had been done before Terence became secretary of state for Europe. He had a lot to do and not much time to do it in.

10.25 p.m. Glasgow/Directors' Dining Room, Ibrox

Roger flushed the olives down the toilet. It had been a busy evening, and there was no danger that anyone would notice what he was doing. As the remaining people went home, they would be stopping by and using the facilities, so his olives would be accorded a fast forward passage into the local drains. On his way out, he made sure Billy saw him. He had just one more thing to do, and that was to collect his money from Alex, who made all such informal transactions for the club.

'What a pity, Roger. We could have won that fair and square. Who knows, the league may yet award it to us. That will make it one more nail in the coffin for those bastards.' Alex's tolerance from earlier in the afternoon was gone.

Roger cared more about the discretion with which he handed over the money. 'Well, that is life, Alex. Thanks. Take care how you go.'

'There are a lot of mad buggers out there. Mind how you go too, Roger.'

There was indeed one man who was very mad, but in the way Americans might use the word. Red was furious that Harry White had escaped his clutches. He had his device in place and it would have been triggered off by the car's motion. Within minutes of the car starting, Harry and all who travelled with him would have been blown to smithreens. Instead, the police were swarming all over and people were pouring out of the posh parts of Ibrox. In the general confusion, he had no time to detach the device. But Red could not see any point in killing an innocent government chauffeur if he was travelling without Harry White. He took out a beer bottle from his rucksack, hurled it at the windscreen and then ran for his life.

Roger was out of the building, and walking rapidly; running would only attract attention. He did not notice Red or anyone else. There were people and policemen everywhere, in a chaotic melee. The police were trying to disperse the fans as quickly as they could, but there were shouts and sounds of fighting all around. He had to be careful. He had to get a taxi to take him to the airport, and then off to Dublin, if a flight was still available. There were no taxis, however. There was not even a bus. Police had cordoned off large areas around Ibrox. Suddenly he heard a horn behind him. It was Calum in his Rover.

'Where are you going? It's murder out there. Can I take you somewhere?'

Oh shit, Roger thought. What is to be done now? He took the line of least resistance.

'Drop me off where I can get a bus or a taxi to get to the airport. I have a late flight to catch. Thanks, Calum.'

'You won't get out anywhere tonight. The airport is crawling with policemen. They are expecting trouble since a lot of the gangs have come over from Belfast. I doubt if any flights will leave tonight. You'll have to wait till tomorrow. Let me drive you all the way home. It is a rough night to be travelling by public transport in Glasgow. Tell my driver where you live.'

10.25 p.m. Glasgow

'Ok, kids, we'll stop at the next junction and go to the Little Chef there. You have been very good so far,' David Byrne said.

He was driving back from the aborted game to their home in Ayr. The nightmare of the match was over. The kids had been frightened, but they had not said a word. He was so proud of them. He had got into the car park ahead of many others who had also been running. He had driven off as soon as he could, and headed south out of Glasgow. But the traffic was bad, and at many places, there were police roadblocks to thwart the rioters. It was not until after nine thirty that they got onto the stretch of A77 which was congestion free. Now, after having driven for an hour, he felt relaxed. Robbie and Alastair had remained silent through the ordeal, and clutched their dad's hands tightly through the twenty minutes it took them to get out of Ibrox.

David thought he had better tell Sophie they were alright. She would have seen the news on TV, and would be worried. So David parked his car in a lay-by and called her. He told her how good and helpful and brave the twins had been. Not once had either of them cried or complained. David let the boys talk to their mum, and they proudly told her that not once had they asked their dad, Are we there yet? Sophie thought they should be rewarded for this, and told David to take it easy, drive carefully, and give the kids a treat. The next rest stop was not far away, and there would be a Little Chef there.

'Look, Robbie, a helicopter,' Alistair shouted.

Robbie was reading his comic. He did not look up at first.

'Robbie, look, it's going to hit the hills.'

Robbie looked up from his book. David Byrne looked up too. He had been aware of the distant noise of a helicopter for the last ten minutes, but hadn't stopped to take note. Now suddenly the air seemed to be ripped apart by the sound of metal smashing into the rocky face of the hill. There was a blaze of fire and then an eerie silence. The noise stopped, and he dialled 999.

10.30 p.m. London/House of Commons

Frank had done his tribute to Terence Harcourt and had moved on to the dreaded subject of Libya. 'Mr Deputy Speaker, I turn now to the question of Her Majesty's Government's policy on Libya. As the right honourable and honourable members know, Libya has been the subject of UN resolutions which have asked the country's leadership to stop aiding and abetting terrorism in the region. We have given Libya ample opportunities to comply with these resolutions, but the response so far has been poor.'

Eric stood up.

'On a point of order, Mr Deputy Speaker.'

'The right honourable member for Nonesuch North knows that no point of order can be allowed during a statement.' Sir Reginald Bassett, the deputy speaker, was firm.

'Is it in order that the right honourable gentleman tells the House a blatant lie?'

'I warn the right honourable gentleman that he is out of order. I shall overlook his breach of parliamentary behaviour this once. I warn him, if he persists, I will have no option but to name him.' Sir Reginald was losing his cool.

Frank was glad about the interruption. Every minute wasted kept the news off the air. He wished there could be more interruptions from all sides.

'Mr Deputy Speaker, tonight at twenty-two hundred, American F-16 aircraft were launched from their base to attack Libyan airport facilities and Libyan planes in retaliation for the terrorist attack by Libyan aircraft on US aircraft carrier *USS Ronald Reagan*. RAF aircraft were engaged in support of the US F-16 as refuelling reserves.'

10.30 p.m. Glasgow/Glencoe Hotel

And now on BBC2, *Newsnight* with Jeremy Paxman.

Margaret saw the futuristic platform move around, and on the screen appeared Jeremy Paxman. It was obvious from the sardonic twist of his mouth that he was going to enjoy savaging whichever minister he had in his sights tonight. Margaret had already seen the Libyan bombing announcement trailed on the news on BBC1.

The headlines played out on *Newsnight.*

America bombs Libya as RAF planes assist with refuelling.

Terence Harcourt, Secretary of State for Europe, has died in Vienna.

Riot and mayhem at the Old Firm game in Glasgow. Was there a plot to attack the prime minister?

Good evening. The American government announced at ten o'clock British time that American planes have taken off from their base in Fakenham in Norfolk. RAF planes are engaged as refuelling reserves. As I speak, Deputy Prime Minister Frank Thompson is making a statement to the House of Commons from where our correspondent Nyta Roberts reports.

There was a cut to Nyta standing in the Central Lobby.

Yes, Jeremy. Frank Thompson is still making his statement. The unrest on his back benches was already evident when he was twice interrupted by Eric Thor, whom the deputy speaker, Sir Reginald Bassett, had to warn that he could be expelled from the Chamber. The mood here is a mixture of sadness about the death of Terence Harcourt and anger that once again Britain has been found playing second fiddle to American policy in the Middle East. Over to you, Jeremy.

Thank you, Nyta, for that. The American attack on Libya will cause major ructions in the country, and even perhaps in the Government. With me to discuss this question is Defence Minister Mary Duggan.

'Mary Duggan, what possible ground in international law can you claim for this blatant and unprovoked attack on Libya? Is Harry White again playing America's lapdog?' Jeremy was not one to start softly.

'That is total nonsense, if I may say so, Jeremy. But before I answer your question, let me say how sorry I am about Terence Har…'

'Hang on. We shall come to that later. First, about Libya, if you don't mind.'

'Of course I mind. I have lost a valuable comrade.'

'With the greatest respect, Secretary of State, can we deal with Libya first, and then talk about Terence Harcourt?'

'I am not going to be bullied like this. Good manners require that we mourn the loss of a high ranking British politician, an outstanding Scotsman.' Mary was determined to have her way.

'Don't you think we should mourn the collapse of British sovereignty in matters of foreign policy before we do that, Secretary of State?'

'There is no collapse of any kind. If you recall, Jeremy, we were joint movers of the UN Security Council Resolution which denounced Libya.'

'Which was only passed because Russia and China abstained, and even then it was eight for and five against.'

'What matters is that we have UN backing for our actions.'

'Tell me, how does the government, or should I say, how does Harry White get away with such illegal actions?' Jeremy was enjoying himself.

Mary Duggan opened her mouth to retort but before she could say anything, Jeremy put up his hand to silence her.

'Just a minute,' he said, 'we have some breaking news.' He pressed his ear phones closer. It looked like minutes passed in silence but it was just thirty seconds. Jeremy was solemn when he resumed.

'We have just heard from our Glasgow studios that the helicopter carrying the prime minister and Oliver Knight, his press officer, has crashed near Kilmarnock. As of now, we don't know whether the prime minister is injured or safe, nor do we know who else was travelling with him. We go immediately to our Glasgow newsroom, and talk to George Trump. George, what is the latest?'

George was in the BBC Glasgow newsroom.

'Jeremy, all we know as of now is that a driver on the road to his home in Ayr from Glasgow, saw the helicopter crash in the south uplands. This is just along the A77. He called 999 and a rescue team is on its way and should be there any minute now. I have spoken to our sports correspondent Ivan Lawrence who was at Ibrox. He told me that the prime minister managed to avoid the press and took off in a private helicopter. He could not confirm this, but the helicopter may have belonged to the Scottish media magnate Calum Kennedy. It is not clear as of now why the prime minister was in a private helicopter, and where he was going. He was in Glasgow earlier, where he addressed a party rally and then watched the game at Ibrox which, as you know, had to be cancelled even before half-time due to crowd violence. Police have made several arrests and there is a rumour that many of the rioters had come across from Northern Ireland for the occasion. It has been a bad day all around for Glasgow and for Scotland, and indeed for the United Kingdom, what with the riots and the death of Terence Harcourt, and now this.'

'Thank you, George. It has been a terrible day for Scotland and now, it seems, for the nation. Mary Duggan, this is indeed a shock, wouldn't you agree?'

Mary Duggan had gone completely white. Twice, she tried to speak but no words came out. Jeremy saved the day for her and said, 'Let us go again to Westminster and Nyta Roberts. Nyta?'

'Jeremy, the House is in a state of shock. The deputy speaker was given the information by the clerks on the table, who were told by the Serjeant at Arms. He was himself distraught as he read out the message. John Altrincham, the Conservative deputy leader and foreign affairs spokesman, was just about to reply to Frank Thompson's statement when the deputy speaker interrupted him and read out the news. He then suspended the proceedings for fifteen minutes while they try to ascertain what has happened. I saw Frank Thomson sitting on the front bench and he was in tears. Austin Mills was also hiding his face in his hands. It is a shocked House of Commons tonight, Jeremy.'

'Thank you, Nyta.'

10.50 p.m. Glasgow

Five ambulances had converged on the site where the helicopter had crashed. The local police from Kilmarnock and Ayr and

Prestwick had rushed to the scene. The Glasgow situation meant that all across the region, police and ambulance staff were stretched. This was the last thing they had expected or needed. The fire which had ignited had been hosed down but the difficult task of rescue remained.

David Byrne had got out of his car as soon as he called 999. He had told the children to stay still and told them not to speak to anyone, nor open the door. He had some experience of emergencies. He tried to get close to the main body of the helicopter. There were bits scattered everywhere. He felt the heat as he got closer. But he could also see someone scrambling to get out. He shouted, 'It's alright. I am here. Grab my hand.' A tall man covered with blood dragged himself forward on his knees and grabbed David's proffered hand. It was Barney.

'Thanks, mate. Can I use your mobile? It is the prime minister in there.'

David gave him the mobile. Barney called an emergency number while David tried to shift the broken shafts of metal to create a passage through the debris. He could hear someone moaning inside.

'Hi, this is Barney Jones. We are on the…'

David said quickly, 'A77 near Kilmarnock.'

'…on the A77 near Kilmarnock. This is a red alert. It is the prime minister's team. The helicopter we were travelling in has crashed. Send all help. Immediately.'

Barney handed the phone back to David and said, 'Let's see what we can do.'

10.50 p.m. London

Lisa was in the mini-bus, having just dropped off Annie at the Savoy. Before that, she had dropped the locals to Waterloo or to Victoria, from where they could get to their homes. She looked at her mobile now and saw six missed calls and five text messages. She had forgotten that she had switched her phone to silent mode when they left The Archduke. She reset the ring tone, and the phone rang immediately. Lisa saw it was Margaret calling from her own phone this time.

'Margaret, how are you, darling? Are you alright? Margaret, why are you crying?'

'Lisa, darling Lisa. How can you not know—such a terrible thing has happened. It is Harry. His helicopter has crashed.'

'Is he, is he…? Oh God. I had my phone switched to silent and they must have been trying to call me. What is the news?'

'We don't know yet. BBC has just heard about the crash, but no one knows anything more. He was in some private helicopter. He was probably trying to get to Belfast, away from the mess that Glasgow is in.'

'Why? What has happened?'

'Haven't you heard anything? It's been a terrible evening. Oh, of course, you've been at your post-rehearsal dinner. Well, the match here broke up because of some violence on the pitch, and then the fans fought each other. Four people have died, and many are injured. Fighting is still going on all over Glasgow. And we heard earlier that Terence Harcourt died of a heart attack in Vienna, where he had gone for an EU meeting. Poor Dorothy. Oh, Lisa, I hope it all turns out alright for you. We can only pray.'

'I must call Dorothy and give her my condolences. Oh God, what a tragedy. I'll call Christine and find out about Harry.'

10.50 p.m. London

Ian called Hilda.

'Have you heard, Hilda?'

'Yes, my dear. I reckon you will be very late back tonight.'

'I think you are right. Sleep well.'

11.00 p.m. Glasgow

The car stopped by the estate. Roger got out and thanked Calum.

'Don't mention it, Roger. Stay put now. Don't go out anywhere tonight.' Calum was most solicitous of his old mate. He was feeling generous. Despite the abrupt end to the football, he'd had a good evening and made an impression on the PM. His mobile phone rang.

'Hello. Oh God. What? When? I'll be there.' Roger thought it best to slink away and not ask if something was wrong. Calum rushed off without waving.

Roger was confused. Having got this far, he had no choice but to go up to the flat and face Deirdre. Hopefully she would be asleep, and ask no questions. Roger had to think about his escape strategy carefully. He did not know how soon he could get out of town.

He rang the bell. Samantha opened the door. She was small for her age but had lively brown eyes and a clear complexion.

'Hi, Roger. How's things?'

Before he could answer, Deirdre appeared in her nightie.

'Have you heard, Roger? Harry White is probably dead.'

'What? How did that happen? Who says?'

'He was in a helicopter, and it crashed. Just outside Kilmarnock. It's on the news. Come and see.'

Harry dead in a helicopter crash? How amazing. Did that mean they would never find out? Would the body be recovered and examined by doctors? Would they discover the poison he had administered? Roger's head was swimming. He slumped on a chair. Harry was dead. He tried to recall Melissa's face. He wanted to tell her, I did it for you, but everything seemed distant and hazy.

'Are you alright, Roger? You look worn out. You shouldn't work so hard. I wish you would take it easy. Go off on a holiday somewhere.' Deirdre was seriously concerned.

'God, I could do with a holiday. Let's try and get out of here, and go off somewhere. Shall we? Where do you think?'

'You choose. It's your holiday and I am afraid you will have to pay for it.'

'Don't worry about that. I made good money tonight. Why don't we go somewhere close by? Like Dublin. We can set off tomorrow. Will you come, Sam?'

'No, sorry, I got too much on. But you and Mum go. You could both use a holiday. When did you last have a holiday, Mum?'

11.10 p.m. London/Drew House

Lex was in despair. He had never known a night like this. He had scrapped the Terence Harcourt edition. That was a lot of money down the drain. Those pictures would now remain in the strong box forever. He had prepared a new front page with pictures of the referee, Peter Houston, with a bandage over his brow. Across his face was a big bold headline in red letters: SAVAGES. Inside there were full-page pictures of the riot in Glasgow, but he had restored the nude on page three. Gisella, as she was called, was holding a football in her hands. A balloon from her lips said, Gisella thought it was wrong for fans to attack referees, and that Paul Houston (whom she had never laid eyes on) was her hero.

He had put the news of Terence Harcourt's death in a small entry on the top right corner beside the masthead and continued the story on page nine with the article Chris had sent in. The first print run had gone for outstation delivery by ten thirty. Now he had to rethink the front page. Should he take Paul Houston off? Would Harry White be found alive and unhurt? The first pictures of the helicopter were beginning to be shown on Rainbow, which got there before anyone else. Good for our side, Lex thought. He knew that the Rainbow pictures would be fed through to him. The question was, could this be the night two big political figures bit the dust?

11.25 p.m. London/10 Downing Street

The phone rang and Christine answered immediately. She had been holding Lisa in her arms. Lisa had come back to Downing Street and found Christine waiting. Christine normally went home by nine but she had stayed back to deal with the aftermath of Terence's death. She'd had all the three TV sets on with BBC, CNN and Rainbow, watching the news as it broke. She was preparing a note for Harry about what the choices were for replacing Terence, and the impact of his death on the Scottish elections. She also had to monitor the media about Libya, but that story had begun to fade because of Terence's death. Then she heard about the crash. She tried to contact Lisa, but her phone just kept ringing. So she stayed behind.

Lisa was pale, but bearing up stoically. Nothing was said. Lisa knew Christine was fiercely loyal to Harry. She also knew that for all practical purposes, Christine was Harry's one constant mistress. In many ways, Lisa and Christine were similar. They had risen from humble backgrounds, were able and good looking. They had both faced a lot of criticism for being stroppy. Christine was like a sister, a big sister, for Lisa. Now more than ever they clung to each other, waiting for the news they hoped would never come.

'Yes, this is 10 Downing Street. Christine Brown here.'

It was Police Superintendent Richard Erskine.

'I need to speak to Mrs White, please.'

'She is here, but you can tell me. I am the prime minister's special adviser.'

'No, madam. I must speak directly to Mrs White.'

Christine knew what was coming, as did Lisa. Lisa took the phone.

'Yes, this is Elisabet White.' Her voice was barely above a whisper.

'Madam, I am sorry to say this on the phone. Someone should come personally and say this. But I want to tell you before it is announced on the TV news channels. I am Richard Erskine of the

Strathclyde police. As you know, we have just had news of the crash
of the helicopter in which your husband was travelling. We have
recovered his body. I am afraid the news is very bad.'

'Tell me, please. I want to hear.' Lisa was calm.

'We found the body with some difficulty, and the doctor on hand
has tested the pulse and heartbeat. I am sorry to say there is no hope.
Your husband, the prime minister, is beyond recovery. He died in the
crash. I am sorry.'

'Thank you, Inspector. I know it cannot be easy for you to say this.
Can you speak to my friend Christine Brown as well?'

Lisa passed the phone to Christine.

'Tell me about the other passengers on the helicopter—Mr Knight
and Miss Disney. Also Barney Jones, the PM's security officer,'
Christine said.

'Madam, Barney Jones has escaped unscathed. We have taken Mr
Knight and Miss Disney in an ambulance to the nearest hospital in
Kilmarnock. Barney Jones was able to identify them, and confirm
their names for us. The pilot Mr Angus Stewart has sadly died as well.'

'Tell me, are the two survivors very badly injured?' Christine was
feeling responsible for Sarah being caught in the crash.

'I could not honestly tell you, madam. They were unable to move
on their own but were quite aware of what had happened. Mr Knight
was most anxious to speak to the assembled newsmen, but we had to
forbid that. It would have been too risky to delay their removal to a
hospital. Would you like the number of the hospital, madam?'

When Christine put the phone down finally, she was pale but
composed. She took Lisa's hands in hers and they sat together quietly,
thinking of what lay ahead.

FIVE MONTHS LATER

10.30 a.m. London/10 Downing Street

Frank Thompson could never get used to working in 10 Downing Street. He had tried his best not to move Lisa White from her home. But Lisa was insistent. Rules, she said, were rules. She had taken just twenty-four hours to move out. She had insisted on not changing the date of her play's opening and went through the first night stoically. She received a standing ovation. And it was not just out of sympathy for a newly widowed woman. The play itself was a success. The reviews all made clear that they were praising *Ubu Roi* on its merits, and not because they were sorry for Lisa. But, after that first night, she moved out and took a flat in Kensington. Fiona Hartley, Roscoe Hartley's wife, had come to her rescue, and rented her one of the three flats that her family owned in London, besides giving her unlimited access to their country mansion.

There was a double funeral for the party to deal with. It decided to first have Terence Harcourt's funeral. Jamie Hencke went to Vienna to bring back the body. Dorothy, accompanied by Adrian Andrew and her three children, had stayed behind and was on hand to receive the body when it arrived in Edinburgh. A huge crowd gathered at the airport and all along the route to Edinburgh Castle, where permission had been given to put the coffin on display for people to pay their respects. It was as if all of Scotland had decided to turn up for the event. The funeral took place on the Friday following, and Dorothy could not complain that her Terence had not been given the most splendid send-off.

It took longer to arrange Harry White's funeral. The crash had to be investigated, even if only for insurance purposes. Once the posthumous examinations were done, Christine orchestrated the detailed arrangements to bring the body back to London. Lisa wanted a private funeral away from the political and media crowds. Her will prevailed, and Harry White was cremated very quietly at Mortlake. According to his wishes, his ashes were scattered over the Fenners cricket ground in Cambridge. He had always said that but for his myopia, he would have been a Cambridge Blue. Now he would be there forever.

The party had unanimously asked for Frank Thompson to take over as prime minister. The conference at Brighton later in September was more like a wake than the usual ideological gang warfare. The comrades were still in a catatonically depressed state about the double death of the two stalwarts. So even his worst detractors were glad to see Oliver Knight when he attended the conference. He was still in a wheelchair, after four months. It was public knowledge that he had received a two million pound contract to write his memoirs, but he had been too fragile to put pen to paper or finger to laptop.

Frank had gone back to an old-style Cabinet with the treasury back in a powerful position and European affairs with the foreign office. He had decided he could not hold two portfolios as Harry had. He said to Nick Davies that he had to sober up and take over as Chancellor, and Nick had quietly gone off to the Priory to seek a cure for his depression and alcoholism. Now, as deputy prime minister, he was getting ready to walk along with John Altrincham at the state opening of Parliament.

Christine came into Frank's office. She had stayed on to help with the transition. They had agreed that she could leave after the Queen's

Speech. She had been put on the list of peerages for her services to politics. Lisa had refused a title, as she was not at all interested in being cast as the party widow. She was going to tour Europe with her production of *Ubu*, and then settle in Glasgow where her friend Margaret had decided to live.

'Are you happy with your diary today, Prime Minister?' The words were still difficult for Christine to say and for Frank to hear.

'Aye, Christine. I have the egregious Calum Kennedy to see in the afternoon. I don't know what I can say to him, except that we don't blame him for what happened. He persists nevertheless.'

'You know why. He was hoping Harry would give him a peerage. All his plans came unravelled that fateful night in Ibrox.'

'Well, until Gideon tells me that he recommends Calum, I am not going to proceed. He is now first minister, and I intend to leave all Scottish matters to him. Less worry for me. Anyway, thinking of that, how is Sarah doing? Is she better?'

'Yes, she should be out of the hospital next week, we hope. But she is alright and in good spirits. She did not enjoy attending the inquest, but she bore up. She still feels guilty that she survived and Harry did not. I tried to tell her that so did Oliver and Barney. Only the pilot died besides Harry.'

'So will she be back at her job? She has the right to resume, and I could do with someone who knows this place.' As a former trade unionist, Frank had not forgotten Sarah's right to resume her job.

'I'll ask her. She has a new boyfriend now. The doctor James Hencke who accompanied Terence's body back from Vienna. I believe he was Terence's protégé.'

'Aye, I met the lad. Terence was going to bring him to London to work with him. Oliver told me that when Jamie met Harry after they heard about Terence's death, Harry said he could come anyway and work here at No. 10 for him. I came across him at the party conference and renewed the promise. Don't know if he is coming, though.'

'Well, it will all depend on her. If she comes back, so will he.'

'That would be good. What else?'

'Oh yes. You have the chief police constable of Strathclyde to see in five minutes.'

'What does he want? Do I tell him we don't blame him either?'

'Something like that, I guess. Maybe a gong was to come to him and has got delayed due to the fracas that evening.'

'Aye, everyone wants gongs and honours. I only wish I was back at number two.'

'Now, Frank—I hope you don't mind me calling you that—this is no time for self-pity. You are where you are because of all your work and your ability. Remember, Harry too got where he was, not because Stan died, but because his time had come. Now, it is your time. Courage, *mon ami*.'

'Thank you for that, Christine.'

Christine stepped out, and returned a moment later.

'Prime Minister, the chief police constable of Strathclyde, Douglas Mackie.'

'Hello, Commissioner, come in. Have a seat. Thanks, Christine. So, Chief Constable, what's up?' Frank's conversational gambit had survived his promotion.

Douglas Mackie waited for Christine to leave. He then shut the door behind him and sat down.

'Prime Minister, I do hope our communications are secure, and that we cannot be overheard because I have some very sensitive information to give to you. It is only for your ears. It is about the prime minister's death.'

'You mean Harry White, since I am still here.' Frank thought he had to put the pompous ass in his place.

'Oh, yes, of course, Prime Minister. It is about the verdict at the inquest. Although it concluded that the ex- prime minister died as a result of injury in the helicopter crash, we have further evidence that he was poisoned. We believe he was given a poisoned substance, an olive, as part of a drink. We believe we know who gave him the drink, though we don't have a motive yet. We would like your permission to pursue the line of inquiry.'

Frank thought for a minute. Christine was right. Harry White was dead and should be allowed to rest in peace. His time, Frank Thompson's time, had come.

'Forget it, Chief Constable. The man is dead. He only needs to die once. Leave him be.'

The chief constable was surprised, but he hid it well.

'Is that your final decision, Prime Minister?'

'Yes, it is final.'

Douglas Mackie wondered if he should stick to his guns. As a policeman, he hated to see a case remain unsolved, and this one was especially important. But then he asked himself whether some advantage would not come to him if he listened to the new prime minister.

'As you say, Prime Minister. Thank you.' He got up, saluted and made a smart exit.

Christine walked in, a half-smile on her face.

'Matt Drummond called. I told him you were busy.'

Frank nodded, then asked, 'Did you hear what the chief constable had to say?'

'Yes. You did the right thing, Frank.'

Their eyes held for a moment, then Christine bent to kiss his cheek.

As she left, the door shut quietly behind her.

The Prime Minister sat back in his chair, and for the first time in a long while, relaxed.

Walter Raleigh's statue has subsequently been moved from its original place.